MONTANA STU

COWBOYS & CAMPOUTS

Time O. Day

LEARNED & HERSHAL
PUBLISHING

Montana Stu – Cowboys and Campouts
Written by Time O. Day
(The Sequel to *Montana Stu—Cowboys and Bridges*
by Time O. Day)

Copyright ©2016 by Time O. Day
Published 2016 by Learned and Hershal Publishing
ISBN: 978-1-933151-06-9
Printed in the United States of America

To the fine memories of Sonny Jones, my stepdad,
my real dad – what a gem!
We never had campouts till you came.

CONTENTS

CHAPTER 1

W ithin the darkened Texarkana forest, at the edge of a clearing, black eyes of a creature intently watched a glowing plastic lean-to flap in the storm. The Southern storm was so fierce it prevented any moonlight from breaking through the dark canopy. Below the heavy clouds, unceasing rain assaulted the lean-to. Lightning was the only light that pierced the firmament. Its jagged lines fingered out, rumbling over the trees, brightening, reflecting off the creature's eyes.

Under the lean-to, flashlights revealed the men and boys of Scout troop 409.

A fifteen year old junior commander stared up through the clear plastic, watching the remnants of the burning electric arc streak across the darkness. "That's awesome!" he exclaimed. The glow of his flashlight bobbed.

"As long as the lightning doesn't hit us," moaned a younger kid.

Behind him, one boy's finger flicked another boy's ear.

"Cut it out Daniel." Without looking back, retaliation was delivered with a punch to Daniel's shin. His red wavy hair shook from the hit.

Behind them, an African American boy asked a kid from Kentucky, "But how does your friend know that Sasquatch eats meat?"

"'Cause he lives in the woods." Virgil touched the plastic above him, liking the sound of the rain. The lean-to had the feel of a tree-fort, and the many faces and chatter under the plastic reminded the twelve-year-old of his family hunting and camping in the backwoods of Kentucky.

With rising fear, Rubin pawed his arm, "But how does he know?"

Feeling confronted, Virgil gazed into Rubin's face. The whites of his eyes seemed to glow. "My friend's not a liar, he can worm a hook and he's got a good hunting dowg."

Commander Charles looked over the shadowy area then bellowed, "Virgil? Rubin? I don't want to be hearing anymore of that eaten stuff."

Joey mimicked the Southerner, "Got a good hunting dowg." He shared a chuckle with another Californian while thumbing back at Virgil. "Hillbilly's talkin'."

"Joey?" The big Commander continued, "I find your comments demeaning, you owe me ten push-ups."

"Now?" Joey looked about the crammed lean-to for a spot to do push-ups.

"No. Wait till we get outside."

Junior Commander Alan flashed his light at Commander Rex. "Commander Rex, why don't you tell us the story about the Sasquatch?" Alan's head bopped around in glee, looking as if it would spring off. "We need to hear about the big spooky." He looked over the troop, which was made up of nine Scouts from ages nine to twelve and two senior Commanders, Commander Charles, 45 and Commander Rex, 64.

Commander Rex tiredly answered, "I don't think that's a good idea."

"I do." The Junior Commander's voice was mischievous. "The boogy-man story will do us good." Alan swung his head around in delight, wanting to scare the heck out of them.

"Not before they go to their tents." Commander Rex took in the many faces, "I doubt they'll get any sleep."

A chorus of voices piped up, "Oh, please, Commander Rex."

Junior Commander Alan's flashlight exposed the beggars.

"We won't be scared," said Katz.

"I didn't cry when Old Yeller died," said Joey.

Rubin was silent.

"Well . . ." Commander Rex felt a slight roll of pain from his innards, ". . . it was a rainy night much like tonight." He cleared his throat. "Back then, my home was in Arkansas. I really wanted to come here because I'd seen the Bigfoot movie on Boggy Creek and it gave me the creeps."

Liking the story, Junior Commander Alan gave an uneasy grin.

Going back in time, Commander Rex blankly stared at the end of the lean-to. "So I talked to another Commander, Commander Wheeler, and we planned a trip out here."

"How long ago was that?"

He paused for a moment, considering. "About ten, twelve, who knows, maybe sixteen years back. I know it was fall, real pretty, the leaves were just turning. I remember hiking in, past this abandoned cabin. It's too bad we don't have more time to look for it. It'd be neat to see if it was still there." His head dropped in disappointment; he was 64 and now living in Los Angeles, and he doubted he'd ever get another opportunity to come back to Texarkana. "We set up camp and went out looking for Sasquatch prints." Again pain rippled through his midsection. He paused to let it pass, running his hand over his moist brow. "That evening, I got back to camp but Commander Wheeler wasn't there." Feeling his temperature rising, he unzipped his coat.

"What happened?" asked Rubin, worriedly.

Commander Rex winced as another shot of pain rolled over his stomach and back.

The troop shifted forward to better hear him.

He quietly groaned, "It's no good."

"Boooo!" Junior Commander Alan grabbed Israel.

Katz and Rubin jumped. The rest chuckled, relieving their tension.

"Dddddon't . . . you nnnnut," protested Israel. Because of his cerebral palsy, his movements were awkward, his hand pulled into his chest like a brontosaurus. "Ssssscared me half to ddddddeath."

"Are we finished?" Commander Charles glared at Junior Commander Alan.

"Sorry." Not sorry at all, the Junior Commander gave Israel a goofy pat on the shoulder while gazing at Commander Rex. "What happened to the other commander?"

"He didn't make it back. I looked and looked but . . ."

"Did you see anything?"

"It was around dusk, getting dark when I felt like I was being followed. After I crested this hill I came down its side and looked behind me." Commander Rex had a painful, faraway look. "Right near the top I saw the silhouette of something big come over. It walked upright."

"We shouldn't have come here," Rubin's mouth hung as he gazed at the plastic. It vibrated, pelted by the rain.

"What color was it?"

"Its fur was brown, dark . . ." Abruptly, Commander Rex rose, heading, trance-like for the opening in the lean-to. "Excuse me," he gasped, and tried to get out of the crammed lean-to. His face met rain as he stood in the plastic opening.

Commander Charles flicked his flashlight on and could see fear in Rubin's eyes. "Gentlemen, we know that Sasquatch can't be real."

"Commander Rex said it was big, real big . . ." said Rubin, frightened, ". . . brown."

"Bears are brown too, you know?" Commander Charles shuffled after Commander Rex.

Rain pelted Commander Charles as he lifted his head through the plastic opening. Looking over his friend, he thought it odd that his coat was open. "Don't you want to stay dry?"

"I'm burning up."

"Are you okay?"

Commander Rex groaned, "Something is really hurting. I think it was the shrimp gumbo."

From inside the lean-to, Rubin reached out and pulled on Commander Charles' coat. "We saw the Sasquatch prints."

Bending into the lean-to, Commander Charles snapped his fingers and looked directly at Rubin, "It had to be a bear print." His flashlight glowed upon Lakalo, a big Hawaiian kid. "Lakalo, get the skit started."

"Okay." Lakalo gave his best buddy, Adam, the eye.

Adam, a big Hispanic boy, nodded.

Behind them Junior Commander Alan gleefully chattered, "Sasquatch like deer guts. Actually, they like any guts." He happily whacked Katz on the chest. "They're going to like your guts."

Katz looked troubled.

Outside the lean-to, the creature stood in darkness and watched Commander Rex move toward the trees.

Sweat bled off the big Commander's forehead and mixed with pouring rain. The block of a man leaned over, readied to vomit. With his hand clutched to his innards, he waited. The pain came strong and he heaved. Wind and rain swept over him. Burning up, he righted himself and opened his raincoat wider. Rain covered his face.

Moments passed. Commander Charles sadly watched him from the lean-to opening. He half listened to Lakalo and Adam finishing their skit before he ducked below the plastic, and bellowed, "GENTLEMEN, do you know what time it is?"

Spencer pressed back his glasses, then touched the button on his watch. It glowed. "It's exactly 9:05, Central time, Texarkana time."

"It's summertime," Daniel said, grinning robustly as he cast out his arm in a theatrical, showy manner. It hit Junior Commander Alan, who slapped it back.

"It's BEDTIME," advised the stern Commander. "And I don't think it wise, on this rainy, stormy night, to do any sleepwalking." His eyes were fixed on Katz, the sleepwalker. The Commander's attention turned to the many eyes beyond Katz. "If you have to go to the bathroom, wouldn't it be prudent to go before you enter your tents?" He shone his flashlight upward, under his chin, the glow illuminating his face then lowered his voice, "That way you won't be disturbing any night creatures."

"I'm going now," Rubin said.

Katz's words could be heard over the rain. "What do you think would happen if the Sasquatch got him?"

"They'd eat your ears first." Junior Commander said. "Ears are a Sasquatch favorite."

"That's bad. That's really bad."

Commander Charles waited for their nervous laughter to subside, then he bellowed, "YOUNG MEN?" He raised his index finger in the air. "What's our code regarding cleanliness?"

Several of the boys responded, "Clean mind, body, and speech."

"For those who don't brush their teeth, I want you to know that Sasquatch can't stand the smell of toothpaste. So, if you brush, you're safe." His grin held sarcasm.

"I'm bbbbbbbbrushing my tttttteeth," Israel said, fearing a Sasquatch.

"I'm brushing the heck out of mine," Katz agreed.

"I'm going to brush mine so good they're going to shine," Rubin said.

Junior Commander Alan teased, "Some say it will also keep the werewolf away."

Katz frowned. "Werewolf?"

"GENTLEMEN, it's time to head off to your tents."

Rubin pulled on Commander Charles's shirt, his voice cracking, "I'm scared."

Commander Charles watched Lakalo and Adam exit. "There's no need to be scared, Sasquatch only take men. That means Commander Rex and myself."

"What about Junior Commander Alan?"

"He's a young man, so they would take him, too." He grinned at Junior Commander Alan who hopped about like an excited goon.

Outside, Commander Rex struggled with the pain as he staggered toward the lean-to.

Commander Charles popped his head out of the lean-to and watched his approach. "Are you feeling any better?"

Holding his side, Commander Rex shook his head.

"I'm scared." Rubin edgily pulled on Commander Charles's sleeve.

"Rubin, there's no Sasquatch. That's only make-believe."

Israel yanked on Commander Charles's other sleeve. "I'm sssssscared, too."

"GENTLEMEN, there's no such thing as a Sasquatch." Commander Charles smacked his hands together. "Let's get going now."

Virgil, Spencer, Lakalo, Daniel, Adam, Joey, and Katz filed out, brushing by Commander Charles. Inside, Rubin and Israel stayed, too afraid to go outside,

While Commander Charles spoke to Commander Rex, Junior Commander Alan sent Israel a puckered brow. "Sasquatch are smelly."

Disturbed, Israel moaned.

"You want to know what they smell like, don't 'ya?" Junior Commander Alan put his face right into Israel's and nodded. "If they're eating garbage, then they smell like garbage."

Rubin swallowed and looked up at Commander Charles who was still talking to Commander Rex. Wanting to get his attention, Rubin again pulled on his coat. "Can't we all sleep in here tonight?"

Commander Charles keenly stared at him. "No, get to your tent."

The rain attacked Junior Commander Alan as he stepped out. Israel and Rubin wouldn't budge.

Commander Charles bent lower to assured Rubin, "There's nothing to be scared of. Commander Rex only told that story for entertainment." He could see that he wasn't getting through, so he poked his head out the plastic. "SPENCER! VIRGIL! GET OVER HERE!"

A few moments passed, then two pairs of boots slopped their way back to the lean-to. Spencer and Virgil stood at the doorway beside Commander Rex.

"Take your buddies to their respective tents and reassure them if they brush their teeth they'll be fine."

Israel pulled at Commander Charles's coat. "I sssssaw the ffffffffoot print."

"Yeah," Rubin added. "It was real."

"Rrrrrrreal bbbbbbig," Israel whined.

Taking on the rain, Commander Charles impatiently directed, "Let's get moving."

Hurting, Commander Rex leaned into the plastic.

Commander Charles addressed Commander Rex. "See all the trouble you caused with your silly Sasquatch stories." He flashed the light upward and could see anguish on Rex's large face. "Shouldn't you come inside?"

Rex gasped, "I don't know what this is but it sure feels like a hospital."

"Is it that bad?" Commander Charles saw Rex's eyes roll. "It'd be a good to hang in here, for . . ." He pulled up his sleeve and angled his watch toward the flashlight. ". . . say, twenty minutes. That way I can make sure these boys are settled in. Maybe by then that gumbo will . . ." Rain wet his lips. "I can't imagine going back to town tonight. That'd be some journey."

Commander Rex nodded, then huffed –another shot of pain hit him.

"If need be, we'll get you to town . . ." Commander Charles worriedly added, ". . . Give me a minute." He was quick to break away.

Wet ground splattered beneath his boots . "JUNIOR COMMANDER ALAN?" His flashlight worked until it captured the tallest figure. "We need to talk . . . " He closed on the Junior Commander. ". . . privately." Rain blanketed the two.

Ever goofy, Junior Commander Alan chuckled, "Did you notice that every kid was brushing his teeth?"

Commander Charles gathered his thoughts, readying to explain that Alan was soon to be in charge of the troop. "Commander Rex isn't . . ."

Junior Commander Alan smeared the rain across his grin, interrupting, "Rubin says he's going to brush his teeth at different times during the night." To quell a chill, he hunched his shoulders and hopped up and down, splattering soil beneath his boots. "In listening to the rug rats, I was starting to feel a little spooked."

"Are we done?"

Junior Commander Alan looked out into the dark, rainy night at the quivering trees, then eyed Commander Charles's wet face. "What's wrong?"

"Commander Rex isn't doing well. He's in a lot of pain. I might have to get him to a hospital. If I take him, that will leave you in charge. If we leave, I don't want you to tell anyone that we're gone; that will scare them even more." A sweep of wind blew rain across his face. "Most importantly, I want you to keep a watchful eye on the troop. Look after them."

Alan's fear rose. "What are you talking about?"

"If we have to leave, I should be back by morning."

Alan was stunned. "Are you saying I have to stay out here by myself the entire night?" He glanced past the Commander toward the dark silhouette of the forest.

"You'll do fine, Commander Alan." Commander Charles started to walk toward the tent where Israel was bent over, struggling to untie his laces. Virgil sat inside the tent, aiming a flashlight back at Israel's shoes.

"Goodnight, Israel . . . Goodnight, Virgil."

"Goodnight, Commander Charles," replied Virgil.

Israel's voice echoed, "CCCCCharles."

Commander Charles pointed at Virgil. "Look after Israel for me."

"I will," Virgil's Southern accent drawled.

Commander Charles's boots splashed through a puddle. They slid as he neared the next tent, where Rubin was untying his shoes. Spencer sat inside the tent, his flashlight bobbing about. The Commander patted Rubin's shoulder. "Goodnight, Rubin. Goodnight, Spencer."

With his toothbrush hanging from his lips, Rubin lifted his chin. "Can't we just all sleep together in the lean-to?"

Commander Charles paced toward the next tent. He could easily view their silhouettes from their flashlight reflecting off the tent walls.

Junior Commander Alan was following. "What if something goes wrong?"

"You'll do fine," Commander Charles reassured him then tapped the top of the tent. "Good night, Joey. Good night, Katz."

"Good night, Commander Charles," they replied in unison.

Commander Charles tapped the tent fabric again. "Joey, you make sure you're sleeping in front of the door. I don't want Katz doing any sleepwalking."

Inside the tent Joey called out, "Okay," and sent a serious eye to Katz.

Outside, Commander Charles asked, "Katz, did you take your medicine?"

Inside, Katz started to rumble through his belongings. "I'm going to."

Commander Charles's boots sloshed to the next tent. "Goodnight, Lakalo. Goodnight, Adam." He could see the silhouette of a licorice stick hanging out of Adam's mouth.

Lakalo quickly poked his head outside the tent. "Hey!"

Commander Charles spun in the mud and looked back.

"You're supposed to give us some candy."

"Let me think about it." Commander Charles pointed his index finger into his skull as if he were deep in thought. "Noooo."

Junior Commander Alan came up beside Commander Charles. "But what if something really bad happens?" He rocked back and forth, working himself into a higher state of anxiety.

"The only thing that could be construed as bad would be Lakalo and Adam running out of food." Even in the dark, Junior Commander Alan could see Commander Charles's grin.

"But what if . . ."

Commander Charles cut him off. "JUNIOR COMMANDER ALAN, in this country, we still have freedom. You know what comes with freedom?"

The Junior Commander shook his head.

"Responsibility." He lifted his finger in the air. "Now, I need you," he aimed his finger at him, "to be responsible for their welfare and their safety, and we won't re-visit this again."

Junior Commander Alan defended, "I'm only fifteen."

"YOU'LL DO FINE!" Commander Charles tapped on the last tent. Even with the pelting rain, he could hear Daniel's harmonica drifting through the tent's fibers. It was a mournful tune. "Goodnight, Daniel."

"Goodnight, Commander Charles."

They started to head back to the lean-to when Daniel popped his head out of the tent and yelled, "Hey Alan, when you coming?"

Alan glanced back at him but was so overwhelmed by his new command that he only shook his head.

Commander Charles walked back to the lean-to, the junior commander trailing.

Commander Rex hadn't moved from his position outside the plastic doorway. Though rain continued to hit his open raincoat, soaking his shirt, he took no notice; the pain in his midsection was too great.

Commander Charles came up behind him. "How is it?"

In agony, Commander Rex shook his head.

"It's no small endeavor to go down that trail." Commander Charles shone the light down at the wet earth. "It's way past slippery." Watching Commander Rex, a long moment passed.

Aching terribly, Rex bent over.

Feeling for his friend, Commander Charles patted his soaked coat. "Give me ten." His boots splattered across the mud, heading toward his tent.

Junior Commander Alan followed, his voice begging, "Don't go!"

At his tent, just inside the zippered opening, Commander Charles knelt on all fours and went through his pack. Rain water dripped onto his sleeping bag as he grabbed a water bottle and some energy bars.

Outside, Junior Commander Alan wouldn't give it up, "I don't want to be here by myself."

Rain covered Commander Charles back as he exited his tent, zipping it closed. "Do you want to offer up your flashlight for said journey?" In the distance, the sky was illuminated by another crack of lightning.

"My flashlight?" Fearful, the Junior Commander shook his head. "Are you crazy?"

"I don't know what you're so worried about . . ." Commander Charles gazed beyond the junior commander, toward the plastic lean-to while buttoning the last button on his raincoat. Above the plastic lean-to, the branches of dead tree swayed in the wind. The commander's eyes returned to Junior Commander Alan's. " . . . I'll be back by morning."

CHAPTER 2

T his was the second time on a plane for the thirteen-year-old Montanan. Excited, Stu walked down the aisle of the Boeing 757 and glanced at his ticket, seat 17E, then stared up at the row numbers. Finding 17, he viewed the window seat, the one he'd asked for. He scooted across to capture it.

With a grin, he lifted the armrest up, down, up, down, then pushed it into the upright position to give him more room. He stared out the window, viewing the tarmac and various colored lights of the LA Airport then rubbed his palm over the seat's fabric. At last, he bounced up and down like a kid about to take his first ride on a roller coaster.

Down the aisle came a man no one could miss, so large that his girth touched both sides of the aisle. Stu frowned when this man placed his luggage in the open bin above. Then the big fellow glanced at his ticket and sent a small grin at Stu, the type of grin that had one of those postscripts attached that read, "You get me."

Passengers couldn't help but watch this huge man angle around the seat to somehow sit in the helpless chair. It was a curious spectacle. He didn't sit down, nor did he flop down. It was a blend of squat-flopping, with the side of him pressed into the Montana kid like a wave flowing over the shore. Finally settled, the man leaned toward him and said, "Hello."

Squashed, with his arms pressed upward, Stu simply nodded, wishing he hadn't lifted the armrest.

"Where you headed?" The huge man asked.

"I'm going to Jamberama."

"What's Jamberama?"

"It's the best campout ever."

"What makes it the best?"

"It only happens once every four years and Scouts from all over the world go." Feeling mashed, Stu took a quick breath.

"Where is it?"

"It's in Missouri."

"Misery? . . That's a hot and sweaty place. What part of Misery?"

"I think it's in the south."

"That's even a hotter and sweatier place."

Stu tried to squeeze upward but couldn't.

"You flying into Kansas City?"

Stu shook his head. "My uncle's plane's in Houston."

"What type of plane?"

"I don't know." Again Stu tried to squeeze upward but couldn't. He looked like a canary stuck in glue. The canary finally cheeped, "It's my second time on a plane."

"I can tell you a thing or two about planes." The big man carefully glanced to the side to see if anyone was listening, then moved his large head back. "These things are a death trap. If anything goes wrong you're doomed." He peered down the aisle as if he were gazing into the future. "You think about it." His gaze returned to the canary. "Once they lock those doors, you're locked in. If things start going south you can bet them stewardesses won't be handing out parachutes."

Thumbing toward the exit door, he continued, "You get that many people trying to get out that small hole it's going to be dog eat dog."

The big man's words hit the wide-eyed Montanan like bullets.

"They give you these seats that float." The guy gave a monstrous frown. "Now you tell me, what good's a float out in the Nevada desert? And for that matter, the rest of this godforsaken land?" His eyes rolled. "A float? They must think we're going to use these seats to bounce or something." Distraught, he shrugged. "These are nothing more than flying cattle cars." He reached up and twisted the air knob then fanned his face. "You ever see the movie *Dumbo*?"

The pale kid managed a fraction of a nod.

"Well, Dumbo wasn't an airplane designer. But if he had been, he would've made them a whole lot bigger." He gave a deep clearing HURRUMPH, then saw a stewardess raise a mask, beginning to go over the plane's safety information. "This is the part where they tell 'ya . . ." His chin rolled back and forth. ". . . it's sad. It's sad, but I know a thing or two about planes." His gaze found the innocent bird. "And I'll tell you the first thing right now. If the stove pipe gets backed up on this baby, you scramble like a monkey over the top of the seats. Don't wait for anybody in the aisles; they'll be tangled up." He flicked his finger forward like one tosses a lure. "No, you scramble over the top of the seats after the closest stewardess." Then his finger trembled upward in the air as if he were on to something. "You can bet your bottom dollar she'll be the first one out. Them broads ain't going to be hanging around here for nobody. Them broads know better." He nodded assuredly. "I know a thing or two about planes."

***

With the beam of the flashlight fighting the dark storm, the senior commanders began their journey. In no time their boots were caked with mud. Twenty feet down the drenched path, Commander Rex slipped and went down.

Standing atop the muck, Commander Charles tried to help him up but he could feel his own boots sliding. With great struggle he got him standing.

Moments passed as Commander Rex tried to catch his breath.

"You should zip that coat up." Commander Charles' flashlight illuminated pouring rain.

In the distance, lightning peeled and snapped, arcing through the clouds like a neon whip lighting up the sky.

***

In the turbulent stormy night sky of South Texas the 757 began to jerk up and down. Rain shot through the two Pratt & Ashley engines. Stu tried to sit up, but the big man's weight was too pressing, so the canary slumped and watched water bleed across the darkened glass of the airliner.

Looking out the window, the extremely large man commented, "A bad night for flying." The plane gave another sudden jerk up, then down. "I wonder how many planes won't make it

With rising fear, Stu asked, "How often do planes go down?"

"You mean crash?"

The canary nodded.

"They say planes are safer than cars as far as accidents, but I don't buy that, I don't think they're telling us the full story." He squashed Stu even more when he leaned over to see flashes of lightning. "What are you thinking? That maybe the lightning is going to hit the plane and knock off a wing?" He rolled his fingers as if playing a piano. "And we all get sucked out and fall thousands of feet?" He leaned away but his girth remained. "Is that what you're thinking?"

Petrified, Stu's mouth hung open.

"Or were you worried that when we landed there would be so much water on the runway the wheels would snap off and we'd slide through, flip . . ." he twirled his hand, "and burn?"

On cue, the plane jerked up and down, then dropped as it hit another air pocket. Locked-in, the overheated Montana cowboy felt his stomach drop what seemed three hundred feet. He panted, wanting to puke, and his hand came up to his lips.

"No, son, they don't crash too often."

Stu swallowed, trying to hold his stomach down as the entire craft shook.

"But when these planes go down . . . everybody dies."

* * *

Inside his tent, Rubin switched off the flashlight and gazed toward the lightning. Even through the nylon, he could see it glow. Darkness held but a second, then with a flip from Rubin's thumb the flashlight again exposed the shifting, rain-pelted tent. Fearful, he swallowed and grabbed his toothpaste.

Beside him, Spencer lay atop his sleeping bag. "What do you think Jamberama's going to be like?"

With dread, Rubin moved toward the tent's entry. "I don't know. I just hope the Sasquatch don't eat me. My uncle says the Bigfoot is going to get me 'cause Sasquatch likes dark meat better than white." A resounding crash of thunder jolted him. "Ohhh!" His white eyes glowed. Fearful, he glanced around the dark. The tent shook from the wind. He began to unzip the tent.

Spencer flicked on his flashlight, put his glasses back on, and sat up to watch him. "I can't see how he'd know that unless he did scientific tests on it." He pondered. "One could use five Caucasians and five African Americans and set them out in the forest in different locations and see if a Sasquatch would like one more than another. But I don't believe there are Sasquatch, and I doubt there would be enough people to volunteer for such a silly test." He considered, "Your muscle mass is certainly the same red color as mine, we are the same color inside, so I find his statement unfounded. There's nothing scientific about that." He grew perplexed about why Rubin had unzipped the tent door. "What are you doing?"

The wind shook the tent door, and rain found its way in. "I'm going to put some . . ." Rubin unscrewed the cap on the toothpaste, leaned forward, and aimed it out the tent opening, then squeezed it into the mud.

"What are you doing?" Spencer aimed the flashlight at the white toothpaste atop the spattered ground. "That's perfectly good toothpaste."

Rubin zipped the tent door halfway up, then fingered a dab of toothpaste and ran it down a portion of zipper. "If the Sasquatch smells the toothpaste, he's going to know that we're good-smelling people, and he's going to go on to the next tent."

Spencer gave him the most exasperated look.

Rubin zipped the opening up and sat for a moment, intently listening to every sound. "I think something bad's going to happen." He pointed toward the tent's zipper. "The Sasquatch is out there." Giving Spencer a pleading look, he asked "Would you pray with me Spencer? Would you pray?"

Spencer had never understood prayer and felt uncomfortable about praying to something he couldn't touch, feel, or sense but he could see Rubin was scared. Finally, he said, "You shouldn't be scared because there's no such thing as a Sasquatch."

In the next tent Israel sat upright, motionless, his ears alert to every sound. Virgil, the best woodsman of the bunch, pleasantly lay inside his sleeping bag, staring at the top of the shifting tent. He enjoyed the sound of the rain hitting the fabric, it reminded him of hunting and fishing with his dad, when he lived in Kentucky. His eyes went to the terrified one, then to a drop that hit Israel's sleeping bag.

The wind was relentless, forcing itself upon the tent, and Israel tightened his coat around his shoulders. "If a Sasquatch cccame, wouldn't it first ttttake Rubin and Spencer 'cause they're in the first tttent?"

"Maybe so," Virgil's slow Southern accent drawled. "Unless . . ."

"Huhhhh?" Israel moaned frightfully, angling his contorted head.

"Unless, there was more than one."

"Yyyyyou think tttthere is?" He listened to the pelting rain.

"I don't know, but they might run in packs."

Israel's eyes widened as he contemplated the magnitude of *packs*. "That's ttttttterrible."

"You should turn off your flashlight. It's getting low."

Israel's bottom lip pressed forward as he moaned, "I wish I wwwould've stayed home."

"You got a knife?"

Israel nodded and wiped one eye with his crippled hand. His other eye held Virgil in its sight. He was reminded how, earlier in the day, Commander Charles had taken Virgil's knife because he didn't have his Knife and Axe card.

"Give it to me, and if a Sasquatch comes, I'll protect you."

Israel struggled to pull it out. His face contorted from the cerebral palsy. "Tttthat's good. Tttthat's good. Get it a buuunch." A drop of saliva fell from his mouth as he awkwardly handed the small pocketknife to the Southerner. Virgil took it, pleased to have the protection of a knife again.

In the farthest tent, the wind muffled the sound of Daniel's harmonica. Lying on his back, he blew into it while gazing at the vibrating tent. The light in the tent rose as a distant flash of lightning arced. He pulled the harmonica away from his lips and softly sang, *". . . a hundred miles."* The wavering harmonica enticed the rain and wind to play along, they shook the tent in a rolling orchestra. Quietly he sang, *"Lord I'm one, Lord I'm two, Lord I'm three, Lord I'm four, Lord I'm five hundred miles away from home . . ."* Again his harmonica picked up the tune. Its sound rang true, made him feel far-away and lonesome.

Neither wind, rain, nor lightning could quell the party going on in the next tent. Adam grinned and pointed the flashlight up from his chin, exposing his brown face, black eyes and hair as he listened to the end of Lakalo's joke.

". . . so the third guy wakes up 'cause he heard something and notices the other two guys are gone. Then he gets up and goes to the corner of the cave and sees this ghost on the toilet, and the ghost is picking his nose and pulls out this big booger." Lakalo chuckled, and barely composed himself. "And he looks at the booger and says, 'I got you where I want 'ya. Now I'm going to eat 'ya.'" He broke into a laugh and laughed so hard that his sides hurt.

Adam had heard the joke before. "I'm not going to laugh." To keep from laughing, he bit down on a piece of licorice, chomped, then pulled it out with gusto. "Mmmmm. Tastes good." The large kid pressed his lips forward to stop a chuckle. "I'm not going to laugh." He couldn't help but grin.

Finally gaining composure, Lakalo flashed the flashlight into his backpack to grab a licorice. "Say . . ." A worried frown encompassed his face. He rapidly searched the backpack – nothing but empty wrappers. "This is bad. This is very, very bad. There's no more candy," he said theatrically, turning toward his Mexican buddy. "And no Gummy Bears." They chuckled. "Booooh hooooo hoooo."

"Only thing badder was Commander Rex's Sasquatch story."

"'You know? I think he planted that footprint."

"You think?"

Lakalo nodded. "Remember how he stopped when we got near it?"

Adam listened to the rain hitting the tent. "He did stop; said we needed to rest."

"You ever hear the one with the three hunters?"

Adam grinned. "You just told me that." He rummaged though his backpack.

"There should be a law that if you run out of Gummy Bears you can immediately run down to 7-Eleven and get some more. That should be a law, no matter where you are."

"Maybe we could go ask Commander Charles if they'll let us go to town."

Lakalo chuckled at the ridiculousness of the statement. Then he became serious. "He'd let us go twenty miles through the rain if we brought him back a box of Krispy Kreme doughnuts."

"You think they're going to have any Krispy Kremes at Jamberama?"

"Jamberama is going to be so much fun, we won't need no Krispy Kremes."

"You really think Montana Stu or Johnny Revv will be there?"

"Commander Charles says so." Lakalo's index finger touched the rain-soaked nylon and immediately moistened. "I'm going to go right up to Montana Stu and tell him that we're cousins, 'cause I got a distant relative that's married to Johnny Cash and sings like a blue bird."

"I loved his movie. I've got every single pog they made."

Lakalo pulled his cap off his head and pointed to a Montana pin shaped in the outline of the state, with a mounted cowboy tearing across the landscape. "Same state Montana Stu is from. I got the Scout emblem, too." He pointed at the emblem. "It's a rare one. I got this on-line. It's got the . . . "

Adam interrupted, "Jamberama is going to be so much fun. I can't believe that tomorrow we'll be there!"

"You think there's any more food in that lean-to?"

"Maybe we should find out."

* * *

The hazy blue lights of Houston International beckoned the oncoming plane. Stu felt a heavy lump in his stomach as the plane shook, vibrated, and pitched. Hydraulics whined, pushing the wing flaps down. Streams of rain flowed across the small window. Peering out, Stu saw the plane's lights reflect off dark water, trees bending in the distance. It appeared the landing strip was coming up at him, fast. A thud—the plane's tires hit; wing flaps angled down and down, forcing themselves upon the storm as the jet engines reversed, thrusting powerfully.

Fearing the plane would flip, Stu closed his eyes, he felt his hair rising on the back of his neck.

* * *

Inside his tent, Joey cheerfully called, "Rummy!" He tossed a card down, then raked his hand out, taking the three pieces of candy he and Katz had bet on. "I like this game. Boy, just think what Jamberama's going to be like!"

"I want to get all the States' pins." Katz said.

Joey ripped the foil off a Hershey. "Spencer said Texas has got a pin that's worth a lot of money."

"Those Texans know it, too, and they'll be wanting three California's for one Texas."

"They're going to want a lot more than that. He was telling me they have this really rare Texas pin. It's black. He said it could be worth thousands."

"Yeah, well, no kid's going to trade you black Texas for a Southern California pin."

"Unless you run across a stupid kid," Joey said with a condescending air.

"No stupid kid is going to have a pin like that."

"Spence says they're going to let out fifty of them."

"I hope I get one."

The wind moved the tent back and forth while rain continued its assault.

"You got to know how to trade. That's the key. You don't just go up to another kid and say let's trade my state for your state. You got to tell that kid that you're not interested in his state unless he gives you two of his."

Katz frowned. "Why would he give up two for one?"

"Because he thinks yours is more valuable, you just have to, like . . . trick him." Another flash of lightning cracked, and Joey turned off the flashlight and gazed up to see if he could see it through the nylon ceiling. Outside, the sky brightened, then went dark.

Katz smirked. "How are you going to do that without cracking up?"

"You got to be serious! You know TJ?"

Katz nodded.

"He went to the last Jamberama four years ago. And he came back with a bunch of pins and one from Ohio that had a tiny little battery in it. It had a car on the front and the headlights glowed when you pushed the button."

"Whooee." Katz listened to the rain shaking the tent and the protective rain cover flapping about. He wished they had secured the cover better.

"They call it a Blinky. Anyway, he came back with all those pins plus seventy dollars in his pocket from selling pins."

"He's a good con man."

"That's not all. He told me he got a kiss from one of the girls who does the food service."

"Was she pretty?"

"I don't know, but he got a kiss."

"What was so special about him?"

Joey shook his head, then chuckled. "He's not afraid to ask anything, that's all. He wants to be a lawyer when he grows up."

"Sounds like he'll be a good one."

"He will, 'cause he'll take the shirt off your back. Anyway, look at this." Flicking the switch on his flashlight, he displayed a red pin on his hat. The pin was shaped like a heart with a gold leaf outline and a parrot in the middle. "He told me that this pin was extremely rare." He snorted. "Told me that it was a Hawaiian pin." His finger pointed to the orange parrot in the middle. "You see that? Isn't that a parrot something? And I never even heard of a Hawaiian pin. I don't even know if we have an outpost over there. So I traded him for my white Texas pin, and a white Texas is worth some big bucks." He frowned, disappointed. "I found out later that the pin wasn't from Hawaii at all."

"He got you, then."

"Yeah, but I still liked his story. It was kind of funny and the pin's not bad. But everybody wants a white Texas. Kids were selling them for twenty-five dollars. I knew this other kid who made eighty-five." He grinned, "You're going to like Jamberama; you get to trade all these pins."

"How do you know which one to trade?"

"It's simple. Like this year, 'cause of Montana Stu and Johnny Revv, Montana and Nevada are good ones. But you don't trade the ones you like for them, you trade the ones you don't like."

They heard a distant crack. Again, Joey flicked off the flashlight and looked in the direction of the lightning. Through the nylon, they could see the sky light up. "You wouldn't get a rainstorm like this in California, least not in the summer."

Katz turned his flashlight back on and lifted his hand to touch the rain sodden tent. A drop of water appeared on his finger. He dragged it across the nylon, making a large Z. "Look at that . . . *Zorro.*"

Joey glanced about the tent, noticing dampness on the seams. "Look at that." He pointed to a small puddle near the tent's zipper and examined the bottom seam. "Your sleeping bag's getting wet."

Katz pulled it away from the edge. "I'll just have to sleep with my socks on. Look . . ." He pointed to Joey's side of the tent. "Your sleeping bag is getting wet, too."

Joey snatched his bag away from the edge and stared at it in astonishment. "Stupid thing. We're going to be floating if this keeps up." Then he noticed another puddle near the back. "We should've put that rain cover on better. I can hear it flapping."

"It's too late now, I'm not going outside. Anyway, this side's good over here, and still, water's getting in." Katz pointed at the puddle. "Maybe we should cut a hole in there. That way the water can get out."

"That's a good idea. And cut a hole in the bottom over here, too. Otherwise, there's no way for that water to get out." Joey pulled out his pocketknife. "Here, flash the light over here."

Katz flashed the light on the puddle. Joey leaned over and carefully cut a slice in the gray poly bottom. "It's going out. You see that? It's going out."

"Cut one over on this side."

Joey shifted his position, aiming the blade toward the other side of the tent, then leaned toward the puddle by Katz's sleeping bag. He cut a one-inch cut through the poly floor.

"There." Closing the blade, he sat up, leaned back, and looked at the first hole he'd cut. A frown covered his face. There was more water than before. "It's getting back in."

"Maybe we need to cut the hole bigger."

* * *

Inside the lean-to, Junior Commander Alan sat transfixed, staring through the flapping plastic. Rain and wind shook it back and forth with violent jerks to the supporting branches. Earlier, when lightning lit the sky, he thought he'd seen a large form walking near the trees. Now he sat petrified, awaiting the beast's approach. In one hand trembled the camp axe; in the other trembled his pocketknife. The storm raged upon him, working him into a paralyzing, chilled frenzy. On his lap sat his flashlight, but he dared not use it, lest he be exposed. On and on, the wind and rain attacked, shaking the plastic in a wild, rhythmic battering. His pocketknife quivered so violently, it appeared the young Junior Commander was orchestrating the cruel heartbeat of the storm. Above him, the dead tree rocked back and forth, back and forth, as if suffering.

A small branch snapped, falling into the plastic. Alan jumped and looked wildly about.

With a crack, lightning streaked across the eastern sky. The teen jerked forward, his frantic imagination searching for the beast. Into his view came the dark silhouette of an approaching figure. In the ten fragments it takes to make a second, Alan felt his hairs standing, charged, then saw a blinding glow and heard an ear-splitting sound so loud it rivaled a cannon. The plastic exploded outward as the bolt of lightning blasted the dead tree, frying it to the core. As the light diminished, the panic-stricken teen glimpsed the dark outline of a body, the arms and upper chest silhouetted clearly against the tents. His vision blurred, then shattered branches crashed through the plastic.

Alan bolted. The axe fell as he tore to get out the ripped opening. Smoke followed, swirling around his churning legs. The plastic clung to him, dragging behind. "AAAHHHH." He fell and slid atop the wet plastic. The knife lay in his wake. Behind him the tree snapped, giving way.

"AAAHHHHH." Alan tried to rise. Around him branches hit the ground, one limb smashing across his arm. Down again he slid. Sheets of rain swept over him. Terror stricken, he madly scrambled up—something behind him was coming, coming, something huge. He ran toward the dark forest, straight into the bush. Scared out of his wits, he rushed through the thick brush, moving as if the devil drove.

Darkness, wind, and rain blanketed the sparks. The rain attacked Lakalo and Adam as they slowly approached the crumpled lean-to. Awestruck by the lightning strike, they silently stared at what was left of the dead tree.

Lakalo's hand came up to touch his pounding chest, his ears ringing. He gasped, "Oh man," but no sound came out.

"That was the biggest blowout ever." Adam's trembling finger pointed up. "That lightning came right over the top of my head." Rain hit his face. "I'm lucky I'm alive!"

"Why are we out here?"

"I don't know." Adam tried to collect his thoughts, but it seemed a century ago since he'd left his tent. Finally, he recalled, "I was hungry and wanted to see if there was any food in the lean-to."

They looked toward the tents of Commander Charles and Commander Rex.

"We'd better not tell them that."

"You think I should tell them that the lean-to got it?"

"No. Commander Charles wouldn't like it none to see us running around."

"It's cold out here." A gust of wind and rain blew through his statement. "What's that?" Adam stared toward the dark silhouette of the trees.

"You see something?"

"I thought I did."

"I'm going back."

* * *

Commander Charles struggled to steady Commander Rex. The flashlight shook back and forth as he tried to get a better grip on Rex's slippery raincoat. It was covered with mud from all the falls they'd taken, and he leaned into him for support. Just to walk upright was a terrible struggle, and both were sore from hitting the ground so often. Commander Charles felt like he could never get his footing. His boots were so caked with mud that every time he took a step, they would slip. Sometimes they would slip a little, sometimes a lot, but they always slipped. This slow and cumbersome task was made more difficult by the slightly downhill angle of the narrow path.

Finally, Commander Charles got a better grip on the side of Commander Rex's raincoat. His muddied knuckles pressed into it, and for a second he thought he wouldn't fall. But on the next step, his lead foot slid over the path's edge. Down they went. In pain, Rex lay there, then rolled in the mud to get up. The mud-covered flashlight weakly illuminated the rain which pelted his face. Charles grabbed Rex's arm, and pulled. "HERE we go again!"

Soaked and mud-caked, Commander Rex winced as a sharp spike of pain hit him in the lower back. Trembling, he weakly fought the pain, mechanically sliding his boots under him to rise.

Though his back ached, Commander Charles struggled to tug him forward. Their journey was so tiring and slow that he wondered if they would ever make the van. A faint light glowed through the muddied plastic lens of his flashlight. He stopped for a moment and moved it about but couldn't make out the path. He was so focused on the step-by-step journey, he didn't spot their van twenty feet beyond until he was upon it.

* * *

Leaning over his sleeping bag, Joey attempted to push water out of the hole they'd cut in the gray poly. His flashlight illuminated the bottom of the tent where water pooled.

Katz sat upright and gazed down on Joey's doings. "It's not going to work. We just got to sleep sitting straight up." He glanced around the tiny, two-man tent. "That's all we can do. Otherwise we're going to get wet . . . really wet."

"We should've never cut this hole in the tent."

"What are you saying *we*? I didn't do it. You did."

"You said so." Joey noticed the flashlight dim. "This is running low on batteries." A gust of wind and rain pelted the tent, shaking it.

Katz frowned and stared into the flashlight. "That shouldn't be going out. It's an Eveready. That's not right. It should stay on all night. Give it to me."

Joey handed over the flashlight. Tired and frustrated, Katz shook it. It brightened, then again dimmed.

"Maybe we should cut a slice from there"—Joey pointed at the first cut— "to there." His finger drew a line across the bottom of the tent to the last hole they'd cut.

* * *

Neither wind, rain, nor beast could keep Virgil awake. He was out. Next to him, Israel sat straight up, wide-eyed, and back in possession of his knife. Wind and rain assaulted the tent. Tilting his head toward the tent's fabric, he listened. The sound of rain, bouncing off the tent was unceasing. *Where was the beast?* He moved slightly, listening for any sounds or movements from outside the tent. *Was that the creature?* Distant lightning lit the skies, and the glow in the tent exposed Israel's worried countenance. Thunder rumbled then cracked.

The kid with cerebral palsy kept his vigil, straining to hear sloshing footsteps or the high-pitched cry of a Sasquatch. When Virgil gave an odd snore, Israel madly waved his awkward hand. But he might as well have tried to raise the dead—Virgil was out.

CHAPTER 3

Inside Houston's airport terminal, Aunt Valerie was so excited about the arrival of her famous nephew that if she had a tail she'd be wagging it. A round pudgy thing, she jerked a large Montana Stu sign up and down, not subtle in the least about being Montana Stu's aunt. Beside her stood her shy, six-foot, five-inch husband, who every so often leaned down and quietly said, "You should put that sign away."

"Oh nonsense," she replied, casting a possessive eye over a large group of teens and youngsters that had gathered.

A boy from the group asked, "Is Montana Stu really coming?"

Aunt Valerie proudly nodded. "Oh, yes. Montana Stu is my nephew, and he's going to visit me." Pert, she minced on her heels, taking in the crumbs of glory, then looked beyond the group toward the exiting tunnel where passengers were filing out.

Her husband once again glumly suggested, "You should put that sign away."

One boy hopped up and down, trying to see the star. Just then a teenager poked him on the back, saying, "I was waiting before you." He thumbed backward. "Get behind."

The boy wouldn't budge, he kept his eyes glued on the exit where passengers were filing out.

Ghostly white, Stu staggered through the doorway, his stomach still hadn't landed. The intensity of the landing had stolen his equilibrium; angling sideways, he put his hand on the wall in hopes of regaining his balance. His uncle frowned because Stu looked like he'd just gotten off a ship that had been through a hurricane.

In front of him, there came a huge shout: "Montana Stu!" And a wave of fans stormed past Aunt Valerie to get at him. They surrounded him and rammed their pens near his face, begging, "Can I get your autograph? Can I get your autograph?"

Aunt Valerie had never seen the like. They were relentless. "Stuee?" she said in a very lady-like manner. "Stuee?" She took two steps toward him, but the crowd was too aggressive.

Her tall husband leaned over and said, "You should've never made that sign up."

She glanced at him, her determination brewing hotter and hotter as she rolled the cardboard up in her hand. Then she smacked the cardboard across her palm. He knew what was coming and stepped away from her.

"Stuuuuuuuuuuu-eeeeeeeeeeeeeeeee!" she cried, then charged toward the boy, slapping the cardboard atop the head of anybody who was in her way. Thunk! Thunk! Thunk! When she reached the overwhelmed cowboy, she enveloped him, pulling him in with one arm, then turned on the crowd, smacking any and all who came near.

The closest were taken aback at her action, but aggressive ones from behind pushed toward her. She charged right through them, pulling Stu along, smacking them on the arms and ears and whatever she could hit. An airport Security man appeared and they scattered.

Safe from the predators, she turned toward Stu, who, still ghostly white, stood wavering without his land legs. "Stuee."

She took his face between her palms and planted a big wet one on his cheek. "I missed you terribly."

He displayed no emotion; the agonizing scare from the plane still gripped him, his stomach still hadn't landed.

His tall uncle patted him as if he were a bird dog that had just brought in four ducks. "How you doing, Stu? You have a good flight?"

Stu slowly shook his head. "Is there a bathroom?"

Uncle Hawthorne didn't hear him.

Aunt Valerie was warding off another pen-pushing autograph seeker. She swung her cardboard. "You . . . you . . . get."

Uncle Hawthorne had been looking forward to taking Stu up in his plane. "Stu, I'll tell you what, you talk about fun. Buddy, you haven't had any fun till you've gone up in my plane."

Stu's nerves were so spent he couldn't lift his eyes toward his uncle.

"Stuee . . . dearee, you look a little pale," Aunt Valerie said, looking his face over with concern. "Are you okay?"

Stu put his hand over his lips to try to stop his stomach from coming up.

CHAPTER 4

T he lights of the hospital were a welcoming sight to Commander Charles. He steered toward the red glow of Emergency. "We made it, Rex. Thank God, we made it!"

He glanced at his mud-covered friend. Rex was rocking back and forth in pain. The van came to a stop outside Emergency. Charles didn't waste time. He headed around the front of the van to open the passenger door.

Commander Rex struggled out. Supported by his friend, he staggered toward the Emergency doorway.

In her time, the nurse behind the check-in desk had seen just about everything, from bloodied foreheads to mangled legs, but these two mud-covered beings gave her an immediate fright. Perhaps it was the way Commander Rex held his free hand. The end of the finger was so covered with mud and protruded from the cuff in such a way that it looked as if it were the end of a pistol. Believing this, she slid her chair back. Every step, the two muddied beings took toward her she slid farther back, until she hit the wall. With her eyes fixed on the imagined gun, she said nervously, "We . . . don't have any money in Emergency."

* * *

Though Spencer was fast asleep, Rubin was wide awake. Carefully listening, he leaned toward the zipper. The patter of rain met his ears. He jerked, *Was that a high-pitched scream way in the distance?* Lightning shot over the storm, thunder rumbled, vibrating the sky.

"You hear that?" Rubin hand trembled as he shook Spencer.

Spencer opened one eye. It closed.

He shook Spencer again. "You hear that?"

Spencer's eyes flashed open, his head clumsily rose.

"Wake up, Spencer."

Spencer's eyes closed, and he fell back.

Rubin shook him again. "They're coming!"

Spencer moaned, "Who's coming?"

Panicked, Rubin bent over and whispered, "The Sasquatch."

"Stop bugging me."

"I'm scared."

Spencer fell back to sleep.

* * *

An owl dug its talons into an oak branch and tilted its head away from the rain. Movement came from below as a terror-stricken teen ran by. The owl's "Awoooooo," followed Junior Commander Alan as he passed. He jerked his terrified mind toward the noise, then tore on aimlessly, his boots splattering the wet and his outstretched arm dropping to run faster. Wind and rain rushed through an opening, forced themselves upon him. Glancing back, Alan didn't see the tree ahead. A branch snapped as he ran headlong into it. His palm rose over his bruised forehead and he staggered on into the dark, spilling his energy out like the storm.

* * *

At the trailhead, Commander Charles braked the van to a stop. He sat for a moment, tiredly watching the sprinkle of rain on the windshield and tried to psych himself up for the return hike. Letting out a long tired breath, he checked his watch—4:37 a.m. He wasn't a morning person but his body went through the motions. As he grabbed his gear, he thought of Commander Rex who he'd left at the hospital. Not knowing what was wrong with him, he prayed he'd get better.

Charles took his flashlight and quietly stepped out the van. Outside, the sprinkle helped to enliven him. He pushed the door shut and looked up at the sky. The half-moon was covered in a misty haze but the glow of stars above the clearing clouds made him think the storm was breaking. Turning on the flashlight, he started down the slippery path.

Just into the trailhead he bent over and picked up a long branch, intending to use if for a walking stick. He broke off its smaller branches, pounded it a few times in the mud then leaned into it. He continued his journey, ramming the stick in on the downside of the path to keep from sliding. The stick worked well and he wondered why they hadn't thought to use them in the first place.

At the rate Commander Charles was moving, the three-and-a-half-mile trek would have been completed before sunrise but his flashlight dimmed. He stopped, shook it, desperate to get it to work, and ran his finger over the glass.

Out it went. It was terribly dark. The slight glow of the half-moon had been taken prisoner by clouds. It would be slow going from now on; his heart sank as he looked about for the path.

He made out the dark silhouette of the trees and the night sky beyond. His stick sliced into the mud, his boots trudged forward and he slid but didn't go down. Bracing his boots, he pulled out the stick and stuck it into the mud ahead, then took a slow cautious step next to it, recalling all the times he'd fallen with Commander Rex.

A bit into this cumbersome journey, he thought he heard something and glanced toward the trees. It was so dark, he couldn't make it out. A foreboding sense came over him. In the back of his mind was Commander Rex's unfinished Sasquatch story. He had seen something moving, something dark and much bigger than a man, and it stayed near the trees.

For a long moment, he peered into the dark, trying to see beyond a tree.

"Awoooooo."

He jerked when he heard the owl.

CHAPTER 5

S un light moved over the top of the forest, exposing the seven two-man tents that sat above the trail. Farther up, the dead tree, or what was left of the main trunk, still stood, jagging upward. Its branches were scattered across the crushed plastic lean-to. A whisky jack hopped about the plastic looking for food, then a crow swept down, landed, stuck his chest out and strolled toward the whisky jack.

Down the slope, Israel moved in his awkward manner, his body angled, hunched sideways, half dragging one leg, heading up the rise to look over the fallen lean-to. The whisky jack noticed his approach and flew five feet, landing on the damp ground. The crow flew up into what was left of the dead tree, his black eye studied the young man with cerebral palsy.

Israel stared at the plastic lean-to, then looked toward the Commanders' tents. "Commander CCCharles?" he pointed down. "Thiiiisssss"—He glanced back at the lean-to—"Got itttt." His awkward hand drew near his chest as he moved toward the Commanders' tents. "Commander CCCharles?"

The morning sun reflected off Daniel's wavy red hair as he rose from the creek, his toothbrush in hand. He glanced up at Commander Charles's tent, half expecting movement. The only movement came from Joey and Israel. The whisky jack and crow flew off, and a mouse ran out of the bottom of the lean-to.

"Hey everybody! . . .The tree fell over." Rubbing his tired face, Joey gazed over the shattered tree that was strewn across their campground.

One by one, the other boys piled out of their tents and meandered over to peer at the remains of the lean-to.

Deep in thought, Spencer adjusted his glasses, walked to Commander Charles's tent and rustled the fabric. "Commander Charles, the storm knocked down the dead tree and a mouse has got into the bread." Again he rustled the tent, then rubbed his arms. It was a cool morning. Everything was damp, washed clean by the storm.

Lakalo closed on the tent with Katz chattering at his heels, reliving his night's fears.

Lakalo wasn't listening. He shot an inquisitive glance at Spencer. "What did Commander Charles say?"

Spencer shook his head, "I don't think Commander Charles is awake yet."

Adam, Joey, and Israel pressed against the tent.

Adam sang, *"Commander Charles. Commander Charles? Here we wait like birds in the wilderness, birds in the wilderness . . ."*

The others joined the singing. *"Here we sit like birds in the wilderness, waiting on Commander Charles."* Higher voices picked up the chorus. *"Waiting on Commander Charles, waiting on Commander Charles. Here we sit like birds in the wilderness waiting on Commander Charles."*

Daniel came up from the creek, pulled out his harmonica, but the song ended. Drawing near, he gave Katz a good morning flick of the ear.

Katz swung a tired hand his way but was too weary to give chase. "Cut it out, Daniel."

Big Lakalo asked, "Did you guys hear that huge thunder last night?"

"How could we not hear it?"

"Rubin said he heard a scream, but I think he was imagining things. How could he hear anything over the rain and wind? Everything was blowing so hard."

"And the huge thunder."

Lakalo looked about. "Where's Rubin?"

"He didn't get any sleep at all, now he's out."

"I didn't sleep much 'cause the tent was so wet." Katz said. "We had to sleep straight-up." He tiredly rubbed his palm across his face.

Behind them, Adam reached over and rocked Junior Commander Alan's tent. "Junior Commander Alan? Get up, Junior Commander Alan."

"He's not in there," Daniel said, wiping his harmonica on his shirt.

"Where is he?"

"I don't know. He wasn't there when I woke up, and he wasn't there when I fell asleep," Daniel said, glancing toward the lean-to. "Last I saw him was in the lean-to."

"Maybe he went to the bathroom."

"Maybe he's at the creek, brushing his teeth."

"I didn't see anybody down there," Daniel said.

Katz faced Daniel. "How long have you been up?"

"I got up to go to the bathroom."

"Commander Charles, are you in there?" Lakalo grabbed the side of Commander Charles's tent and shook it. It was so lightweight it perplexed him. "It doesn't feel like anybody's here, either."

A worried look spread over Israel's face. "Hhhhhe's not therrrrre?"

Spencer unzipped the tent and peered in. Others poked their heads in.

"Uh-oh."

"This is really different," Lakalo said, surprised at the empty tent.

In unison the group moved to Commander Rex's tent, encircling it.

"Commander Rex, are you in there?" Katz's voice had a ring of panic. "Are you in there?" They shook his tent, and several eyes widened. They knew from its lightness that it was empty. Spencer unzipped it, and everybody closed in to look.

"Uh-oh."

"This is really, really different," Lakalo said, feeling edgy.

"Maybe they all went to brush their teeth."

"Commander Charles wouldn't do that. He always leaves someone in charge," Spencer said, matter-of-factly.

Lakalo yelled, "Commander Rex! Commander Charles!"

Katz started to say, "I just wish I would've . . . "

But Israel interrupted, "Shhhh."

They listened.

Katz's hand started to tremble. "The Sasquatch only take the older ones. That's why they're gone."

"Shhhh."

"Shut up," Joey demanded.

"Shhhh," Israel said, more emphatic than ever.

Spencer addressed Joey. "Don't say shut-up."

"I'll say shut up if I want to. Who put you in charge?"

"I've got my First-Class rating. That puts me above everybody else here." Spencer looked about.

Joey sneered at Spencer. "Well, who's to say everybody's gone. They might be right around the corner."

"What's that?" Katz pointed to a long smeared footprint in the mud. Beyond it was another. "I bet they could only take three at a time, and as soon as they lock them in their cave, they'll be back for us."

"Commander Rex!" yelled Daniel. "Commander Charles!"

"Don't yell. A Sasquatch can hear it. They'll come," Katz said with panic.

Upon hearing this, Rubin poked his head out of his tent. He tiredly stared at Katz.

Katz angled his thumb toward the empty tents. "The Commanders are gone."

"Gone?" Rubin's white eyes flashed as the nightmare he'd had the night before jarred him awake.

Spencer adjusted his glasses then countered, "There's no such thing as a Sasquatch."

Everybody gave him a wary glance, then all eyes turned to the three vacant tents. Their emptiness shouted at them.

"There has to be a logical explanation to this."

"Commander Rex! Commander Charles!" yelled Daniel again.

Fearful, Israel pushed him. "Stttttttop!" he whispered. "You're ttttttelling them Sasquatch . . . wwwwwe're here."

"They already know we're here," Katz said. "They took the Commanders, and they're coming back to get us."

Rubin approached, his voice came like an ill omen. "They get the mens in the nighttime, and the boys in the day."

"I bet they make you dance around the fire, then poke you in the rear with a pitch fork before they put you in the pot."

"We're all gonna die," Rubin said, wide-eyed, tossing the comment in as one would toss a dead chicken into a pot of gumbo.

Virgil came out of the forest and approached the group.

"Virgil, what are you doing running around the forest? There's Sasquatch here."

"I've looked around," Virgil frowned, "the Commander's are gone."

"Last night, I heard the Sasquatch scream their high-pitched cry. I heard them!" Rubin pointed east, casting a fearful eye past the creek.

"Are you sure that wasn't the wind whistling through the trees?" Spencer asked.

All eyes looked east to where he pointed. Suddenly a flock of crows burst out of that area. They flew right at them.

"Something's coming!"

"Oh, my gosh! Oh, my gosh!" Rubin took two steps backward and bumped into Katz. Their fear was contagious.

The rest retreated, their eyes glued in the direction the birds had escaped.

Lakalo glimpsed something in the distance. It was moving around the trail they'd come in on. His head pressed forward as he tried to make it out. But there was too much bush. The brown thing appeared again, moving along the path. He pointed. "Look at that!"

"It's a Sasquatch!"

Hearts pounded at the ominous sight. Even Spencer, the logical, scientific one, was taken aback by the brown being that appeared to walk upright like a man. It disappeared behind a clump of red bud bushes and hardwoods. Spencer's lips mechanically mumbled, "Couldn't . . ." He adjusted his glasses.

"What's it going to do?"

"It's going to eat us!"

"Ohhhhh!" moaned Israel, frantic, looking about for something, for anything, then up at Virgil.

"Let's go!" Virgil grabbed hold of Israel and shoved him forward. "We got to run for it! Com'on! Go! Go!"

Scrambling up the bank, the troop passed the crushed lean-to, gained firmer ground where pine needles lay, and tore toward the shadowy timber.

Near the rear of the pack hustled Adam, red-faced, so panicked that he might end up last and be the first captured by the beast that when he sloshed through a wet patch, he slipped and went down. Hot on his heels, Lakalo fell on top of him. Up the two big boys clambered.

Forty yards ahead, Virgil came to a small knoll. The rising sun brightened the hardwoods beyond the knoll, revealing the vastness of the forest that went on and on as far as the eye could see. Breathing hard, he stopped and looked back. Rubin and Israel ran straight at him. Virgil sidestepped them, still looking for the last of the troop. At last, he spotted Lakalo and Adam.

"What are we waiting for," gasped Rubin.

"It's gooooing to getttt us," moaned Israel.

Down the knoll, Virgil led, heading west through the bushes into the shadowy forest.

Holding his aching side, Adam finally attained the knoll and gazed downward at the disappearing troop. His chest heaved. Certain he would die if he took another step, he bent over and panted.

Knowing he was dead last, Adam shot a searching, fearful eye at the lurking timber behind.

The morning rays filtered through pines, exposing dripping branches, enhancing the cool freshness. All seemed calm. Then, from where they had started, a squirrel gave a shrill shriek, alarming the forest of an intruder. This scared Adam onward. Down the knoll he trotted.

* * *

Junior Commander Alan ran his trembling hand over the gash in his forehead, then clasped his arms to his stomach to stop his shaking. But he couldn't stop shaking. Exhausted, he blankly stared, taking in the endless trees.

His voice was weak, "Commander Charles?"

The morning forest was damp and cold. Dark shadows hung on the outside edge of the pines where the early rays hadn't penetrated. "Commander Charles?" Dizzy and dehydrated, he shivered, and gazed at a maple tree—the tree seemed to be moving.

* * *

The mud-covered brown being slogged into the camp and studied the open tents. Wiping his hand across his muddied cheek, he called out, "BOYS?" Commander Charles found Junior Commander Alan's tent and gazed in, then glanced quickly back at the creek. "IF THIS IS A JOKE, LET'S END IT NOW!"

His tired eyes drifted to Commander Rex's tent. "I don't appreciate anyone getting into our tents."

He gave a heavy-eyed search about the vacant area. The creek was much higher than yesterday. Leaves on the trees still dripped from the aftermath of the storm. Strange that all the boys' tents were unzipped, and the dead tree lay about in scattered pieces. He started toward the bushes, anticipating some sign of life, then stopped, half-expecting the troop to leap out of the bushes and yell **Surprise**. He resignedly said, "It's not going to work. I'm too tired for this. I'm far too tired."

Exhausted, he flopped down on the wet soil outside his tent. It didn't matter to this extremely proper, generally clean man that his mud-covered pants would get further gooked. Knowing the root cause of hyperthermia, he was determined to get into dry clothes. He began by trying to find his shoelaces amongst the mud caked boots. Finally, he dug enough mud away to expose a mucky lace. His right leg began cramping from the cold. He took on the harsh pain and laid back to press it out. A skinnier man would have been shivering to the core.

Sitting up, he yelled, "JUNIOR COMMANDER ALAN!" His fingers unzipped his muck-covered coat. Off it came. There wasn't one part of his outer coat that wasn't smeared. Even beneath his shirt, the bottom of his former white T-shirt was amber in color, stained from the earth. He was growing weaker with each piece of clothing he took off.

Perplexed at his troop's disappearance, he stood up and swayed, off-balanced, then shouted again, "JUNIOR COMMANDER ALAN!" Once again his searching eyes glanced about the vacant camp.

Fifteen minutes had elapsed since he began taking off his soaked clothing. He ended by stepping into the tent and zipping it up to change his personals. Not having slept in twenty-six hours, his puffy eyes blinked and his legs throbbed. They ached as if they'd pushed a wheelbarrow through mud and rain for a hundred miles. There was an abrupt cramp, this time in his left leg, and he lay back on his sleeping bag, jerking, trying to press it out.

The morning sun was now on the rise, evaporating the moisture on the outside of the tent. Inside this cocoon, the warmth eased his cramped leg, and melted into the exhausted one. Its heat captured him, pulling down his heavy eyelids. He rolled sideways atop the sleeping bag. Sleep overcame him.

* * *

"Hold up Virgil." Spencer hurried toward him.

Virgil turned and stopped. Other boys pulled up behind, panting, bending over to catch their breath. No one could see Lakalo or Adam.

"We're getting too far ahead," Spencer gasped, bent over, feeling his lungs burn. "We got to wait for Lakalo and Adam."

"We got to keep going." Rubin's eyes widened. "It's going to get us."

"No, we're a troop . . ." Spencer admonished, ". . . and we have to stay together."

"What if Lakalo and Adam got lost?"

Rubin threw up his palms in frustration. "That's their problem. They should've kept up."

"No, we have to wait for them." Spencer stood upright, shaking his head.

"We can't go back," Rubin said, fearfully.

"We got to stay together. That's what troops do."

"He's right," Virgil said, nodding. "Let's wait a minute."

"Then I'll go back." Spencer was determined.

"Good," Rubin said, too afraid to go anywhere but forward. "You go back. But we shouldn't yell, that'd be no good, Sasquatch would know where we are." He ran his hand across his damp forehead.

Katz approached, adding, "You shouldn't yell at all." He eyed Rubin. "Did you see that Sasquatch? He was huge."

Rubin gasped, "Promise you won't yell, Spencer."

Spencer adjusted his glasses and stepped toward Virgil, giving him an instructive nod. "You look after them."

Virgil returned his nod.

Sweat beaded off Spencer's brow as he went over a small rise, returning the way they'd come. Farther on, he stopped and looked back. No longer able to see the six, he suddenly felt vulnerable, alone in the woods. A nervous hand pulled out his compass. Turning it toward north, he noted his return route of ninety-eight degrees. But it was little relief for the twelve-year-old. He was out of eyesight of everyone and in a thick forest that looked somewhat the same whatever direction he turned.

He continued over a small knoll, then went down where the bush became thicker and the trees more numerous. No tall mountains or hills were visible to use as landmarks. He walked farther, wondering if the two had taken off in a completely different direction and grew frustrated that they hadn't kept up. *Was one of them hurt?*

Up a slight rise he went, down the other side, then up again. Finally, he looked back at the spot he thought he'd come from. His head turned and sun's rays came through the hardwoods just so, and for a second, he wasn't sure if that was the spot at all.

Panic-struck, he spun quickly, glancing at another group of trees. They looked the same. He spun again, and his alarm grew as the forest closed in on him. He spun and felt dizzy, sinking, lost . . . totally lost. Sweat streamed down his forehead. His fingers raced into his pocket in search of the compass. He lifted it, adjusted his glasses, and his hand trembled as he waited for north to settle. It seemed to take forever. He wanted to yell but he'd promised not to. Quickly studying the compass, he glanced back at ninety-eight degrees to where he thought he'd come from but wasn't sure if that was correct. Yet he knew he had to trust it. He stood for a moment to settle down, then took long breaths and slowly looked about. A feeling of heaviness came over him. Half a minute passed. *Would he get more lost if he kept searching?*

It frustrated him that he was too afraid to keep searching and he determined if they ever got back together, they should have rules. He took two steps toward ninety-eight degrees and his eyes widened with joy when he saw Daniel appear, seemingly out of nowhere, standing atop a small rise. Spencer grinned and waved, feeling like he'd been saved from a prison cell. Daniel returned the wave, and Spencer covered the forty or so yards back to him.

"Was I ever glad to see you!" Spencer beamed. "I thought I was lost."

"It's bad out here, the way the land rolls." Daniel gave him a friendly punch. "You can get lost real easy."

Spencer glanced back from where he'd come. "We have to find Lakalo and Adam."

"We'll find them." Daniel looked beyond Spencer. "Rubin and Katz aren't going back for nothing. They're too scared."

Spencer quietly advised, "We have to keep one of us always in sight of the other. You see that high spot over there?" He pointed.

"Yes."

Spencer glanced again at his compass then pointed. "If you come up to that spot with me, then I'll go ahead. That way I can keep going without getting lost."

They set off together. Fifty yards farther, Daniel positioned himself on a ridge and Spencer took off from there.

He hadn't gone far when his eyes lit up—there were Lakalo and Adam.

The good-sized, dark skinned boys looked like brothers, sitting at the base of an oak tree.

Spencer was pale-faced when he marched down the knoll toward them.

Seeing him coming, Lakalo appeared very apprehensive, thumbed behind him and whispered, "It's around."

Spencer gave him a perturbed nod and quietly said, "What are you guys doing just sitting? Everybody's waiting for you."

"We couldn't keep up," Adam softly said, pulling his sweaty shirt away from his chest.

Lakalo urgently thumbed back. "Quiet, it's around."

"We weren't going to yell." Adam abruptly scratched a chigger bite.

"We shouldn't talk," Lakalo whispered. "It's terrible." He ran his hand down his sweaty arm and glanced back from where they'd come. "That creature's around."

From behind, some thirty yards back, a twig snapped. This sent a chill down their spines. Spencer bent lower and motioned for them to follow. With the image of the brown beast fresh in their minds they quietly rose and followed Spencer, crouching low, careful to step over any branches.

So intent were they on their escape, they didn't notice the doe and fawn that slowly browsed up the hill.

CHAPTER 6

Stu dragged his feet into Aunt Valerie's kitchen and headed toward the breakfast table. There was nothing modern about the kitchen; even the refrigerator was over forty years old. The appliances owed their existence to Uncle Hawthorne. He was a tinkerer, and she was a cook.

From the tiled counter, Aunt Valerie watched Stu rub his tired face. Tickled to have him, she expectantly awaited his reaction to her table. It was decorated with a bowl of fresh strawberries, whipping cream, a glass of orange juice, bacon, and waffles from which heat was rising. Behind this, two delicate yellow roses displayed themselves in a purple vase.

Stu closed his eyes and sniffed. The bacon smelled heavenly.

She grinned, then chirped, "Good morning, Stuee."

He tiredly glanced over. "Good morning . . . Aunt Valerie."

She lifted a brown egg. "How do you want your eggs?"

"Over medium."

"Did you have a good sleep?"

"All I could dream about were problems with a plane. I woke up a lot because it was going to crash."

"Probably from the scare you took on the plane last night. That's how it works with dreams sometimes." An egg cracked and sizzled as it hit the hot bacon grease.

"That dream was so spooky that it made me jerk."

"That sounds more like a nightmare than a dream." She examined the whitening edge of the eggs as they cooked. "Sit down, Stuee. Sit down."

He again sniffed the bacon then sat at the table. Looking over the fresh strawberries nicely cut up in a green bowl, whipping cream, the flower beyond, his sprits began to rise.

"Today, Stuee, I'm going to have a little get-together with my friends here at the house, a little tea social. I bet you couldn't guess who the main attraction is?"

Stu shook his head. "Barbie?"

She smiled, dishing an egg out of the frying pan, onto a plate. "It's you, honey. It's Montana Stu."

"Me?" He looked at her mournfully. "Couldn't you pick someone more exciting?"

"There's no one more exciting than you, Stuee, and I'm very happy you're here. And all my girlfriends are excited, too."

He picked up a piece of bacon. "Are there any guys coming?"

"Oh, heavens no, dear. This is for women only. This is a tea. Teas must be proper. Teas must be formal." She raised her head proudly, and pressed her chin out in a noble manner as she walked the plate of eggs his way.

"Why do you want me, then?"

She gave him an overly pious look. "Because, you are the main attraction. And the main attraction can be who he is." She set the plate in front of him. "In fact, I've picked out some clothes for you,"

"Clothes?"

"Yes. I've purchased some clothes that I want you to wear."

"I thought you said I can be what I am?"

"Yes, but you must make your Aunt Valerie happy just this once." She placed her hand on his head. "You're going to like this outfit. You wouldn't believe where I found it."

He lifted a doubtful eyebrow, not knowing how to deal with her theatrical ways.

"I found it at the Sally Ann."

CHAPTER 7

The Scouts were gathered at the place where Spencer had left them.

Spencer quietly began, "We're a troop, and we have to have rules."

Lakalo couldn't hear him so he waved and quietly said, "Com'on; let's get in a huddle, so we can be quiet. Com'on, huddle up."

The troop formed a circle, with their arms over each others' shoulders. Katz, Rubin, and Israel kept looking around, fearful, watchful.

Spencer continued, "It's not right to leave anyone alone, by themselves, out in the woods. We can't do that again."

Exasperated, Rubin whispered, "That's not our fault. They have to get away faster." Rubin shot an accusing finger at Adam. "You should've kept up. We could've gotten eaten."

Spencer quietly continued, "From now on, I vote we stay together. All in favor, raise their hand." Everybody raised a hand but Rubin. "Okay, that's settled, then. We'll always stay together. And don't let anyone get out of each other's eyesight. It's real easy to get lost out here with all the trees. Another thing, we've got to make long sticks to fight off"— he glanced back the way they'd come—"whatever that thing was."

"Good idea. We'll smash their teeth out," whispered Joey.

Lakalo gave a nervous chuckle.

"And poke their eyes out."

"If it grabs one of us, he's going to get hammered by all of us," Katz said with a rising sense of strength.

"Not so loud. We have to whisper."

"Nine Scouts swinging clubs is a powerful thing,"

"Yyyyyeah." Israel nodded, relieving his stress. "It's a ppppowerful . . . tttthing." He mechanically leaned into Lakalo.

Spencer continued, "The sticks have to be made of good strong wood that won't break on the first hit. And we have to get back to the van today. That's our mission. Another thing . . . we have to have a leader." He paused, making eye contact. "Now, I've a compass." He brought his arm down to pull it out.

Virgil, who'd been quiet until now, pointed south. "The van's in that direction."

"How do you know without a compass?"

"I just know."

"I vote for Spencer; he saved me," Adam raised his hand.

"I vote for him, too," Lakalo raised his hand.

Rubin's hand shot up. "I vote for Virgil. He got us away from the Sasquatch."

"He's new in Scouts and doesn't have his First-Class rating yet." Joey protested, scorning Rubin with a frown. "Hillbilly can't lead."

"I don't care." Rubin shrugged. "I vote for him anyway." He bent over and scratched a chigger bite.

"I vote for Vvvvvvirgil." Israel gave him a hopeful look.

"I vote for Virgil," Katz said. "He got us away from the Sasquatch."

Joey addressed Rubin, Katz, and Israel. "Legally, you can't vote for someone to lead if they don't have their First-Class; you can't do that."

Last to vote was Daniel, who pointed his index finger toward Spencer.

"It's settled, then." Spencer offered his hand to Virgil. "You did good to get us out of there." They shook, and Spencer turned with a new sense of leadership. "Okay, we need to get our sticks and get moving if we're going to make it back before dark."

They began foraging about, looking for solid sticks that would make good clubs.

Katz proudly lifted a heavy short hunk of wood. "Look at this. Look at this. This will knock them out." He glowed.

"Yyyyeah!" Israel loudly replied. "Kkkkknock 'em ooout!"

"Quiet you nut!" Rubin hissed, staring straight at Israel. "They're going to come."

Israel slipped behind an oak tree, hoping he wouldn't be seen.

Sporting his new-found club, Katz swung it up and down.

Five minutes into their search, Spencer advised, "We need to get going. We can't be looking for clubs all day."

"I'm hungry," Lakalo advised Spencer.

"I'm thirsty," Israel moaned.

"We need to get some water . . . "Rubin groaned. ". . . or we're all going to die,"

"That's not true. The book says we can last for three days without water and three weeks without food."

"I don't care what the book says. I'm thirsty."

"You'll have to find it along the way." Spencer studied his compass, then pointed southwest. "We need to go in that direction."

Virgil shook his head. "No. It's . . ." he pointed straight south, ". . . over there."

Joey sneered. "How do you know without a compass?"

Virgil didn't know how to explain about the sun and the shadows it cast and the way it came up and went down.

"Well, how do you know?" Lakalo asked.

Feeling everyone's eyes, Virgil felt like the outsider, the Southerner, the Kentuckian. So when he finally said, "I just know," his voice held little conviction.

"Well, it's this way," Spencer adjusted his glasses then pointed southwest, "'cause that's what the compass says. Let's go." He began walking southwest and the others quickly fell in line.

Frustrated, Virgil was the last to fall in. He trailed behind Israel, who walked with a hunched gait. The Kentuckian gave a long studied eye to the way they were going, and the slight shadows at the base of the trees, then glanced upward at the noonday sun. He slowly shook his head, disturbed that Spencer was taking them in the wrong direction.

CHAPTER 8

Down the hall Aunt Valerie marched. She carried an all-white rhinestone cowboy suit, hat, and boots. The ensemble was truly one of a kind. "Stuee, will you look at what Aunt Valerie has for you to wear!"

Stu turned away from washing his hands at the sink and took in the sight. He gawked at the costume. The jacket was ultra-smooth, white leather, with one side covered by a sparkling rhinestone cowboy. This cowboy was tossing a rope at a running steer. The pants were also white leather. Curious, Stu reached out and ran his fingers over the jacket.

"It's even got a cowboy hat." She displayed the white cowboy hat as one would display something precious. "It must've cost a fortune to make." Proud, she thumbed toward herself. "There's no better shopper in all Texas than your Aunt Valerie. You put this on, and I'm going to have to call you Roy." She rubbed his head admiringly. "You put this on, and you're going to have to sing us ladies a little cowboy song."

Stu balked. "I'm not singing no song."

"Oh, yes. You have to. The little ladies will like that."

"I'm not singing no song. I'll put the suit on, but I'm not singing no song."

"I'll pay you money."

"How much?"

"I'll pay you five whole dollars."

"No way. That's way too low, and you know it."

She blinked, enjoying the moment. Her head waddled back and forth, and her rump followed. "I'll pay you a whole ten dollars."

"No way. Ten dollars is way too low and you know it."

Her head drew back, her fingers moved close to her chest. She rolled them as if she were playing the piano. "Twenty?"

"Aunt Valerie, I feel like I'm being used. Twenty dollars? You know how much they pay me in Hollywood?" He cast her a hard eye.

She was taken aback, and her hand covered her mouth as she gathered her thoughts. Antsy, she glanced over at her purse, then back at him. "Stuee, your Aunty's not a rich woman." Her countenance changed to sorrow. "I guess you don't have to sing." Her voice broke, signifying forthcoming tears. "But I hope you like the suit." She sniffled – her movements would have impressed the top producers in Hollywood. "It's just . . . Stuee . . . " She sniffled again. "When I was a little girl I had a dream of a cowboy who came and saved me after I got shot by a band of bank robbers."

Stu carefully watched her.

"And he sang a little song for me while I lay there bleeding."

Feeling bad for her, Stu patted her on the arm. "It's all right, it's okay, I'll sing for you, and you keep the twenty. Heck, your breakfast was worth more than twenty. It was really good."

She blinked away her tears, instantly brightening, then tenderly cupped his cheek. "Thank you, Stuee. You make me so happy." As she stared at the top of his hair, it came to her. "You know what I can do for you?" She tousled his hair. "And you're going to like it."

"What's that?"

"I can make it so none of your fans will jump you."

"Do you have some skunk sauce or something?"

"I can dye that hair of yours," she buffed up his hair, "so nobody will know who you are."

Elated by the suggestion, Stu touched his hair. "That's a good idea! Can we do it now?"

"Do you have any movies you'll be doing?"

"In four months. But my hair grows fast, and it'll be grown out by then. Can we do it today?"

"No, good heavens no. Today's the tea social. You'll be on display today for all my the ladies." She smugly touched him on the chin. "We don't want you looking like anybody but Montana Stu."

CHAPTER 9

It was greenhouse weather, the time of year you could hear corn growing. The noonday sun beat down on Commander Charles's tent. Inside the temperature was over a hundred. Outside, the sun's rays vaporized the damp soil, raising the Southern humidity unbearably.

Commander Charles's eyes flashed open, closed, then opened—for a moment he didn't know where he was. He squinted, and his heavy eyes slowly scanned the nylon fabric. Suddenly, he sat up and glared straight ahead at the tent zipper, his entire being branded with a question, *Where's my troop?*

Next to the shattered tree trunk, a whisky jack hopped from the lean-to and cast a curious eye on one tent that shook and vibrated. A man forced himself out of the tent with a towel tightly wrapped around him, and marched toward the creek. It was 11:50 a.m. The sun was straight up. Looking like a bear coming out of his winter den for the very first time, Commander Charles tilted his palm to shield his eyes from the blazing sun. His pinky white body seemed to glow. He didn't slow when he came to the ten-foot wide creek that was four inches deeper from last night's storm. His head shook as he tried to grasp something that was too huge to grasp— *Where's my troop?* His big toe caught a rock, and the reaction that followed was an instantaneous belly flop into the creek. Water splashed up the banks. The big man slowly rolled over and sat up, then leaned over his girth and stared back at the empty tents. Water flowed around his side and he cupped his hands and splashed his eyes several times, hoping to clear them, hoping to see his boys running about. Water dripped off his chin as he stared at the vacant camp. The boyless camp was sobering. He blinked, and pressed his frustrated fingers through his sandy-colored hair.

His rising anguish burst out in a mighty shout. "JUNIOR COMMANDER ALAN?" The blast sent birds flying out of trees.

Now wide awake, he tightened the towel around his waist and marched back, making a beeline for the boys' tents. He looked in one tent after another, picking up speed as he searched. "JUNIOR COMMANDER ALAN?"

Junior Commander Alan's was the last tent he looked in. If his heart wasn't low enough already it sank even further when he walked toward the crushed lean-to. The whisky jack flew off. Nearing the lean-to, he ripped the plastic open and saw a field mouse scurry for cover. Flies buzzed last night's leftovers. The Commander picked up the axe and studied it, then looked about for any sign of blood. Backing away from the plastic, he examined the fallen tree, its scattered branches then carefully stepped over the debris in search of a clue, any clue. He stopped and gazed up at what was left of the dead trunk. There were scorch marks that clearly showed the burning of lightning.

Seeing a spot where someone may have slid, he bent lower and attempted to piece the puzzle together. The prints he found were smeared with pine needles pressed through them. He searched till he had completely circled the fallen tree. His finger gripped the T-shirt that covered his belly as he stared again at the lightning strike.

"JUNIOR COMMANDER ALAN!" He looked toward the trees and listened—not even the flight of wings responded. A sickening feeling enveloped him, his troop was gone. Anxiety attacked from all angles. How could he explain this to their parents, let alone the District Command? He dropped to his knees, his hands rose toward the heavens, and his soul begged, "Please God . . ."

* * *

The troop's progress was slow. Even under the canopy of trees the oppressive heat and humidity made them sweat. Spencer led, on occasion glancing down at his compass, keeping his heading southwest. Behind him, Joey followed, casting a tired eye at the small hills in front; it was a continual hike up and down similar landscape. It all began to look like the same moss-covered trees they'd passed before.

"I'm starving," Adam said. "When are we going to get back on the trail?" His finger ran down his sweat-soaked shirt.

"We're not going to hit the trail," Virgil said matter-of-factly.

"Why not?" Lakalo glanced back at him.

"The trail's in that direction." He pointed southeast.

"How do you know?"

"'Cause it is," Virgil said with assurance.

"Then why are we going this way?" Joey angled his chin in the direction they were heading.

"Because he's going in the wrong direction," Virgil answered.

Rubin looked haggard. "I'm so thirsty I could die."

"Spencer?" Lakalo asked. "How long is it going to take to get back?"

"Shhhhh!" There was fear in Rubin's voice. "You guys shouldn't talk so loud. It can hear us."

"Spencer? How long is it going to take to get back?"

Spencer stopped by a small oak and turned toward the troop. "It took us three hours and ten minutes to go in, so it's probably going to take us at least that to get out, and maybe more 'cause there's no trail."

"We're never going to get out of here heading in this direction," Virgil said with conviction. "We're going in the wrong direction."

Taken aback by his remark, Spencer adjusted his glasses. "You know . . ." he caught Virgil's eye, ". . . it's improper for you to be talking like that."

"Why? You're taking us in the wrong direction."

Katz tossed his club. "That thing's too heavy. I can't carry that everywhere." He bent over to scratch a chigger bite.

Spencer stepped toward Virgil. "You don't know that."

Katz was so tired he thought Spencer was speaking to him. He answered, "I know, 'cause I've been carrying it for miles."

Spencer paid no attention to Katz, his eyes were fixed on Virgil, "How do you know your way is the right way?"

"'Cause I've been out in the woods all my life, and I always know where camp is, and I always know how to get back to the truck."

"But you don't have a compass."

"I don't need a compass."

"You don't have a Cut-and-Chop card either, or your First-Class rating," Spencer said.

Hoping to quell the situation, Daniel pulled his harmonica from his pocket, placed it against his parched lips, then gave it a tiny blow. The quiet sound was settling, but couldn't cut the tension between Spencer and Virgil.

Israel awkwardly angled his head toward Virgil. "He gggggot." His contorted neck muscles shook. "He gggggot us away . . . from the Sasqqqqquatch."

"That's a whole lot different than guiding us back to the van," Joey stated.

"That's right," Spencer said. "If you don't have a compass, you should keep your directions to yourself."

Virgil tightened his fist. He tried to swallow but felt a lump in his throat, a lump that wasn't caused from the blistering humid heat or the lack of water, or the fact that he was the new guy—he knew Spencer was taking them in the wrong direction.

Daniel quietly sang, *"When we all get to heaven . . ."*

Spencer turned and walked back to the front. "Let's go, then."

"We'll . . . ggget there." Israel stuttered.

Frustrated, Virgil shook his head, knowing that wasn't about to happen. As the troop moved away from him, he turned and gazed in the direction he figured the van was, then he looked back at Israel, the awkward one, the one he'd promised Commander Charles he'd look after. His gut felt hungry and hollow, and his thirst had sucked his lips dry, but it didn't negate his promise to Commander Charles.

* * *

Flat on his back, Junior Commander Alan viewed the leaves moving above him. He dumbly rubbed the swollen gash on his forehead and struggled to sit up. His head swayed as he stared at the oak tree next to him. Something seemed odd about the bark and his hand mechanically moved forward to touch it. Pressing one hand into the damp soil to steady himself, he ran his other palm over the bark and focused on it as if he'd never seen bark before. Unable to concentrate, he gazed beyond the oak into the endless forest. A chigger bit into the back of his hand, but he didn't feel it—his skin was numb.

Finding the forest's movements bizarre, a slurred grin crossed his lips. Again, his eyes stared blankly at the oak tree. It was a curious sight; he'd never seen the base of a large tree shift and move. His eyelids grew heavy, and he tiredly yawned. In his hypothermic state, he dumbly patted the ground as if it were his bed. When he lay back down, the decomposed oak leaves didn't feel damp. The view of the trees, the glint of blue, and the noonday sky beyond—all seemed to dizzily sway.

His mouth hung open as he viewed something black that landed in the limb above. A crow cast a black eye down at him. The Junior Commander gazed past the black one to the leaves, the ever-moving leaves.

Commander Charles squatted to better study the pine needles. Figuring they had been freshly displaced, he ran them through his fingertips, then rose and followed the disturbed needles farther into the forest. Two and a half hours earlier he had begun his search, yet he still wasn't sure he was following his troop's tracks. At this slow and tedious pace, he reasoned he would never catch the makers of the prints before dark. Ahead, he heard a snap. He stopped and searched the rolling landscape. From behind a hardwood a doe appeared. Beside her wagged the small tail of her fawn.

The Commander's second-guessing continued. *Were the displaced needles made by deer or were they from his troop? Or could his troop be back at camp?* The sun was beginning its decline—time wasn't on his side. They should've been packed up and on the road to Missouri by now. It was over two hundred miles and he didn't want to miss Jamberama's opening ceremony. *Could the boys be back at the van?*

Time and time again, he had tried his hand-held FVR radio but to no avail. Desperate, he shouted, "SCOUTS?"

The doe and fawn bolted. A squirrel dashed up a pine, then stopped and looked back at him. It chattered.

Commander Charles listened, hoping to hear a faint cry from the boys. None came. "SCOUTS!" A creepy stillness blanketed the forest. The calm spurred the Commander to action, spinning around, he headed in the direction he'd come. After ten quick steps, he stopped. *Was that the boys laughing?* He turned back, his eyes madly roving, searching the rolling landscape. For a better view, he went up a small rise. "JUNIOR COMMANDER ALAN?"

The forest was silent.

CHAPTER 10

Delicate tea cups sat atop lacy doilies. Their many colors and patterns accented the dessert table which stood in the middle of the living room. Although the room was small for socializing seven ladies, there was nothing small about the variety of sweets and pleasing desserts. Aunt Valerie wasn't sure if God created ladies for teas or if He created teas for ladies. Regardless, this would certainly vault her into the highest social status—she was actually related to Montana Stu, and if all went well, he would sing. Basking in this glory, she giggled, then dabbed her lips with a colorful hanky, mumbling to herself, "Oh, my. Certainly this will be a poo."

The chatter was thrilling. To her right, a stately woman, clothed in a puffy lime-colored dress, bragged to a woman, clad in a peach-colored outfit opposite her, about how sweet her grandchildren were. On the other side of her, a thin-faced woman, costumed in a burgundy organza suit, elaborated on how much money her daughter's husband made, then bragged about their new house that had marble this and granite that— he was a lawyer. Sipping her tea, a yellow-dressed belle listened impatiently to this rant and only hoped to get her two bits in. At opposite ends of the couch sat two Southern belles, who held a conversation about camellias, with Aunt Valerie in the middle. Both seemed experts on the latest varieties. Aunt Valerie didn't know camellias but continued to dab her lips with the hanky, for she'd read somewhere that it was the dainty thing to do. The chatter was pitched above the soft music that wafted from an antique stereo.

Aunt Valerie suddenly blurted, "It's a wonderful white suit."

One belle thought she was talking about a particular camellia and added, "Oh, yes. White Empress has a gorgeous white suit that I believe the judges are partial to."

Aunt Valerie was so enraptured with the event, she seemed to be floating on Tinker Bell dust as she dreamily responded, "It's the Western suit that I bought for Stuee. It's just adorable." She took a bite of her chocolate tort and dabbed her lips with the colorful hanky.

"How delightful," commented camellia lady. "It sounds like a Leucantha."

"Yes," Aunt Valerie said assuredly, nodding, pleased to finally reign atop her social order. "They're custom-made."

"All suits should be so pre-formed," interjected the other lady. "There is such a difference between buying it off the shelf as opposed to measuring the lines." The belle proudly pulled on the see-through sleeve of her baby-blue gown and continued, "When I had this made . . . "

Down the hall in the guest bedroom, Stu struggled and sweated to put on the white leather pants. They were at least three sizes too small, but he was determined to please his aunt. He pulled and wiggled and pulled and wiggled at the pants until his fingers ached. The pants had a sucking effect, tightening, constricting around his thighs with each stretch, much like a wetsuit. Finally, he got them up to the bottom of his rump. His eyes bulged when he stared down at the straining seams. Panting, he shook his head, frustrated that he hadn't stopped growing a year ago.

Feeling too constricted, he changed his mind, and tried to take them off. His legs stumbled forward, but the pants pressed in and wouldn't obey, wouldn't even budge. There was a knock on the door.

"Hurry up, Stuee. The ladies are waiting." Aunt Valerie rapped the door again.

Bewildered at his Houdini predicament, he madly struggled to pull the pants up. This time he got them over his rump and sucked in his gut to zip them. The zipper came up a third of the way and stopped. He pulled on the metal but it wouldn't budge. The door rapped.

"Stuee?"

"These pants are too tight, but I think I got it!" Red-faced, he grabbed the shirt. "I just got to put on the shirt and boots, and I'll be out."

The shirt shuffled through his fingers as he lifted it. Examining the size, he grew concerned, it was way too small. H doggedly slid his arm in one sleeve, flailing his hand to grab the one behind his back.

After the fifth attempt, he snagged it and dug his fingers into the opposite sleeve. Scrunching his shoulders, he pulled the shirt together, then grabbed a button and forced it through a buttonhole. The button flew off, pinging across the room. Snagging another button, he rammed it through another buttonhole. It popped off and did a rubber-ball bounce across the carpet. Panicked, he mumbled, "It's not my fault," and glanced toward the door. Finally, he tied the bottom of the shirt into a knot to hold it together; the end of the shirt just covered his half-open leather pants. Grabbing the belt, he haphazardly wrapped it around his midsection and buckled it to cover the open zipper. He was starting to look like a 1970s Elvis Presley—bare chest, sporting white leather pants.

He bent over to grab the boots and heard a ripping noise as the pants tore smack down the middle of his rump. Disheartened, he tried to glance back but couldn't turn his shoulders far enough to look. He felt around and his finger poked through the two inch long slit and touched his underwear. Maybe he could cover it with the coat. Again, he bent over to put on the boots. It was a terrible challenge because the back of the shirt stretched so tight, he couldn't move his arms forward, and the pants were even tighter.

Finally, he got his foot down into the boot, his poor toe scrunched and pained as he pressed and pulled it into place. He limped around to deaden the pain, one boot on and one boot off. Then he grabbed the other, forced his foot into it, and stomped on it, but it was tighter than the other and as much as he stomped, it still wouldn't slip all the way in. So he bent over to grab it. There was another ripping sound as his pants ripped higher up the backside. This had an instant releasing effect upon his buttocks.

Grabbing the top of the white leather boot, he pulled with all his might. The foot slid in. The sides of his foot throbbed from the overwhelming squeeze. Red faced, Stu wiped perspiration from his glowing brow, and grabbed the rhinestone coat. The coat fought him, too, and he stopped more than once to take a breather. Finally, he pulled it up over both arms. The tightness of the suit had a straightening effect on his shoulders. Grabbing the hat, he stumbled toward the door, then opened it with a stiff arm.

For a moment he stood, searching for breath and felt like he was in a straightjacket. If he could only get this thing over with! Down the hall he went, boots stomping, bee-lining for the living room, putting on the cowboy hat as he went, and pulling the back of the coat down to cover the rip in his pants. He curved into the living room, stopped, and gave a respectful nod to the peach attired belle. "Howdy, ma'am."

She was taken aback to see such a flamboyantly dressed showman and returned his acknowledgment with a welcoming smile. The chatter immediately ceased, and the ladies came to full attention. They looked as if they were vying to sit up straighter than he was standing, but that was impossible—his suit was tighter undeniably than their dresses.

"Come in Stuee and sit next to Aunt Valerie."

He was reluctant to do so because of the rip in the back of his leather pants, but his legs found themselves scuffling over to her, then with a quick spin, he flopped down. His eyes widened as he felt the pants rip even more.

The awestruck belle next to him unconsciously ran her fingers over the white leather of his rhinestone coat. She was stunned by its creativity.

Aunt Valerie rested her hand on his back as if she owned him. "Stuee, why don't you tell us about your Hollywood exploits?"

Stu shrugged, extremely worried, conscious of the rip in his pants. "It's not much. We were working on a *Pure Sun* commercial."

"How do you like acting?"

Stu barely moved. "It's all right."

"What would you rather do, ranching or acting?"

"Ranching."

A few ladies giggled.

"What do you like best about ranching?"

"I like roundup." Stu's total consciousness was on the hole in his pants. What would happen when he got up?

"What do you do in roundup?"

"In the fall we kick them out of the woods for the feedlot." Forced to sit bolt upright, he shifted his uncomfortable position, but his legs, ankles, and feet felt numb from the constricting pants and boots.

"What do you like best about roundup?"

"Generally, we stay out a night or two, and Pops brings this old sheepherder's wagon along, and at night there's a fire and the fellas tell stories."

"Do you have any stories to tell?"

"No, I'm too young."

"I don't know of any boys that went all the way from San Francisco to Montana by themselves," observed the lady in the burgundy dress.

Aunt Valerie rubbed her hand across his back, proud as a button. All the ladies would look up to her now.

Stu commented, "Well, Johnny Revv was there and so was Poncho."

"How's Poncho doing?"

"He's doing good, came up and stayed with us this spring, and we took him out fishing." His feet throbbed as he shifted again.

"How'd he do?"

"He caught more bull trout than anybody."

Aunt Valerie dabbed her lips with the hanky, wagging her head, her fingers pianoing over his back, displaying him as one shows off fine jewelry.

The peach belle asked, "How's his heart?"

"His heart's good."

"How's your pony?"

"Gray's good."

"What would you rather be doing?"

He glanced her way. "Than being here?" he asked and pointed at the green shag carpet.

She nodded.

"No disrespect, ma'am, but . . ." He thought of a lot of places he'd rather be but there were so many he was afraid to say. At last he just shrugged.

The belles smiled, feeling indebted to Valerie for being invited.

"How's your driving?" asked the peach belle.

"Good. But, lately . . ." he appeared perplexed, ". . . every time I've wanted to drive the tractor, my dad says he's got something wrong with it or somebody else lined up."

Immediately understanding, the belles giggled.

Stu gave the burgundy belle across from him a curious glance then added, "But I'm going to see about getting on it, just as soon as I get back."

"Do you still sing?"

"Sometimes during calving when a cow's a little jumpy. Just to settle them down. Old Smoke Junior taught me that."

The lady costumed in the burgundy organza suit turned to the lady in lime green. "Isn't the way he talks just like a Montana cowboy?"

"How's your father doing?"

"Dad's good, happy that Mom's back."

"What advice does he have for you these days?"

"Tells me to watch every word I say, 'cause it could come back and haunt me."

"Do you ever wish people didn't know who you were?"

"Yep."

"When's your next rodeo?"

He thought they asked more questions than the TV people. "Next one is in September."

"What a lovely suit. Where'd you get it?" questioned the lady in peach across from him.

Stu thumbed toward his Aunt. "My Aunt Valerie bought it." He felt a nudge on his back that meant for him not to tell them where she bought it. Not getting it, he proudly continued, "She's the best shopper . . . bought it at Sally Ann for a whole twenty dollars."

Aunt Valerie rolled her eyes, feeling like her social status instantly dropped into a black hole. No matter how far she reached, she'd never recover. She nudged him, theatrically teething, "Why don't you sing us a song, Stuee."

"Oh, yes. That would be wonderful," said one of the ladies. "And please stand up dear, and let us take a good look at that lovely suit."

CHAPTER 11

A gentle wind blew through the forest, but the hint of coolness offered no hope to the disheartened Commander who entered the camp. Glancing up at the changing sky, he noted the drifting clouds. Static came over the walky-talky attached to his belt. He lifted it, turned up the volume, and heard Commander Rex's distinct voice: " . . . der Charles. Come in, Commander Charles. Over."

He was quick to answer. "Commander Rex, it's so good to hear your voice! Obviously, you caught a ride back. Are you feeling better? Over."

"I'm approximately halfway down the trail. Yes, I'm feeling a lot better after the shot they gave me. It turned out to be a kidney stone. Over."

"So it passed? Over."

"Yes, thank God. How are the boys? Over."

"I was hoping you'd tell me that they're back at the van. Over."

"I can't say they are. Did some of them go ahead?"

"I'd like to give you some good news, but we have a serious problem." Commander Charles gazed at the collapsed lean-to. "I found the camp abandoned. No sign of anyone. I've spent the day following trails that may or may not have been theirs. And I hate to turn back and give up the pursuit, but I believe we need to call in search and rescue. Over." He reached down to scratch a chigger bite.

"Copy that. But tell me, my friend, is this a joke?"

Commander Charles sorrowfully pressed in the "Talk" button of his walky-talky. "I wish it was. Ohhhhh, how I wish it was. Over."

There was a long pause before Commander Rex asked, "Any sign of foul play?"

"No, but the tree we tied the plastic to was hit by lightning, and the lean-to is no more. Over."

"Lightening?"

"Roger that."

A moment passed. "It's six thirty-four now, I'll head back to town, and get things rolling. Over."

"Roger that. Could you call their parents and National and tell them the situation?"

"Roger that. How's Commander Charles doing?"

"This is," Commander Charles paused, tired, considering, "too big." He pressed his hand into his aching temple.

* * *

"Anybody have a flashlight?" Spencer adjusted his glasses then squinted at the compass, but was unable to see the magnetic needle. "Anybody have a flashlight? I can't see the compass."

Virgil's angry voice could be heard at the back of the troop. "Maybe it'd be better that you can't see the compass. Then maybe you'll go in the right direction."

Sad chuckles rose amongst the discouraged troop.

Spencer took three steps toward Virgil and retorted, "You're being disruptive. You shouldn't be disruptive."

"Good!" Virgil said with frustration. "You shouldn't lead if you don't know where you're going. The van is way over there!" He pointed east. "You've taken us way off."

"How do you know? You don't have a compass."

"You're reading it wrong, or something's wrong with it, 'cause it's over there!" Again he pointed, but the darkness made it a useless gesture.

"I think we're almost there."

"No way!" Defiant, Virgil shook his head. "You've taken us too far this way." He thumbed west. "We must've walked at least six miles by now, and the trail was only four. Even if you went straight that way," he pointed, "we would've hit the trail."

"We'll get there soon."

"You've been saying that allllll day."

There was a chorus of agreement from Joey, Rubin, Katz, and Lakalo.

Spencer adjusted his glasses and looked into the darkness. "It doesn't matter, we're almost there."

"No, we're not!" Virgil said belligerently and stepped near him, pointing. "The van is over there!"

Lakalo moaned, "It's too dark to walk."

Joey whined, "Now we got to stay the night."

"I'm so thirsty." Rubin touched his parched lips.

"We're almost there," Spencer reiterated.

"You don't know where you are!" Virgil's teeth bared as he angrily pointed east. "It's over there!" He was so intense in his movement that Spencer stepped back, believing he was going to strike him.

"This is too much," Katz complained. "I'm not going any farther. It's too much." With no thought of chiggers, he flopped down. Rubin shifted forward and accidentally stepped on him. "Watch where you're stepping, you nut head."

Joey whined, "I'm starved,"

Virgil took Israel by the arm. "We need to talk."

Israel followed him into the dark, his shoulders rolling from right to left, his right leg dragged at an awkward angle.

"Don't let him have your knife," Spencer called after them. "He doesn't have a Knife-and-Axe card." The chirps of crickets covered the forest.

Out of earshot of the rest, Virgil stopped and faced Israel. He whispered, "You know that Commander Charles told me to look after you?"

Israel swung his head away from him toward the dark silhouette of the others, then swung it back. His mouth hung as he nodded.

"This guy," Virgil pitched his chin toward Spencer. "This guy's taking us wrong. He's getting us lost more and more. We didn't walk this far when we came in . . . you know that?"

Israel's lower lip came up over his upper, after which he managed a dry swallow and nodded. He brought his awkward face near Virgil's. Virgil leaned back from Israel's bad breath.

"Come tomorrow, we're going to have to go back on our own. You know?"

Israel was slow to nod. To his side, a firefly glowed green.

"If others want to come, they can come, but I told Commander Charles I'd look after you, and we have to go."

"Okkkkay," Israel said, pulling his chin down. "But how dddddo you kkkkknow where you're gggggoing?" He struggled to swallow. "Wwwithout a cccccompass?"

"I know the woods. And I know the way the sun comes up and goes down and the way the shadows are. I know the woods. The van is over there!" Virgil pointed.

"Are you ssssure?"

He nodded. "I been out in the woods all my life. I've never been lost."

"Okkkkkay."

"Can I use your knife?"

Israel eyed him warily. "What dddddo you need it for?"

"I'm going to start a fire."

"Yeah. Sssure."

As Virgil and Israel approached the troop, Spencer saw the knife in Virgil's hand. "Israel, you shouldn't have given him your knife. He doesn't have his Knife-and-Axe card." Spencer glanced at big Lakalo for some help.

Lakalo kindly asked, "What are you up to, Virgil?"

"I'm going to get a fire going."

"A fire would be good," Katz commented.

Virgil bent over and ran his fingers through the pine needles, gathering some.

Still hoping to hang on to his command, Spencer adjusted his glasses and advised, "You're supposed to have a radius of six feet cleared before you start a fire so you don't burn the forest down." The hum and chirping of locust and cicadas quieted as Spencer continued, "You shouldn't start a fire unless you have water."

"It rained last night, and everything around here's damp," said Lakalo.

"Fires are good," Katz said and rose to help. "Virgil, you got any matches?"

Virgil replied, "I got a stick of magnesium."

"What's that?"

"It'll start a fire if we have some paper. Anybody got paper?"

"Yeah. I do," Adam said, feeling almost too fatigued to get up and give it to him.

"If we have a fire going . . ." Joey's voice had a spark of hope. ". . . other people will see it and come find us."

Virgil took the paper Adam offered, then went to his pile of needles and tore the paper into strips. "We need more dry sticks." Rubin handed him two small sticks.

"Chiggers are everywhere," said Joey, scratching a bite on his ankle. "They're everywhere."

Katz looked about the darkened forest for firewood. "I can't see."

"We should've stopped before it got dark and built a shelter."

"How do you build a shelter without a tent?"

"You can build it out of big branches," Virgil said.

"I'm going to die without food! I'm just going to die!" Adam moaned.

"You don't have to die if you don't want to, 'cause a person can live three weeks without food," Spencer responded.

"Tell that to my stomach. I thought you said we'd be back to the van by now."

"It has to be real close."

"We're going to miss the opening ceremony at Jamberama," Joey whined. "Here we come all the way across country and miss the opening ceremonies."

"Here's some more wood." Daniel dumped some branches beside Virgil.

Virgil broke up sticks, arranged them in an A-frame, then placed his paper next to the edge and brought his tinder near. Satisfied, he ran the aluminum piece down the magnesium. Sparks shot off, illuminating the paper he was attempting to light. He did it again and again, and a vapor of white spraying sparks blasted off the magnesium into the paper, singeing it. A green mist rose from the paper until a tiny flame appeared. Carefully, he fed the flame more paper. It ate it up, asking for more. Virgil placed a small stack of pine needles atop the little fire, then took the two sticks and put them atop the needles. The fire continued to grow, feeding on the pine needles, but their dampness didn't enhance the flame. It slowed, threatening to die.

"Com'on!" Virgil pleaded, pushing the end of the paper into the heat. The flame again took hold and licked over the small sticks.

Israel approached, awkward as ever, carrying two small twigs, his eye fixed on the flame. Two steps from the tiny fire, he tripped on a rock. His foot shot forward, landed directly on the small fire, crushing it out.

CHAPTER 12

After supper, Stu followed Uncle Hawthorne into his small office which was crammed with everything from airplane models to beaver tails. Happy to be in his den, Uncle Hawthorne sat down in front of his antique roll-top desk, leaned back in his easy chair, and looked Stu over. "That's some hairdo."He grinned at Stu's blonde hair with orange highlights on the top.

Stu nodded proudly. "Nobody will recognize me now . . . and no more singing to ladies."

His uncle laughed. "But it did make your Aunt Valerie happy." He saw Stu staring at one of his model planes. "That's a B-25." He lifted the green model of a two-engine Army plane and handed it to Stu. "It was used in World War II in the first attack on Tokyo."

Stu held it by both wings to study it, and remembering his experience on the plane, felt apprehensive just holding it.

His uncle took another plane off the roll-top. "This here is a high-wing experimental. It's a humble craft and your uncle owns one just like it." He proudly beamed. "I've owned it for fourteen fine years."

"How old does that make it?"

"It's thirty-seven years old. What do you think? Isn't she a beauty?"

Stu stared blankly at the model his uncle held, considering the word "experimental." "Does it still work?"

"It sure does. That's the plane we're heading to Jamberama in."

Uneasy, Stu asked, "We're taking an experimental plane up?" His voice revealed a rising fear.

"Don't let the name fool you. It's a good plane." He rolled the model plane around in the air. "My little bird can go a hundred and twenty knots."

All the fears of that stormy ride into Houston flooded back for the youth. "What happens if it crashes?"

"For the most part, planes just don't crash. There are things that happen beforehand that give off warnings. If you don't do anything about the warning, *then* there'll be consequences."

"But what happens if something bad happens?"

"Well, if we're up high enough, I've got a parachute, and you can use it. Otherwise, if there's a flat open area or a road that I can land on, I'm pretty good about setting it down."

"But what happens if lightning blows a wing off?"

"Then it's a bad day for flying."

"That's no good." Stu swallowed, more apprehensive than ever.

"What's wrong?"

"All I saw was trees everywhere around here."

"It's nothing to get worked up over. If things get out of hand, I do have a parachute."

"But what if you're flying too low?" Stu looked at him warily.

"Stu, you worry too much."

CHAPTER 13

In a traveling box in the rear of a pickup truck, an excited hound bayed, anxious to get out. A rescue worker undid the latch, and the dog's head popped through the door. A leather strap was snapped onto the black-and-tan's collar. The hound's tail beat against the metal box, wagging its way out.

Behind them, another truck pulled up, its headlights piercing the dark, illuminating the rescue workers and their tracking dogs.

"Hey, Red. What's it gonna be?"

"Looks like some kids are missing. He said an entire troop." Red yanked back on the leash of one rambunctious dog that was growling and straining to get at the black-and-tan. "Get up there!" He pointed at the hound. "Settle down you!" He cuffed the other.

Another vehicle pulled up, followed by another. A man from the Texarkana search and rescue stepped out. "Hey, Jimmy. Looks like you still got the black-and-tan." He grabbed his backpack.

In minutes, the team was ready at the trailhead. The dogs looked as if they'd leap out of their skin.

Commander Rex filled them in on the location of the camp then said, "I could lead you."

Jimmy came alongside and put a reassuring hand on Rex's trembling elbow. "You look like you need some rest. They'll be able to find the camp and the dogs will take up from there." He nodded to Red, who gave way to the dogs' pull and bolted down the trail.

Headlamps flashed as handlers tried to keep up with their hounds.

* * *

The beam of Commander Charles's flashlight illuminated a hickory tree. To his left, a firefly glowed green, then disappeared. Farther along, another one appeared, glowed then blinked out. Crickets chirped, orchestrating their wings making the forest sound as if it were alive. Charles cast a frustrated gaze toward a group of trees; he'd been searching for over nine hours, and the trail had dissipated to nothing, absolutely nothing. It ate at his gut. He blamed himself. Again, he yelled, "JUNIOR COMMANDER ALAN?"

For a moment, all was silent, even the locusts and cicadas didn't move.

CHAPTER 14

Junior Commander Alan lay comatose under the oak tree. In his hypothermic state, his body had shut down. Eleven hours on the damp soil had sucked out what was left of his strength. Crickets quieted as a fox drew near the body. It sniffed his hand, then approached his face. Sensing life, it backed away then sat down to wait.

* * *

Spencer glared at Virgil who approached the fire, carrying a six inch rock.

Virgil dumped the rock, then slid it near the flames.

"You shouldn't put rocks near the flames; they'll crack," Spencer said.

Ignoring him, Virgil walked away from the fire, looking for another good-sized rock. Behind him, Adam stretched out his palms toward the heat. Lakalo sat to the side of him, taking in the warmth. Exhausted, his tired eyelids grew heavy and he fell asleep. Virgil approached with another rock.

Hearing a thud, Lakalo awoke to see Virgil push the rock toward the fire.

"What're you doing? You shouldn't do that. They can blow up," Spencer harped.

"They only blow up if they're really wet, like the ones from a creek. But if you don't like it, then go away from the fire. You didn't build it."

Katz dropped some wood in the flames, then wearily followed Virgil, who was on the hunt for more rocks. "Why do you put the rocks in there?"

"It's too much work to keep the fire going all night, but if you heat up a rock, then take it out and pull it near your stomach, it can keep you warm."

"That's a good idea. What're you eating? You got more?"

Virgil arched his chin toward a tree. "Moss."

With hunger driving, Rubin was quick to head off for the tree.

Lakalo overheard Virgil and responded with, "Moss? Is it any good?"

"Hillbilly," Joey commented, "you can die from that stuff."

"Don't eat it, then," Virgil said, more determined, as he picked up another

rock.

Appreciating Virgil's survival skills, Katz followed, carrying a rock.

Under the dark oak tree, Rubin reached for some moss. "How's it taste?"

"It doesn't taste that good, but my daddy says it's good for you." Virgil dumped the rock near the fire and pushed it in place. Rising he walked toward Rubin.

Rubin picked moss from the bark and frowned when he put a strand on his tongue. He pulled it away. "Tastes hairy and old." Starved, he touched his tongue on the hair-like moss again, then, closing one eye, chomped and sucked a piece into his mouth. He chewed it quickly then swallowed. "I wish I had some water."

"Deer eat it all the time. It's like candy to them," Virgil said. He ducked to get under a fir tree, pulled Israel's knife out then began to cut at the base of some smaller branches.

Rubin asked, "What if there's tiny bugs on the moss?"

"My daddy says bugs are good protein. Better than anything you can buy in the store. You see any ants, you should get 'ya some."

"Poouui," Joey said.

"You get hungry enough, you'll be looking for 'em."

"I'm with you on that." Lakalo said, "I'm starved." But he was too tired to rise.

"What else can you eat?" Rubin asked.

"There's food everywhere, if you know what to eat. Honewort, berries, if you can find them; bedstraw, too. There's lots of plantain and maybe if we're lucky we can get a rabbit. I've found a rabbit trail over there . . . set up a little snare." Virgil continued to cut away on the branches. "It's too bad there's no bullfrogs around, they're good eating."

"That's sick man. You eat frogs?"

"Frog legs are good, snakes too."

Lakalo said to Adam. "I hear rabbit tastes like chicken."

"Who showed you which plants are good to eat?"

"My daddy, granddad, and my uncles know the woods." Virgil bent the branch over until it snapped, then tossed it toward the growing stack of branches.

"Those branches are going to burn for a long time," Rubin said.

"We're not burning them. We're going to sleep on them."

"Oh . . . That'd be good."

"And we'll put them on top of us, too, like a fort."

"You got any for me?" Rubin asked.

"Take those on top. They can be your bed,"

Rubin grinned and gazed over at Spencer, who was on the other side of the fire talking to Lakalo, Joey, Adam, and Daniel. Rubin wondered what he was saying, but Spencer's voice was too low.

On the far side of the fire, Lakalo quietly spoke. "Spencer, why don't you go talk to him?" Lakalo's big Hawaiian way made his counsel appear as if it were coming from a chief. "You and Virgil can get along."

"He's against me," Spencer sadly said.

"You should try to talk to him. See if you can work it out."

The boys were silent; all that could be heard was the musical hum of cricket chirps. A moment later Spencer got up and took a few steps toward the area where Virgil, Rubin, Katz, and Israel were working. Not knowing how to approach Virgil, he watched the robust group. Wanting to help, he walked near, grabbed some branches from the pile and headed toward the fire.

Rubin tore off after him. "Hey, those are mine!"

"I'll help, too." Spencer said, and headed for the fire to toss them in.

"Hey! Gimme that!" Rubin grabbed the branches. Spencer thought he was joking and pulled back. The branches slipped out of Rubin's hands and he went down. By the time he'd scrambled up, Spencer had tossed the branches in the fire.

Rubin bolted after his branch. "Idiot!" He snatched them out of the flames and flopped them down several times. "Dumb idiot!" Finally killing the flames, he cast an angry, hard glare at Spencer. "Trying to burn my bed."

Virgil came over and gave Spencer the most perplexed frown.

Taken aback, Spencer adjusted his glasses.

Katz called out from under the tree, "He's going to sleep on those branches." He stepped out from under the tree and strolled closer to the fire. "Virgil knows. He knows everything. We're going to make a fort and sleep with the hot rocks."

"Sleep with rocks?" Joey's chuckle was mocking.

"You'll see. When we're all warm in our little fort, you'll see." Katz went back to Virgil who was separating the branches into four stacks.

Spencer, Daniel, Lakalo, Joey, and Adam were too tired to do anything but sit by the dying fire. They occasionally watched the others follow Virgil's instructions for building the fort.

Using the tips of their boots, Virgil's group rolled their hot rocks toward a tree, which was forty feet or so across the way. Joey noticed two rocks left behind, so he rose and headed over to ask Virgil, "Can I join you guys?"

"Yep." Virgil nodded. "I'll help you cut some branches."

It irked Spencer that Joey was following Virgil into the darkness. *Was he breaking up the troop?*

The continuous chirping of locusts and crickets encompassed the forest.

* * *

A light breeze softly swayed the nylon tent, and a faint light bounced off of its fabric as Commander Charles trudged into the dark, deserted camp. "BOYS?"

He'd been yelling every five minutes and didn't pause to look around. The response was always the same, hopelessly silent. Earlier, he had taken a flashlight from one of the tents. Now, inside his tent, it glowed, illuminating his backpack. He searched for food. Abruptly, he righted himself at the thought of having to tell the boys' parents.

Snagging the last of his granola bars, he angled his head toward the tent's opening. "BOYS?"

He took his cup and water purifier and pushed out the tent. The flashlight shone, taking him down to the creek. At the water's edge, he loaded his water purifier, shot the water into his cup, and watched a firefly's green flash. His tired fingers reached out to touch it. He swayed, so exhausted that he lost his balance and slammed his foot into the water to steady himself. Straightening, he stepped out, looked about the darkened world, and pressed his fingers into his temple in a weak attempt to compose.

His thoughts returned, and with them came worries. *Was this the work of some crazy?* Suddenly, he blurted, "Boys?" But his call wasn't as loud as before. There was no power in it. Spent from the endless search, his weary eyes fell on the darkened creek. A small moon shone through the trees and danced atop the surface. He wished for some hope, for anything, but even the locusts' chirps weren't calming. *Could the troop have gone back to the van?* For a moment, he took solace in that thought. *The troop is skilled enough to do it. Spencer knows how to read the compass. Surely he could get them back. But why haven't I been informed?* He wondered if they had tried and couldn't find him. *Maybe the radio's batteries were too weak.*

He turned, took an off-balanced step and peered into the distance where the trail angled. 'BOYS!" he yelled. His eyes lit up at what he saw; there, rounding the trail, was the beam of a flashlight, then another, then another. A rush of optimism washed through him as he waved his flashlight back and forth. In the distance, a hound dog bayed.

* * *

Drawn into the damp soil, Junior Commander Alan appeared at peace. The flash of fireflies twinkled like stars above, and the melody of whippoorwills and tree frogs seemed to be singing to his being. Occasionally, the cicadas and crickets joined. Alan's baby finger twitched slightly, then was still. To his side a patient fox awaited its meal. Minutes slowly passed and a slight breeze touched the leaves, then the sudden trill of locusts' wings filled the air. It was as if they could sense the youth's spirit rising out of his body. And if a spirit could rise then hover and look down on its own face, the locust suddenly fell silent.

Far above, clouds had gathered, edging close to the moon, threatening to take it prisoner, to cut off its light. Below, the fox sensed something and with a flick of a shadow it was gone.

With his nose guiding, the black-and-tan closed so quickly it nearly ran into the form on the ground. The hound stepped back, then gave a terrible bay. It panted, nosing over Junior Commander Alan, giving him an anxious lick, smearing the youth's cheek with its wet tongue. The hound gave a mournful whine then, another long moaning bay, calling out to others. It nudged Alan's cold cheek.

Less than a minute passed before a flashlight illuminated the dog. A red- haired man kneeled beside the youth.

"How you doing, son?" The man squeezed Alan's wrist, checking for a pulse. "Stay with me, now." Overwhelmed with the possibility of a corpse, the man's voice cracked. "Stay with me, now!" There was no sign of breath. He squeezed his wrist tighter, desperate to feel a pulse.

Three other rescue workers came up from behind, "What do you got?"

"Not breathing. . .but he might have a pulse." The three broke into a flurry of activity. One began CPR. A plastic apparatus was slid down Alan's throat. Off to the side an injection was made ready. They quickly stripped the body of its wet pants while another pressed heat packs upon Alan's cold chest.

With the injection in hand a rescue worker searched for a vein, his headlight illuminating Alan's arm. Not finding one, he anxiously mumbled, "Com'on, Com'on."

Red's anxious voice spoke into his walky-talky: "Headquarters, come in. Over."

The walky-talky responded, "Go ahead. Over."

"We've found a male. Approximately fifteen or sixteen years old . . ." As he went on, one drop of rain hit Alan's eyelid; the lid didn't flinch and the drop rolled in and lay. Other drops hit the trees, intermixing with the melody of the cicadas and crickets.

* * *

Virgil's eyes flashed open. Awakened by a sound, he lifted his fir branch. A drop of rain hit him on his neck. He sat up and stared across the clearing at the fire. Except for a hint of smoke drifting up, the fire was out. Droplets fell, hitting the gray and black coals like tiny bombs, spattering them, giving a beat to the haunting sounds of the locusts. Beside the fire, Lakalo sat up, Daniel, then Adam, and finally Spencer. Spencer wiped water out of his eye and put on his glasses. Lakalo poked his tongue out to catch a drop, cast a tired, lazy eye toward Virgil and noticed Virgil waving him to come over.

He nudged Adam and Daniel, then rose and headed toward Virgil's group. Spencer reluctantly hung back.

Virgil rallied his troop, "Hey! Wake up! We got company. Sit up, Joey; sit up, Israel." Virgil handed Lakalo a branch. "It's no good to get wet." He handed another branch to Adam, then thumped Rubin's chest. "Get up, Rubin, get up."

The rain hit Spencer who stood outside the tree, waiting, wondering if he should find another tree, still feeling alienated from Virgil.

"Com'on Spencer, get in here." Lakalo slid over to let Spencer in.

Eventually, all nine boys ended up, shoulder to shoulder, with their backs against the tree's trunk.

Virgil lifted a branch. "Take the branches like this and put them in front of you. That way we can make a little fort and keep our heat in." They did so. A long quiet ensued.

Out of the quiet came Katz's voice. "I wonder if the Commanders are alive."

"What dddo you tttthink the Sasquatch will ddddo with em?" Israel asked.

"They're going to cook Commander Charles up, 'cause he's the biggest. He'll go first," said Rubin.

Katz frowned. "Junior Commander Alan will get it last 'cause he's skinny."

"That's no good. Don't talk like that."

Spencer sat deep in thought, contemplating what his eyes had seen that morning. He'd never believed in Sasquatch until the brown being appeared, walking upright. He knew a bear didn't walk upright, and no man would be that brown. Reasoning this out, he finally asked, "Why haven't they found any bones of a Sasquatch?"

"They probably have," said Adam. "But they're not telling anybody because it would scare people."

★ 104 ★

"Mmmmmaybe it's 'cause . . . they live in cccccaves." Israel angled his awkward lips, took a breath, then finished. "And nobody's fffffound their cccccaves."

Rubin stared into the dark rainy forest and whimpered, "Too bad we're here."

The rhythm of the rain increased. "Too bad there's Sasquatch," mumbled

Katz.

"Shhhh!" Lakalo interrupted, hearing a noise coming their way. The boys on his side of the tree stared toward the sound and heard leaves crunching. Hearts raced and boys from the back of the tree leaned around to see. Virgil, Lakalo, and Adam were quick to dig into their pockets for their pocketknives. A skittish doe burst out of the darkness and trotted by.

Rubin continued to stare into the darkness, wondering if he'd seen something move near the dark edge of the trees, thirty feet beyond the dying fire. His tired mind thought it was a black hairy foot. Troubled, he fearfully whispered, "There's something out there."

Next to him, Katz farted. It was loud enough to make Joey and Adam chuckle.

"Quiet." Virgil's whisper was urgent. "Something else could be pushing the doe."

Apprehensive, they gazed across the clearing to listen . . . drizzling rain. Then, a distant thump of a helicopter. The sound grew till its powering rotors filled their ears. Joey began to rise when the craft's lights passed. It thundered on.

Downhearted, the troop listened to the receding chopper sound till all that could be heard were drops of rain.

"I bet they're looking for us."

"Shhhh!" Rubin whispered, gazing into the rainy dark, "We shouldn't talk, something's out there."

* * *

The helicopter's blades shot wind and rain downward in a whirling fury. They beat the trees, the ground, the rescue workers, and Junior Commander Alan. A rescue basket was lowered on a cable.

Through the helicopter's doorway, a technician directed the descent of the basket. "Litter has hit the ground."

The rescue workers wasted no time. In moments Alan's body was strapped into the metal basket. Red stepped away, squinting upward, taking on the rain and wind to give a thumbs-up.

Fifty feet above, the helicopter technician worked the switch, raising the basket. "Litter is coming up . . . Litter is through the trees."

Rain covered Alan's body as it rose above the trees.

Looking down from the helicopter's doorway, the technician worked the cable. "Litter is spinning."

Within minutes, the technician grabbed the basket and pulled it on board. "Litter is on the deck."

In an instant, the helicopter swept away, leaving behind the rescue team.

Red hunched over his log book to keep it from getting wet and wrote, *Helicopter pickup at 3:12 am.* He glanced up to see Commander Charles's haggard face.

"What's it look like tracking down the rest of the boys?" the Commander asked.

Red didn't want to remind him that rain washes smells away, and from here on, it'd be tough for the dogs to catch any scent.

* * *

Asleep against the tree, Katz said a line of gibberish then leaned forward, his hands pressing into the damp soil as his knees guided him out from under the tree. Although his face brushed branches, he didn't awake. The sleepwalker arose and journeyed forward as if his life had purpose. Here and there he conversed with some invisible person or force as he traveled into the dark. The rain had stopped, but the leaves of the red buds still carried rain drops and Katz's pants dampened as he pressed through the low bushes. On he walked, sometimes stumbling, mumbling a language that made no sense.

His wet legs went up and down the rolling landscape; ten minutes passed before he walked headlong into an oak tree.

* * *

Light rose from the eastern sky, blazed over the tops of the trees, casting long, dark shadows. Virgil was up first, moving through the morning freshness toward the rabbit snare. He glimpsed something tan lying still, and his heart pounded with excitement. Nearing the rabbit, he bent and ran his hand over its soft fur, his fingers especially appreciating the delicate ears. He undid his wire snare, took his catch by the hind legs, and carried it back to the dead fire. Setting it down, he went about the task of getting the fire going. It didn't take long before flames were devouring the wood he fed them.

Virgil shifted his attention to the cottontail. Israel awoke and leaned sleepy-eyed against the tree. He saw the Kentuckian working his knife into something. Perplexed at what he was doing, Israel rubbed his eyes, then leaned forward and squinted. He saw Virgil cleaning a lumpy brownish red substance out of a furry body.

"What are you doing?"

Proud of his catch, Virgil grinned with joy, lifting the creature. "I got a rabbit."

Taken aback, Israel moved his hand awkwardly up near his mouth and moaned, "Ohhh."

After skinning the rabbit, Virgil returned to the fire. He cut it in two, thrust a sharp stick through each half, and carefully placed them near the fire.

Ten minutes passed, then Lakalo called out, "I can smell that from over here." He came out from under the tree. "Do I get a piece?"

"We'll . . . I'll split it up for everybody."

"What is it? A bird?"

"It's a rabbit."

"That sure is small." Lakalo eyed the cooking meat and rubbed his belly.

"It's a cottontail."

Walking hunched, Israel dragged his foot toward them. He stopped and stared down at the meat. "Ppppoor rabbit."

Adam followed and drawing near the fire, studied the two small roasting pieces. "What is it?"

Virgil pointed to the bloodied rabbit skin. "It's a cottontail."

"Can I get some?"

Virgil proudly nodded. "I'm going to cut it up."

"Hillbilly, can I have some?" Joey asked and rubbed his cold arms.

"Yeah, everybody's going to get some."

"Ppppoor rabbit," said Israel.

"Would you shut up on that?" Lakalo's hunger drove. "Who cares how poor it is. It's dead. And I'm going to eat some."

Holding his stiffened hand to his chest, Israel shrugged and stepped away. Virgil attempted to calm him. "It's okay . . . don't need to get worked up. The rabbit's gone now." His voice was kind. "Anyway, he'll give us a little energy."

Israel looked through the openings in the trees at the distant blue sky.

Virgil knelt down, took hold of the end of the skewer stick, rolled it over, and leaned it against a rock.

With mounting excitement, Adam sniffed the browning meat. "That's coming along good."

"We made it through another night," Spencer said, nodding his head, trying to cheer the troop. "We should be back at the trailhead soon."

"Not the way you were taking us," the Southerner said.

Rubin walked between them. "We're lucky the Sasquatch didn't find us." He tiredly glanced about. It seemed like someone was missing but he didn't know who.

Joey moved his dry tongue around his parched mouth and watched Virgil pick some moss off an oak, roll it in a ball then pop it into his mouth. He went to a leaf and put his tongue on the bottom to suck off a drop of water.

"Hey, the rabbit fell over." Adam pointed at the brown lump that was laying in the ashes.

"We can't eat it now; it's all dirty," Joey said.

"I'll eat yours then," said Adam, starved.

"Forget it, I'm eating it. Hillbilly, the rabbit's in the ashes."

"Don't call him Hillbilly," Lakalo sneered at Joey, his hunger driving his anger.

Virgil approached, nonchalantly rolling the moss between his fingers, and closed on Israel. "Here, Israel. Try this." He offered Israel the moss ball. "It'll give you some energy."

Israel took it and brought it up near his nose. Virgil watched him awkwardly place it in his mouth. Israel frowned at the taste then spit it out. "It ttttaste tttttterrible." Israel righted himself, his hand drawing near his chest and his fingers pointing down.

"You have to eat something," Virgil said, worriedly.

"It's . . . okkkkkay," Israel said.

"Hillbilly, the rabbit fell over."

Virgil moved toward the fire, his thoughts on Israel. He knelt next to the heat and using two sticks propped the meat back upright. It smoked and seared a burnt burgundy, spitting juices out.

"Anybody see where Katz is?" Rubin asked, anxiously.

"Katz?" Virgil rose from the fire, calling, "Katz?"

"Don't yell," Rubin implored.

"He hasn't had his medicine in a few days," Spencer said.

"Katz sleepwalks," Lakalo said ominously. There was an abrupt seriousness about the troop, it was as if they'd been poked by a needle.

Virgil walked toward the rising sun and called, "Katz?"

"I bet a Sasquatch got him and it's going to kidnap us one at a time till we're all eaten." Fearful, Rubin glanced around the shadowy forest.

"I bet he sleepwalked into the forest," Lakalo said.

"We have to go find him." Virgil said. "He's got to be found."

"The Sasquatch will find us."

Virgil sternly glanced back at Rubin. "If they took Katz, they already know we're here." Turning west he yelled, "Katz?"

"He could be anywhere out there," Lakalo said hopelessly, staring into the forest.

"He could be dead," Joey said, "and you're making a lot of noise for nothing."

"I'm going to find him." Virgil moved toward the tree they had slept under and searched for clues. None presented themselves. He reasoned Katz walked in the same direction that he'd been facing under the tree and perhaps to the right.

Daniel came alongside. "I'll help."

"I want to help, but I don't want to get lost," Adam said.

"I don't get lost," Virgil confidently said while tossing a glance at Spencer. He went to the right of a red bud bush. "If you stay within eyesight of each other you won't get lost."

Adam and Lakalo joined them and the four fanned out into the forest. Spencer wanted to help but he was smarting from Virgil's *getting lost* comment.

"Katz?" Virgil called. To his right were Lakalo and Daniel. "Fan out wider, we're too close."

Daniel swung farther to the right. The landscape rose then dropped. It was comforting to have Lakalo in view. Out of the tree's shade he felt the sun's warming rays and heard Virgil again call, "Katz?" Ahead of them a squirrel leaned over a branch and gave a high pitched chatter. Daniel imagined being totally lost in a vast forest—it was a scary thought.

Ten minutes into the search his eyes scanned the area beneath an oak tree. At first he didn't recognize the body, but then his eyes snapped back. It was Katz.

"Hey!" He hurried toward him. "He's over here!" It was a relief to see him move. "Hey, Katz. You okay?"

Katz moaned, pressing his palm into his swollen forehead.

While helping him up, Daniel noticed Katz's bruised forehead. "That's bad. Wow." Katz stumbled. Daniel grabbed him by the arm to keep him from falling. "You look a little woozy."

Virgil approached. "You got a bump there. You hit that tree?"

Katz stared at the ground. "You got any water?"

"I got a rabbit and there's still some water on the leaves. They're still damp." He pointed toward the oak leaves.

"You got a rabbit?"

"Yea," Virgil proudly said, "I'm cooking it up right now."

On their way back, Virgil snagged a flat stone to use to cut the rabbit on. The rabbit was well done by the time he took hold of the first stick. The rest of the famished troop found strength to welcome Katz and examine what looked like a third eye on his forehead. Then hunger overcame their sympathy and it wasn't long before they were back gathered around the rabbit, waiting.

Virgil rose from the white meat and nodded toward Katz. "You guys go ahead." Lakalo and Adam were immediately down on their knees, trying to figure out which piece was the biggest.

Lakalo took the first piece, Adam snagged his next. Rubin and Joey bumped shoulders when they went after theirs. Katz continued to rub his forehead, watching.

Rubin asked Virgil, "Aren't you going to take any?"

Virgil nodded and pointed to the dirt covered piece. "Go ahead."

"This rabbit is good," Lakalo licked the corner of his lips and stared down at the remaining pieces, coveting them.

"Ppppoor rabbit," Israel said.

Virgil looked at Israel with concern. "They say it's good." His voice was encouraging "A fella needs to eat." Israel's eyes kept drifting back to the damp rabbit fur; the sight of it disturbed him. Virgil tapped him and pointed at the meat. "Take your piece, Israel."

"Nooo . . . you go ahead . . . I dddon't want nnnone."

Lakalo and Adam eyed the two remaining pieces. "If you don't eat it, I will," Lakalo said with glee, "I got first dibs."

Virgil tried to persuade Israel. "You're going to need some strength to get back to the van. It'll give you some energy."

Israel stared at the small piece of ash-covered meat, then swung his head. "It's okkkkay." He gave him a tired look.

Virgil could see the sparkle in Israel's eye was gone. He gently led him away from the rest of the troop.

Out of their hearing, Virgil turned and spoke softly, "Listen, Israel. I can't look after you if you don't eat. I told Commander Charles I'd look after you. You have to eat."

Israel swung his head away from him.

"You like chicken, don't you?"

Israel swung his head back. "Yeahhh."

Virgil lifted the piece of meat. "This meat tastes like chicken."

Israel's took the offered meat, bringing it near his nose, then eyed it as if it were alive.

Virgil bit into his piece to persuade him. "It tastes like chicken, and it'll give you energy. You're going to need energy 'cause you and I are going back to the van today."

Israel swung his head around and looked again at the bloodied rabbit skin, "Vvvvvirgil, you eat it. I ccccan't eat the bbbbunny."

Virgil pleaded, "You got to eat it, Israel." He angled his head toward Spencer. "This guy took us way off-course. It's a long way back to the van now, and you're going to need every bit of that rabbit to keep you going."

CHAPTER 15

Stu worriedly trudged across the tarmac, following Uncle Hawthorne toward a group of planes. Even though his uncle carried two heavy pieces of luggage, he still had a lively step.

The tall man set the luggage down and pointed toward a larger plane.

"That's a Cessna. It's very reliable. It's won several awards for safety and performance."

Stu found his statement somewhat relieving and angled toward it, thinking it was his uncle's plane.

"Stu, it's not that one. My plane's over here." He angled his head proudly toward the smallest plane in the lot. "Isn't she a beauty?"

Stu's mouth dropped. He'd never seen such a small aircraft and wondered how his uncle's six-foot-five-inch frame could ever fit in it. "That's it?" Stu stared at the experimental as if it were a coffin.

"You betcha. I named it after General Custer. I call her Custer."

Surprised, Stu gazed up at his uncle. "Didn't Custer die?"

"Well . . . yes." He placed a proud hand on his nephew's shoulder. "But we all have to die . . . sometime."

Walking toward the high-winged plane, he looked up into the blue sky. "But today we won't talk about dying 'cause we're going flying, and we have the perfect day for flying." He checked his watch: 7:13 a.m. "We got a long way to go."

He unlocked the door and swung it open. "Come up here and take a look-see."

Stu stepped uneasily toward the craft. "You said you have a parachute?"

"Yes. Just right inside." Uncle Hawthorne pointed toward the back of the plane. "It's there, just in case anything goes wrong."

"Wrong?" Stu said, panicky.

Uncle Hawthorne touched him on the shoulder. "Relax, Stu. Nothing is going to go wrong." He pulled the front seat forward to put the luggage behind it. "You're going to be able to sit right next to the pilot. I bet you've never sat in a cockpit before." He glanced down at Stu. "Have you ever sat in a cockpit?"

Stu shook his head. "Does the parachute work?"

"They work like a charm. But you don't want to pull the parachute cord unless you really need to 'cause they cost a fortune to reload." Uncle Hawthorne smugly nodded. "It's going to feel good to get some air under our wings. I love flying. Isn't she a bomb?" He grinned.

The thought of a plane being a bomb disturbed Stu even more.

"Here, let me give you a hand." He helped Stu through the door. "It's going to get hot soon."

Stu held the pilot seat with one hand, the steering column with the other, and looked about the tiny cab. Behind the two seats, the aluminum sides of the plane swept back, leaving a small area just big enough for the few pieces of luggage and a gray lump of fabric with many straps and harnesses that encompassed it. He anxiously pointed at the lump. "Is that the parachute?"

"Yes. It's back there. Scoot over, Stu. Let me in."

The plane rocked, leaning to one side, as the tall man climbed up and angled his frame this way and that until he finally wedged himself into the pilot's seat. "It gets hot down here early." He glanced at Stu. "Let's get that seatbelt on you."

"Shouldn't I put on a parachute first?" Stu stared up at him. Uncle Hawthorne's head came a half-inch short of the metal ceiling.

"You can do that if you want, but generally you put the parachute on if the plane starts to have problems."

"I want to put it on now."

"Okay, Stu. But you might find it a bit uncomfortable on the flight. Head on back there and grab it."

Stu scrambled over the seat top. When he picked up the parachute he noticed a small roll of baling wire caught in it. He unhooked the wire and the plane jerked about as Uncle Hawthorne struggled out the door.

"Com'on, Stu. We'll put it on outside. There's plenty of room outside." He helped Stu back out the door.

After much strapping they finally got the oversized parachute on. "We'd better get under way; it's going to be a hot one."

"What about air conditioning?"

"There's no air conditioning on this bird."

"How's this parachute work?"

Uncle Hawthorne pointed at a pull cord. "You pull that one. But before you do that, you need to count five seconds."

"What if it doesn't work?"

Uncle Hawthorne pointed at another cord. "It takes a few seconds to engage, but if it doesn't open, then you pull this cord"—he touched the lower cord— "there."

"What if that doesn't work?"

Uncle Hawthorne rolled his eyes. "It's going to be a hot one, Stu. We gotta get some air under our wings."

When they got back inside, Uncle Hawthorn saw that Stu was just as wary even with the parachute on. "You want to push the starter button?"

"No."

His uncle glanced at him sideways and pushed the starter button. The engine rolled over. It sounded way out of tune. Uncle Hawthorne adjusted the throttle. The engine rolled over and over. Uncle Hawthorne frowned and let go of the starter button. "I need you to push the button while I go underneath." He bent lower, opening the door to make room to crawl under the dash.

Stu watched him maneuver his long leg outside while bending lower and lower to get under the dash. Finally under it, he commanded, "Okay, Stu. Go ahead. Push the starter." The engine made a series of pops as it rolled over and over. Stu's worries increased when he heard his uncle pound on something.

Suddenly, the engine puffed as it sparked and came alive. "Don't push the starter!" his uncle shouted, quickly crawling out from underneath the dash, admonishing, "No, no. You don't want to do that 'cause it'll wear out the starter gear. But you did good Stu . . . Old Custer's a going now." He revved it. The engine sounded like a band of loud, out-of-tune rocks banging around. Outside, the propeller spun in a blur.

"What happens if the starter goes?"

"What's that?"

Stu raised his voice. "What happens if the starter goes?"

Uncle Hawthorne looked thoughtful, the top of his head touching the ceiling. "If the starter gear goes and something happens up there"—he angled his chin toward the sky, his eccentric eyes telling stories, haunting stories—"then things get real quiet." He began his preflight procedures and stared down at the instrument panel, worked a few controls, and checked the wings. He glanced over at Stu, who appeared disturbed. "Hey, Stu!" he encouraged, patting him on the shoulder. "Old Custer's running good!"

The speed of the engine rose to a deafening noise. The plane rolled forward, and Stu grabbed onto the door handle as it taxied toward the runway.

Uncle Hawthorne took the microphone and talked to the control tower.

Cleared to take off, the little plane gained the runway, revved its engine, and hurled itself down the long concrete.

Stu perched himself upright and stared at the end of the runway, then up at his tall uncle, who gave him a wild grin. To Stu's amazement, the plane came off the ground and slowly rose. He took hold of the parachute pull cord and looked directly down. Uncle Hawthorne's voice rose in a song. *"Up*

we go, into the wild blue yonder, flying high, over the sun!"
Stu could barely hear him over Custer's roar.

CHAPTER 16

Spencer glanced around the small clearing where the troop had spent the night. The fire was dead, the fir branches they'd slept under were scattered about the base of the tree.

"What time is it?" Virgil asked.

Spencer checked his watch. "It's 8:36 a.m. We should be back at the trail soon, then we'll go straight to the van."

"Which direction are you heading?" Virgil asked.

Spencer tentatively pointed southwest. "That way."

"That's the wrong direction." Firm in his conviction, Virgil pointed northeast. "The trail is over there, not over there." He shot a glance in Spencer's proposed direction.

"We're this way of the van now." Spencer fanned his hand toward himself.

"You've taken us way off-course."

Spencer could feel the challenge, and became obstinate. "No. I know the compass. And I checked it, and that's the right direction." He pointed southwest.

"You're not going the right way. Can't you tell from the sun, the direction it came up?" Virgil pointed toward the shadow cast by a nearby pine. "Can't you see from the shadows, the way they are . . . now?"

Katz dumbly looked at the shadow. "What's wrong with the shadow?"

Exasperated, Virgil jerked an accusing finger at Spencer. "You're wrong in going that way!"

"I have the compass. I took the compass course and passed it. Have you passed the compass course?" There was a long pause as he glared at Virgil. "No, you didn't." He offered the compass to Virgil. "Do you know how to read a compass?" Virgil stared at the glass and felt embarrassed at the question.

Joey joked, "Hey, Hillbilly . . . it looks kind of round doesn't it?"

Others chuckled at Virgil.

"Here, take it," Spencer said, extending it toward him.

A rousing anger gripped Virgil. He pushed Spencer's arm away. "You said the same thing yesterday. Over and over you said we'd be on the trail soon. Real soon and we're not! So what good is your compass course?"

"Yeah, we're not," Rubin stated.

"You made us lost," Katz said.

This caught Spencer off guard. "Well, it's . . . well, it's going to work today. You'll see." He turned and shot a demanding glance at Lakalo and Adam, the two he'd rescued. "Let's go." He headed southwest, angling between two pines. Lakalo and Adam fell in behind.

Virgil raised his voice, "I'm going to take Israel back."

Spencer stopped, causing big Lakalo to bump into him. He adjusted his glasses as he turned. His dry lips spoke, "You can't take Israel, we're a troop, we have to stay together."

"A troop that's getting more and more lost."

Rubin asked, "Why can't he go?"

Katz responded, "We'll never make it to Jamberama if we don't all stay together."

"Hillbilly, what's Commander Charles going to say if we don't stay together?"

Spencer shook a trembling finger at Virgil. "That's right. Commander Charles wouldn't go for it."

Determined, Virgil loudly replied, "Commander Charles told me to look after Israel."

Lakalo pulled on Spencer's shoulder. "Are you sure you're going in the right direction?"

"Yes." He nodded assuredly. "Southwest is the way back. And we're

close . . . really close."

Lakalo addressed Virgil, "He says . . . " He thumbed toward Spencer. "He says we should be there soon. I say we just go a little ways and see if we can get there."

"But we're not going to get there, 'cause he's taking us in the wrong direction."

"Hillbilly, how do you know which direction is the right direction without a compass?" Joey taunted.

Angered, Virgil eyed Joey. "'Cause the way the sun comes up and the way it goes down." He pointed west. Joey felt his intensity and looked away from him.

Lakalo pleaded with Virgil, "Instead of fighting all day, let's just try and go Spencer's way. He says it's just a little ways."

Adam added, "Can't you just go a little ways? That way we can stay together."

Behind Virgil, Israel tapped him and craned his awkward neck forward. "Let's jjjjust gooooo with them."

His statement killed Virgil's intentions. Saddened, he looked like a whipped dog that couldn't save its master no matter how hard he tried.

"Well, let's get going," Lakalo said, waving an impatient hand. "Don't want to wait around here all day when we can get back to town and eat some hamburgers."

Holding his compass, Spencer was quick to head to the front of the line and lead southwest.

Virgil stepped out of Israel's way, letting him pass. The tired troop trudged away from him. His anger grew as he cast a troubled glance east.

* * *

The constant roar of Uncle Hawthorn's plane, coupled with the oppressive heat, drove sweat down Stu's face into his soaked T-shirt. Hoping to catch the full force of the breeze, he leaned closer to the plane's open window and stared out at the distant forest. The breeze didn't enliven the exhausted one.

Uncle Hawthorne loudly spoke, "Isn't it great?"

Haggard, Stu turned toward him. "It's so hot."

Uncle Hawthorne gazed at him, perplexed, then lifted his finger as it came to him. "You're not used to Southern humidity. You could take that darn parachute off. It heats you up plenty."

Stu took another look out the window. It was a terribly long way down.

"That's a hot old thing. Anyway, we're going to be in the Black Crow in about an hour."

"I'm not going to take it off."

"Okay, Stu. It's up to you."

Stu took another fearful look out the window. The distant tree tops gave his stomach a hollow feeling.

Uncle Hawthorne's cheerful eyes turned back to look out the window. He sang, *"It's a good day for flying, Mr. Bean. It's a good day for flying, Mr. Bean."*

* * *

The search and rescue crew lay sprawled out under the shade of a pine, sound asleep. Beyond them, the hound dogs slept. One black-and-tan got up and trotted down to the creek for a drink.

A rescue worker suddenly awoke and scratched a chigger bite on his neck. He sat up and looked toward the scout's tents, then glanced at his watch. It was 12:47. The noonday sun was steamy off the tent tops. He had no problem lying back down.

From behind the tents came Commander Charles. Coming in from his search, he looked haggard, famished. Hearing something to his right, he glanced that way to see another group of search and rescue workers coming around the trail. This cheered him, and he lifted his arm to wave.

A bald man in the front of the line returned the wave.

It wasn't long before they converged.

"Here come my heroes," the Commander mumbled to himself. His mind was so fatigued that it was running on nerves, totally spent from endless hours of searching.

"Someone said you lost your troop." The others gathered about the blond, blue-eyed Commander who normally had it all in control.

"Are you the one with the missing troop?"

"Yes." Charles felt a mixture of anxiety and embarrassment.

* * *

Old Custer rattled and shook as it approached the landing strip. Stu looked as if he was in a torture chamber, sitting bolt upright, perched like a caged bird, his eyes glued on the runway. Anticipating the worst, he clutched the door handle. Every deflection of the wind shifted the tiny craft about, making it feel like it was made out of rice paper.

As he worked the controls, Uncle Hawthorne confidently bobbed his shoulders back and forth to an old-fashioned tune.

The lines on the landing strip came up fast. Stu caught his breath, staring wide-eyed at the approaching concrete. With a skid and a jerk the wheels hit and the engine slowed as Uncle Hawthorne pulled back on the throttle and steadied the craft. He gave it a bit more throttle. It roared down the runway. He backed it off again, grinned and loudly spoke, "Old Custer did it again. He won another battle. See, Stu, there's nothing to it."

Stu let out a long breath to relieve his stress, but hung on to the door, for the plane was braking, and anything could happen in the tiny craft.

When the plane finally came to a stop, Stu quickly unstrapped the parachute. The bulk was hot and he was desperate to get it off. Feeling off-balance, he fanned his sweat-soaked T-shirt and more than once put his hand to the dash to steady himself.

Before they left the plane, his uncle had him retrieve a dry shirt. The Black Crow was too fine a restaurant to look as if you were dragged from an old wringer.

Stu's wrung-out body stumbled into the restaurant. What he liked best about the Black Crow was its air conditioning, so cool. He had no trouble melting into the circular cushioned seats. It wasn't long before he downed half a jug of iced tea. The burger and fries were delicious too.

By the time they left, he felt somewhat revived. But it didn't last; outside, the oppressive humidity beat on the Montana kid. A clammy tenseness permeated him as he waited for his uncle to refuel Old Custer. He stared at the winged deathtrap and wished, *If only I could get out of this flight.*

Uncle Hawthorne approached. "You going to put on the parachute?"

Eyeing the deathtrap, Stu ran a hand across his damp forehead and wondered what was worse: dying of heatstroke inside the aluminum cooker or crashing to the ground? "I'm going to keep it on the floor in front of me."

"That's fine, Stu. Whatever you want. Wasn't that a fine lunch?"

"It was good . . . but my stomach's no good. I got to go to the bathroom again."

Coming out of the washroom, Stu gathered what was left of himself and somehow headed back to the plane. How he dreaded the moment. That plane was like a coffin to him.

Careful not to disturb the parachute on the floor, lest he somehow pull the cord, he clambered in.

"Stu, you want to push the starter button?"

Stu shook his head.

Perplexed, his uncle gazed at his passenger and pushed the starter. It klanged round and round. RRRRRRR, KAAPOOF, RRRRRR KAPOOF. The big man pulled his finger off the starter and once again opened the door and angled his awkward six-foot-five-inch frame under the dash. "Could you push the starter?"

Nervous, Stu leaned over and pushed the starter button. Below him was the torso of his uncle, who was pounding on metal as the engine turned over.

Finally, the engine ignited, coming alive. Again it sounded like a bunch of rattling rocks to the Montanan.

Sporting a proud grin, Uncle Hawthorne crawled out from under the dash. "Old Custer's a good old bird."

Stu watched him guardedly as he took hold of the controls.

Uncle Hawthorne thumbed toward the back. "I keep a roll of baling wire in the back just in case things get out of hand." He gave Stu a goofy grin and patted him on the shoulder. "I bet it reminds you of the farm. Huh, Stu?"

Stu swallowed, wanting nothing more than to get off Custer before it crashed. He glanced back at the small roll of baling wire in the back of the plane. The Montanan knew what baling wire was for: fixing things that were broken.

Uncle Hawthorne brought the RPM up, and Stu once again grabbed the door handle. Custer roared down the runway.

* * *

Bitten by a chigger, Lakalo slapped his leg and sat up. His weary eyes took in Adam, Joey, and Spencer, who were spread out under an oak tree. Scratching the bite, Lakalo turned his gaze in the direction of Rubin, Katz, Israel, Daniel, and Virgil, who were clustered under another oak thirty feet away. Lakalo felt the full impact of the Southern humidity. Hot and sticky, he ran his finger down his sweaty brow and gazed at the heat waves rising off a patch of sunlit dirt. Opening his mouth, he touched his tongue to the sides of his dry lips, then tried to swallow. He couldn't.

His heavy head angled toward Spencer. "I thought you said we'd be at the trail by now?"

"Yeah." Joey sat up, vigorously scratching his leg then snapped, "Why aren't we there yet?" He shot an accusing glare at Spencer.

Lakalo tiredly asked, "Is there something wrong with that compass?"

Spencer pulled the compass off his neck and handed it to Lakalo.

Lakalo looked it over, leveled it, tapped the glass, then carefully pushed it away from his chest. He watched the red needle swing back and forth until it settled into one position, which he assumed was north.

Spencer pointed at the needle. "You see, that's north, and we came in heading northeast. Then we came back on the trail on this side of it. And if we want to go back and find it again, we have to go southwest. And that's," he pointed, "the direction we're heading."

"But we're lost, so something's wrong."

"'Cause we're lost," Joey said, smartly. "And you got us lost."

Adam added, "We're going to die if we don't get water today. We're all going to die."

"That's not so," Spencer said. "The book says we can live three days without water. It's only been two days since we left."

"The book!" Joey gazed at him with disdain. "What does that book know about my stomach?"

"I could do with a nice tall Coke and a double, double cheeseburger right about now."

"We're going to miss Jamberama. Can you believe it? We come all the way out from California, and we're going to miss Jamberama," Adam said, a small tear forming in his eye. "Jamberama would've been so much fun."

Across from them Virgil picked at some pale green moss on the tree, carefully removed it, then tasted it, rubbing his tongue over the surface, and finally chewed it. He tapped Israel to get his attention and quietly said, "I told you he doesn't know where he's going." He glared across at Spencer.

Israel asked, "You know how to get back?"

Virgil nodded. "But it's a long way now. At least a five-hour walk." He lifted a finger in Spencer's direction. "He really took us wrong; he really did. We should've gone back this morning. We would've been back there by now."

"I'm sorry, Virgil," Israel moaned. "I'm sorry."

"It's all right . . . Will you come with me when it cools down?"

"Yeah." Israel gave him an awkward nod.

"I'll go with you," Rubin said. "Can you get us another rabbit?"

"I'm going, too," stated Katz. "You know how to get there . . . right?"

"I know." Virgil was definite. "I've been in the woods since I was born and never been lost. Come hunting season, we'd be out every weekend. My daddy and I go out. We hunt turkey or deer. My daddy's gotten a bunch of black bears. We got eight deer just last year."

"Eight? Is that legal?"

"It sure is. We got a tag for each one of them. Tie it to their ear."

"What do you do with all them deer?"

"We eat 'em . . . one at a time."

Katz chuckled. "Is deer any good to eat?"

"It's better than raccoon."

"You eat raccoon?"

"Yeah, raccoon's good, dogs love coon hunts. They get really excited about that." He nodded. "Sleep all day and hunt all night." Suddenly, his grin evaporated and a lump formed in his throat as he stared across at Spencer, the one who'd led them astray. This was the worst situation he'd ever been in: no food, no water, and miles from the trail. It seemed hopeless, but his determination drove. "When it cools, we're going."

* * *

The plane rattled forty-three hundred feet above the Texas landscape. Inside, Uncle Hawthorne pointed toward the distant horizon. "That area's known as Texarkana. It's famous for its Bigfoot sightings." He kindly patted Stu's arm. "Hey, Stu, I know how much you like to drive . . . tractors and the mini-chopper. You want to steer?"

Stu was so convinced the plane was going to rumble apart any second that he didn't respond.

His uncle nudged him, "Stu, you want to be the pilot?" He grinned, staring down on his nephew's florescent white hair with orange highlights.

The way the small plane jerked up and down had worn Stu's nerves, fatiguing him to the point that he sat rigid, staring at an empty rivet hole. Previously, a sinking feeling gripped him when he ventured to look out the window. At times, he felt as if his mind were reeling, spinning faster than the propeller. At other times, seconds seemed to take hours to tick past. Now, as he stared at the rivet hole he imagined the entire structure suddenly ripping apart.

"Stu, you want to drive?"

He gave the smallest shake of his head. Consumed by fear, Stu held tightly to the door handle, his only movement came when he allowed himself to slowly angle to see the parachute. Oh how he wished he'd put it on when they took off from the Black Crow Restaurant. Now, he felt terribly stiff and light-headed, wanting nothing more than to get off the death trap.

"Stu?"

The young man was slow to move his head to look up at his uncle.

Thoroughly enjoying the flight and everything about the tiny craft, Uncle Hawthorne glanced over his compass. "This is a bad area because of its iron content. It makes a compass go screwy." He pointed at his compass. "You see that? We're really heading northeast, but that's off." Running his fingers over the GPS, he continued, "I count on my Global Positioning System when I'm around these parts. You can count on a GPS."

Stu allowed his eyes to go down to the parachute again.

"Last week, I took the boss up." Uncle Hawthorne frowned. "What a puker old Mortis was. Good thing I brought bags." He pulled a plastic garbage bag out from under the seat and shook it about. Trembling, Stu stared at it. "That old boy threw up everything and then some . . . I mean and then some."

* * *

Feeling the day's heat waning, Virgil rose and glanced back at Israel. "We got to get going. It's a long way back." He offered his hand to help. Israel's palm came up slowly, mechanically. Virgil pulled him to his feet.

Dead tired and hungry, Rubin stood, "I'm going."

"Me too," Katz said, on the rise.

At the oak across from them, Spencer also rose, saying something to Lakalo about being really close now. With Adam and Joey, they approached Virgil's newly formed troop.

Watching their approach, Virgil fired the first volley. "We're not going that way anymore." He pointed west. "We're going back to the van. If any of you want to come with us, you can."

Challenged, Spencer defiantly shook his head. "You can't lead." He thumbed impatiently toward his chest while walking toward him. "I'm the leader. We had a vote." He glanced at Katz as if he were a traitor, then back at Virgil. "You're new and haven't even got your First-Class."

The hair on the back of Virgil's neck rose. "You've been getting us lost."

"I can't be lost. I have the compass. It's just a little farther than I thought it was."

"You've been saying that over and over."

Virgil looked past Spencer at Lakalo, Adam, and Joey. "Any of you want to come with us?"

Spencer pressed a desperate hand into Virgil's chest. "You can't take anybody. You can't break up the troop. That's not right."

Virgil pushed his hand down, repeating, "Any of you want to come with us?"

With a tired shake of his head, Lakalo protested, "You shouldn't break up the troop."

Virgil felt bad for them. His eyes met Adam's. Although Adam wanted to change direction and go with him, he shook his head, feeling he owed Spencer his allegiance—it was Spencer who'd returned for him when he and Lakalo were lost.

"It's not that much farther," Spencer argued, pointing southwest. "It's just over there."

"You've been saying that for two days. You keep getting us lost . . . more and more." Virgil addressed the others. "You might not make it if you don't come."

Spencer's voice rose. "I'm the leader. I was voted in. I've got my First-Class. And I've got the compass." Aggressively, he pressed his hand into Virgil's chest. "It's settled then: You can't take them!"

Virgil pushed his hand away and started in the direction he intended to go.

Spencer quickly stepped in front of Rubin, who was following Virgil. "Let him go, Rubin. If he wants to get lost, let him do it." His hand trembled as it pointed at Virgil. "He doesn't know what he's doing. He doesn't even know how to read a compass. He doesn't know!"

"He got the rabbit." Rubin stepped around Spencer. "And I'm going with him."

Spencer put his hand on Katz's shoulder. "Don't go, Katz. It's not right."

"I'm going." Katz brushed by Spencer, heading toward Virgil as if his life depended on it.

Next came Israel, awkward as ever, shoulders rolling wildly up and down with each angled step. Spencer grabbed him by the wrist. "You can't go, Israel. You can't go. He's taking you on a death march!"

With a slow mechanical movement, Israel's other hand reached across his body to free himself from Spencer's grip. "I'mmmmm sorry, Sppppencer, but I . . . ggggo with Vvvvirgil." He tried to break free, but Spencer was too quick.

He grabbed him with his other hand. "You have to stay."

"Let him go!" Virgil came on like a lion, angrily knocking Spencer in the shoulder.

Spencer was relentless and wouldn't let go of Israel. As soon as Virgil pulled one of Spencer's hands off Israel, the other grabbed hold. Finally, Virgil caught Spencer off balance and pushed him.

Stumbling backward, Spencer fell. He rushed up and came at Israel who was being led away by Virgil. Spencer bowled in and grabbed Israel.

Virgil ended up between them and, using the butt of his palm, pushed Spencer's chin back. Israel dodged out and moved closer to Katz.

A reckless frustration came over Spencer—*Virgil wouldn't obey the rules! He was taking his troop! He needed to be brought in-line!* Spencer's clarity of mind left him, his face furled into a menacing, frustrated frown, he stepped back to square off with Virgil, then rushed forward, slamming into him, knocking him backward.

Virgil, stronger, retaliated by batting Spencer's hands down.

Unyielding, Spencer pushed, blocking Virgil like some awkward offensive lineman.

Virgil grabbed hold of his shirt, spun, and flung him to the ground.

"Leave him be!" Adam shouted. The rest of the boys watched in dismay.

Spencer wasn't about to stop. *Virgil needed to be brought in-line!* Down on all fours, he panted, then charged, plowing into the rebel.

Virgil was shoved backward but in no time regained ground. The two stomped back and forth like two rutting bull elk. So much energy was spent that they leaned into each other to get a second wind.

Finally, Virgil grabbed hold of Spencer's collar and again flung him to the ground.

Spencer caught his breath while his fingers dug a fistful of dirt. He rose, charged then flung the dirt at Virgil.

Half-blinded by the dust, Virgil let loose a flurry of desperate punches, most of which hit his opponent in the hands or arms. But the last caught Spencer on the side of his mouth. The impact was heard by all. It knocked Spencer sideways, his glasses flew though the air. Dazed, he stumbled and fell to the ground.

"Stop!" Adam shouted. He picked up Spencer's glasses.

Noticing blood smeared across Spencer's cheek, big Lakalo pointed at Virgil and yelled, "You shouldn't do that!" He tightened his fist.

Joey threw his two bits in, blurting, "Arky, that's wrong."

Breathing hard and blinking, Virgil fingered the dust out of his eyes. "He pushed me first, and he wouldn't let Israel go." He tried to catch his breath.

There was a tense pause. Virgil kept blinking, trying to get the dirt out. He stepped back as the big Hawaiian closed on him.

"Go then . . . just go!" Joey shouted, shooing his hand forward as he walked toward Spencer.

Virgil didn't waste any time. "Let's go." Backing away, he waved to Israel.

Katz, Rubin, and Israel followed, all of them looking back. Israel gave a sad wave.

Katz felt strange, as if he were losing half his family, yet was drawn to his new leader and his ability to punch. He called out to them. "When we get back we'll tell the Sherriff where you are."

A stunned, shocked silence enveloped the remaining group. They watched their friends disappear over a knoll.

Adam felt torn up inside, and groaned, "We got to pray!"

"It's no use," Joey said, "We're doomed."

* * *

Inside the plane's tight cockpit, Stu stared at the tiny rivet hole. The temperature had somehow risen. *How could it have gotten any hotter?* Sweat streamed out of him. Under the constant roar of the plane's engine he felt like a cat with half his body held underwater – the other half on a never-ending roller coaster. Each time the wind jerked the tiny plane; he tightened his grip on the door handle but dared not look out the window to take in the Texas landscape. When the wind slapped the small craft sideways, his nerves frayed, unraveled, spiking his imagination – *Was he going to pass-out? Was he going to die?*

Uncle Hawthorne looked over at his nephew. Stu was obviously stressed, perspiring so much that his wet T-shirt was getting his pants damp. "Goodness, Stu, what are you working yourself up for? Aren't you the fearless one who can do back flips atop a horse at full speed? This should be a piece of cake."

His words were a blur to the formally fearless cowboy. Again the wind caught the tiny craft and again Stu's fingers dug into the door handle. The never-ending strain of being locked in a rattling cage and shaken about, fifty-three hundred feet above the earth, kept poking at him like some cruel keeper of the cage.

The constant engine roar strained him to the point of dizziness. He panted. There wasn't enough air in the cabin. Panicked, he grasped at a last desperate prayer. *Please God, please Lord, please get me out of this.*

The hopeless prayer was just out of his lips when the plane's engine coughed—it was as if it, too, were choking for air. It stalled, coughed—then died. The propeller came to a whirling stop. One end of its blade stuck in the one o'clock position. Stu heard wind whistle through the windows and openings. If the Montanan's heart wasn't already low enough, it fell another thousand feet.

While Uncle Hawthorne pressed on the starter, he looked over the engine gauges. For the first time, he didn't appear so robust, or carry such a breezy confidence. Ducking his head to see out the window, he searched the landscape for a road, a field, or a meadow to land in. A road angled off to the east, but it offered no relief, for it was too winding, too encompassed by trees, and a long way off.

Stoically, he looked down at Stu. "Stu, you might want to put that parachute on."

Any lack of movement from the fearful one burst forth in a blur of motion as the boy bent, quickly lifted the rig, and threw it over his shoulders, moving so fast it would've made a mongoose take a second look.

His uncle didn't notice. He was intent on studying the winding road, determining whether he could make it.

Stu's deathly serious fingers quickly shoved, ramming the strap into the buckle. But it kept jamming.

Uncle Hawthorne glanced down at the blur. "Can you push the starter while I go under?"

Wide-eyed, Stu nodded, then jerked his head when Uncle Hawthorne opened the door. The hundred-plus-knot wind blew in as his uncle's leg went out the opening. This allowed him to get his long torso under the dash. He called out, "Okay, Stu, go ahead."

Breathing heavily, Stu pushed the starter button. The engine went round and round.

Below, Uncle Hawthorne pounded on metal. "Stop!" he yelled.

The terrified boy let go of the button. No time was wasted to get back to strapping on the parachute. Abruptly the plane caught a gust of wind and jerked sideways. Stu rammed his hand into the pilot's seat for balance. Beyond his uncle's leg, he saw the oncoming Texas landscape. Panting, he pushed off of the seat.

His uncle's voice came distant and unreal, "Go ahead, Stu, push the starter."

As the starter engaged, Stu could hear his uncle pound on something, the engine rolling over and over but didn't ignite.

"Okay, Stu, stop!" Uncle Hawthorne popped his head out, hastily adjusted the throttle, then disappeared back under the dash. "Okay, go ahead and push the button."

Again, Stu let go of the parachute buckle to push the starter. He could hear the whine of the engine. The pounding was more desperate now.

"Stop!" yelled his uncle, who quickly crawled out, banging his head on the dash before pulling his long legs back inside. He hurriedly stared out the window at the winding road in the distance, concluding he would be extremely fortunate to make the landing. "Stu, I don't know what happened to Old Custer, but you might have to parachute out."

If the drum beat hadn't been rolling in Stu's chest before, it was thundering now.

Uncle Hawthorne grabbed the hanging buckle on the parachute and ran a strap through then tightened it. Even at that, the adult-sized parachute was too big for Stu.

Stu saw his uncle's thumb aimed toward the rear.

"Go back and get that baling wire." The whistle of the wind was an eerie reminder of Custer's fate as Stu scrambled, parachute and all, over the seat. His feverish mind wondered how his uncle was going to wire up the engine before the plane crashed.

Uncle Hawthorne again pushed the starter. The engine rolled over and over.

Beside him, Stu struggled over the seats. "Here," he called, angling the baling wire toward him.

His uncle took the wire and Stu couldn't believe his eyes when he started wiring the parachute straps tighter with the baling wire.

In finishing, his uncle gave a valiant grin. "Don't want you falling out. It's really for adults, but I think it'll work now."

The words *falling out* flashed in Stu's mind like a Las Vegas billboard.

His uncle gave a final twist to the wire and handed the roll to him. "I can't find anything to cut it with so hang on to the roll." He gave a quick glance out the window. "Don't let it go. You don't want it to get caught up in the parachute. Lord knows what would happen then." He took Stu's other hand and placed it on the pull cord. "Listen, Stu. You have to pull this three seconds after you jump. Got that? . . . Three seconds."

The wide-eyed kid nodded.

Uncle Hawthorne thumbed toward the door as he grabbed his radio mic, his

fingers roving to turn it on. His voice was urgent. "You better jump!" He banked the plane to the left to try to catch the road in the far distance.

Stu didn't know which hand to use to open the door, the one that held the baling wire or the one that held the pull cord, so he turned backward and leaned into it, pushing the door open with his elbow. Then, he froze. Ninety-knot winds howled straight at him. Staring down, Stu saw tree tops, thirty-nine hundred feet below. It took his breath away. Dropping the pull cord, he jerked away from the opening.

Uncle Hawthorne stared at the road in the distance, calculating his speed and figured he'd have only one attempt to land Custer. He glanced over and was surprised Stu was still there. "Stu, you got to jump!"

Stu yanked the door shut and gasped, "I'm not going to jump!"

Uncle Hawthorne spoke into his microphone, "Houston, we've got a problem. I've got a parachuting due to engine problems, GPS reading six, nine, three, one . . ." He shooed the back of his hand at Stu like one would shoo a fly away. "Stu, you got to jump!"

"I'm not going to jump!" The terrified Montanan blurted and shot a fearful glance out the door's window.

"You might die then!"

Stu glanced up at his uncle, who was glaring out the opposite window at the distant winding road. The starter wound the engine over and over, pressing his uncle's statement home.

Uncle Hawthorne banked the plane left, his eyes piercing Stu, his voice rising. "You have to jump!"

Stu's fingers grasped the parachute as if it were connected to the last lifeboat on the *Titanic*. He could feel the walls of the deathtrap close and forced himself tighter to the door, then peeked down. Again he gasped and jerking back toward his uncle, exclaimed, "I'm not going to jump!"

His uncle let go of the starter to relieve the engine. It was an eerie quiet, a poignant sound of wind whistling through the door cracks.

"We're dropping, Stu, and coming to a point where we're going to be too low to jump. So you better jump."

Petrified, Stu's heart pounded into his skull, blocking out the whistle of the wind. Jerking around, he struggled to push the door open. The vastness of space stretched beyond and the fullness of his uncle's statement came home at the sight of the looming trees. Their tops seemed to be rising up from the landscape, extending toward him. Again, the engine wound.

Stu let go of the door. The wind slammed it shut. He glanced back at his uncle, who was madly working the controls and staring out the window at the road.

Knowing the remote possibility of walking away from a landing in the trees, Uncle Hawthorne glanced over at Stu. "Listen, Stu." His finger thumped the glass on the altimeter. "We're losing altitude. Old Custer is falling . . . fast. If you don't jump, you're not going to make it."

Again, Stu looked out the crack at the bottom of the door, and his eyes watered at the blur of trees. Then he swung his head back to his uncle. "I'm not going to jump!"

"Then you are going to die!" Uncle Hawthorne said, with such force and intensity that it pushed Stu away from him toward the door.

With one hand, Stu grabbed the wire and with the other he grabbed the pull cord. The Montana cowboy closed his eyes, leaned into the door, and pushed it till it opened wider. Strong winds met him, but his shoulder pressed further and further till there was no turning back. He opened his eyes and gasped, then tried to spin to grab the seat, but it was too late. Out the opening he fell. Sweeping under the tail wing, he pulled wildly on the baling wire, thinking it was the parachute pull cord. The gravity of his action was rushing toward him in the form of hot humidity. His neck stretched toward the rapidly closing earth. Again and again, he pulled on the baling wire but to no avail.

The wind screamed by his face, pressing his skin, sickening him. Finally, Stu tilted his rigid head away from the ground to look at the hand he'd been jerking. Realizing it held the baling wire, he frantically jerked the parachute pull cord. Up sailed the chute. It caught and sprang open. The jolt was so hard, so instantaneous, it knocked the wind out of him. He hung there, suffocating, fighting for air in a vast sky that offered nothing but air. Little white stars appeared in his vision.

Finally, he inhaled, taking in deep breaths. As he floated downward, his stomach felt like it was a mile above his chin. He was to the point of losing consciousness and angled his sore head back to breathe.

Below him, his feet dangled as if disconnected. He continued to draw in long, deep breaths. His head dropped, and in the midst of the forest he saw an old garage next to a log cabin. Gaining his breath, he arched his head back to see the wide open parachute and the blue sky beyond, then turned sideways and saw the plane angling away in the distance.

For a second, he felt exhilarated, thrilled at being off that tiny craft, but the sensation instantly left him as his eyes took in the many trees. They were getting closer, yearning for his arrival. He caught a glimpse of a person way down the hill from the cabin, then three others came into view. As they rounded a pine, one was pointing up at him. Suddenly, they were gone, for Stu's descent, coupled with the many trees, cut off his view.

A black puff of smoke shot out the rear of the plane. Its engine engaged in a series of weak revs but none strong enough to lift the craft out of its downward descent.

Inside, Uncle Hawthorne frantically worked the throttle back and forth, desperate to gain altitude. The engine roared, then cut out, then engaged, then backfired. It seemed luck was running with him, for the wheels skimmed the tops of the trees, swooping toward the winding road some hundred yards ahead. Then, the engine sputtered and cut out. The plane was heading straight for a truck moving in the same direction. Sweeping over the top of the old truck, the plane's tires banged the cab, smacked the hood, then hit the pavement directly in front of the it.

In the truck, a stunned old man slammed on the brakes and watched the plane power away from him, down the two-lane highway.

"If this . . . " mumbled his stunned wife, lifting her hand to her wrinkled lips. ". . . if this world's not coming to an end!"

* * *

Spencer's group stared up at a parachute in the sky.

"I think it's the Marines. It's got to be the Marines because Marines jump into forests," Lakalo said.

Daniel walked with excitement in his step. "Marines are tough."

"I think it's somebody with search and rescue," Adam said, forgetting his thirst, happily gazing up at the parachute drifting down.

Forgetting his hunger, Lakalo joked, "I think it's Superman."

Joey interjected, "Superman doesn't need a parachute."

"I don't care. I think it's Superman, 'cause he's going to get us out of here."

"He'd be Superman if he could get us to Jamberama."

"He's doing pretty good to come right down where we are. I bet he's a Navy Seal."

"Navy Seals don't parachute; they swim like frogmen. But he could be Army. I've got an uncle in the Army."

"There's nothing tougher than the Airborne Rangers."

Encouraged by the parachute, Daniel pulled out his harmonica and gave it a blow.

Spencer shielded his glasses from the sun as he looked toward the parachutist, then frowned at how small the parachutist was. "That's no Army man. He's too short."

As Stu came into clear view, there was a perplexed look on each face.

"Army people don't have hair like that. That's not allowed."

"That's a kid!"

Stu's parachute drifted past the top of a tall pine, heading for an opening between the trees. But the parachute didn't clear one tree. It caught on a limb, grabbed hold, and yanked Stu sideways into a mass of branches. He hung there twenty-five feet above the ground, dangling like a puppet on a string.

Out of the forest came Virgil, Israel, Katz, and Rubin, all of them looking for the one they'd seen falling, the one they figured was going to rescue them. They would've walked underneath him except they saw Spencer's oncoming troopers, with their eyes staring up. They turned to witness their superhero slide down the face of the pine tree and crash into the ground.

Virgil was quick to close on him. He knelt beside him. "You okay?"

Stu winced. His hand came up and rubbed the back of his head.

"How do you feel?" Katz asked.

The parachutist painfully sat up.

"What's your name?" Rubin asked.

"Stu." He cleared his throat, then arched his chin toward the direction of the plane. "Did you see if that plane made it?" Joey, Lakalo, and Adam shook their heads.

Katz stepped forward. "I couldn't see because of the trees."

"I heard the plane, but I didn't see it," blurted Rubin.

"I heard something . . . like an engine. Who's in it?"

"My uncle," Stu said sadly.

"He probably made it. Uncles never die," Daniel said, encouragingly.

"Mine did," Joey said.

"Did he die in a plane?"

"No."

"Shut up, then." Daniel turned back to Stu. "He's probably all right. Where you from?"

"Montana."

"Montana Stu?" Daniel said, jokingly.

Stu closed his eyes and rolled his sore neck about. "Some folks call me that."

"No, really. Who are you?" Virgil asked.

"Montana Stu."

Virgil glanced over at the troop and shook his head, knowing that this fluorescent blond-haired kid was *not* Montana Stu. He leaned over Stu to examine the back of his head, figuring he must have bonked it pretty hard to think he was Montana Stu.

Rubin came near, looking over Stu's bright hair and his pale, pale face. He pointed at him. "You're the whitest white boy I ever did see."

Still shaky, Stu replied, "I'm just glad to be back on solid ground." He took a deep breath and ran his fingers through the dirt.

Joey observed, "Well, you're not Special Forces."

"Who are you?"

"Just Stu."

"Montana Stu?" Katz asked again, wondering how out-of-it this kid was.

Stu nodded.

Joey rolled his eyes, gaping at Stu's weird blond hair. "Who are you kidding? You hit your head hard." Standing behind Stu, he circled his finger about his own ear, indicating Stu was crazy. There were a few grins.

"You're not Montana Stu," Rubin said. "He'd come to save us on a horse. He don't do parachutes."

Stu started to rise but fell sideways. "Boy, howdy," he moaned—there was a sharp pain that came from his ankle.

"What's wrong?" Virgil asked.

Breathing like he had a hot coal in his mouth, Stu painfully reached for his ankle.

Israel's head swung back and forth, then with an awkward bend toward Stu, "You alllll right?"

Stu lay back down. "My ankle don't feel right."

Katz bent over Stu's foot. "What's wrong with your foot?"

Joey stepped away from Stu, saying, "Montana Stu's not going to hurt himself falling down from that tree. He rides mustangs and flips over big barrels in the rodeos."

Rubin pointed at Stu's fluorescent hair. "That's some hair you got there."

"My aunt dyed it."

Adam frowned. "Why'd she do that?"

"So nobody would recognize me."

"Sure," Joey said with a cynical chuckle.

Spencer stepped behind Stu and looked over his scalp in search of a bruise. There was a long pause as everybody watched him. Stu felt his examining eyes and frowned back at him. Feeling caught, Spencer righted himself, "How's your head?"

Stu nodded. "Fine." He gave Spencer a hard eye. "How's yours?"

Slightly embarrassed, Spencer adjusted his glasses and nodded.

Joey swung his hand back and forth in front of Stu's face. "How many fingers do you see?"

"Forty," Stu said sternly.

Joey had had enough of this cat-and-mouse on the kid's identity and took a bolder approach. He knelt beside Stu, declaring, "You ain't Montana Stu. What state do you think we're in?"

Stu looked about at the different trees then joked, "Hawaii?"

"Well, smarty, what's your real name?"

"Just Stu."

"Where you from?"

"Montana."

Joey continued, "I think you saw his movie one too many times. You must be from Texas. But we're going to give you the benefit of the doubt and call you Idaho . . . Spud . . . something."

Lakalo leaned over Stu and quietly asked, "You got any food . . . candy

bar . . . anything?"

Stu shook his head.

"We'll just have to call you Spud then . . . Spud out," Joey said.

"Guys from Idaho don't have hair like that." Spencer's finger extended toward the fluorescent hair.

"It's silly." Joey frowned. "You from Florida?" Stu didn't respond. "Miami?" Stu wanted to punch him. "You look like a Miami."

"We were hoping you were with the Seals and coming down to save us."

"Save you? Why you got to be saved?" Stu asked.

"'Cause they just got in a fight." Katz pointed at Virgil and Spencer. "They're going that way." He pointed to his right. "And we're going this way." He pointed to his left. "And both of us are lost and out of food and haven't drunk anything for a week."

"Why you going in two different directions?"

"'Cause we're lost and they got in a fight," Rubin said.

"You got a canteen?" Rubin asked, his thirst gnawing at him. Stu shook his head. Rubin looked up into the vacant sky. "Is there someone coming in behind you?"

"What do you mean?"

"Are they going to drop another guy down that has some water and can get us out of here?"

"And has some food?" Lakalo added.

"There was only one parachute on the plane." Stu's thoughts turned to his uncle.

"You come down here to save us and you got no food and no water?"

"His leg's hurt, too," Katz said.

"He's good for nothing," Joey added.

"What type of commando are you?"

"I'm not a commando."

"Montana Stu. Yeah, right."

"We know who you are." Joey threw an accusing finger at him. "You're messed up."

"It's sad," Rubin said mournfully, "'cause you're worse off than us."

Troubled, Stu lay back on the pine needles and stared up at the tree. Virgil looked over at the baling wire. "You want some help to get that parachute off?" Stu nodded and Virgil began to unwire him.

On Stu's other side, Spencer began to pull at the tangled cords and straps.

Stu examined Spencer's cheek, noting the dried blood. "Why'd you get in a fight?"

Virgil and Spencer wouldn't look at each other.

"'Cause he," Katz pointed at Spencer, "has been getting us more and more lost and . . ."

"That's not it!" Joey arched his chin toward Virgil. "He thinks he knows better, even though Spencer has his First-Class and the compass, and was in charge."

"Least he got us a rabbit."

Stu's eyes met Virgil's. "You got a rabbit?"

Virgil swung sideways and proudly tapped the rabbit fur hanging under his belt.

"We ate it this morning," Katz said.

Israel's face contorted as he gasped, "Poooor . . . rabbit."

Stu gazed at the purplish bruise on Katz's forehead. "You get in a fight too?"

Joey thumbed toward Katz, "He fought with a tree and lost."

Katz grinned and said to Israel, "Montana Stu's pony is Gray."

"Montana Stu wouldn't hurt his foot if he jumped out of a plane," Joey assured them. "He's smarter than that."

"I said a prayer that someone would come and help us," Katz said.

"Great!" Joey exclaimed. Tired, dirty and starving, he gazed at Stu, who appeared to be a total liability. "Here we get a guy who's all mixed up . . . thinks he's Montana Stu, and now we got to save his sorry hide." He cast a hard eye at Katz. "Do me a favor?"

"What?"

"Don't pray anymore."

Still lying on the pine needles, Stu looked the weary group over, and realized they were all wearing uniforms. "Are you Scouts?"

Katz proudly straightened. "Yeah, I'm a trailblazer."

"What happened to your Commander?"

"The night before last it stormed and they got taken by Sasquatch," Rubin said.

"We saw one." Adam said. "It was bad."

Struggling to sit up, Stu stared at him, perplexed. "You saw one?" His parachute fell off, and as Virgil rose, Stu leaned forward and ran his hand over his ankle.

"We all saw it," Adam said with a solemn note in his voice.

"It was coming after us."

"It was brown and big and walked upright."

"We barely made it out of camp."

"They came and got the Commanders at night." Rubin threw a concerned eye toward the bush.

"You got any water?" Katz asked again.

"Why don't you just go to the cabin that's over that hill?" Stu pointed toward a nearby hill. "They have to have food and water."

Rubin's eyes lit up. "There's a cabin over that hill?" The troop stared at Stu in astonishment.

"I saw it when I was coming down." With an awkward lunge, Stu rose, but found his one foot couldn't support his weight. He hopped a bit before Virgil came alongside to support him. Stu rested on his good foot.

"Walk it off, walk it off," Rubin suggested.

Stu leaned on Virgil. "How long you been lost?"

"Over a month," Rubin moaned.

"No, we haven't."

"We're going to die soon if we don't get water," Rubin said.

Stu hopped free of Virgil. "If you determine to make it, you'll make it. Anyway," he grabbed Virgil's shoulder again, "I'm a Scout, too."

Katz excitedly welcomed him. "Hey, hey."

As Katz went on, Joey whispered to Adam, "I wonder if this guy is like those guys that always have to one-up-you? I bet he'll say he's going to Jamberama if I say it first."

"Go ahead," Adam whispered.

"Yeah." Joey spoke loudly. "We were heading for Jamberama."

"Well, what do you know? I was, too," Stu replied.

"That's where we were ggggoing," said Israel.

Joey rolled his eyes, mouthing to Adam, "I told you." Then he spoke out loud. "But we're not going to make it."

"We can make it," Stu responded, taking a few hops.

"Jamberama's is over four hundred miles away and it only lasts a few days."

"I know. I ride my pony in the closing ceremony. We can make it," Stu said.

"There's no way," Joey protested.

Stu challenged, "What's our motto?"

Katz, Adam, Rubin, and Spencer instantly responded, *"Ready, ready for anything."*

Tired and sweaty, Joey fanned his face.

"Okay!" Stu looked over the haggard troop. "We just got to work together, and we'll make it."

Spencer came up on Stu's other side. "I can help you, too." Stu put his arm around his shoulder, balanced on one foot between him and Virgil, then eyed Israel. "Who are you?"

Israel's face contorted as he struggled to say, "I am . . . IIIsrael." He extended his awkward hand, angling it toward Stu.

Leaning on Virgil, Stu shook Israel's hand. The introductions went down the line.

Joey eyed Lakalo. "Now we got to take Idaho Spud up the hill."

"I'm going to call him Miami 'cause I can't see somebody doing that to their hair in Idaho," Adam commented.

There was renewed vigor in the troop now as they followed Spencer, Virgil, and the so-called Montana Stu toward the hill.

Though Stu's foot hurt, he didn't need two people to help him up the hill but it pleased him that Spencer, the kid with dried blood on his face, and Virgil, the kid with the rabbit skin, were working together.

Katz walked near Stu. "How's your foot?"

"It'll be all right." Stu took a deep breath, masking his pain.

"Poor little foooot," said Israel, bringing up the rear.

"I bet you it's not even hurt," piped Joey.

There was no complaint from Spencer and Virgil. Step by step, they sweated as they journeyed up the slope.

Lakalo didn't notice his dry, thirsty lips nor his lack of energy as much as he had earlier. Even Israel, the weakest, figured if the two leaders could somehow help this Spud up the hill, he could get there, too.

Despite his sore ankle, being off that plane had a releasing effect on the Montanan. He felt somewhat giddy when he leaned into Spencer and joked, "Did I ever tell you about the mountain blue bird?"

Coming up from behind, Joey mockingly rolled his eyes. "No, Miami. Why don't you tell us?"

"There was this mountain blue bird that flew into the window of the cookhouse . . ." As Stu went on, the boys forgot about their hunger and thirst; they had their hands full with their own wounded bird, helping him up the mountain.

"Are you sure there's a cabin up this hill?" Joey asked.

"I saw it when I was coming down," Stu replied, looking up at the darkening sky.

By the time the exhausted troop crested the hilltop, the sun had faded. Their footsteps were slow and cumbersome but they weakly pressed on.

Spencer noticed the cricket and locust chirps had intensified. In the darkness near the underbrush, the faint green glow of a firefly could be seen. It blinked out.

"Where's that house?" Rubin asked, tiredly.

"It's down that-a-way." Stu pointed. "I saw a road down there, too."

"We came up this hill earlier in the day," Joey pointed in the opposite direction. "And you're telling me it's just down the hill?"

"It's so dark, how do you know we came up this hill?"

"That's where I think I saw it," Stu said, angling his head downhill. Darkness had fallen so much that he could barely see his shoe, let alone a cabin. Around him a constant concerto of chirps filled the air from locusts rubbing their wings, calling for mates. The rhythm vibrated the dark forest, drowning out the scuffling of dried leaves that the troop trudged through.

The lack of light made their journey awkward, each step an adventure, and any energy saved going down hill was used in wariness of the unknown.

As Rubin trailed along at the end of the group, he constantly looked back, feeling like something was watching him. Not a hint of moonlight—nothing was offered to dispel the dark forest.

"Are you sure it was this hill that you saw the cabin on?" Lakalo asked.

"I think it was," Stu said, perplexed why they hadn't seen it yet.

Trudging downhill, Joey walked into a bush and got a face full of branches. Put out, he pushed the leaves away from his face and stepped back. "We should stop. It's too dark. We're just going to get lost more and more."

Disheartened, Katz responded, "What does it matter? We're already lost."

"We should stop. It's too dark to go on."

"There it is!" Rubin pointed to a faint light. A rush of excitement followed.

"I hope they got food!"

"Water! I'm drinking a gallon of water."

"I'm drinking five gallons of water." Katz brought his dried lips together.

"I hope they have lots of good food, like a warm apple pie and maybe a nice turkey."

"I don't care what they got as long as it's food."

Outside the cabin, a dog barked, then another aggressively joined. The troop stopped and listened.

Stu quietly said, "Them dogs are right ahead." Then, from a distance came the distinct baying of hounds.

Surprised at the cry of the hounds, Virgil pointed in the direction they'd come. "You hear that? Those dogs are behind us."

Katz swallowed, his nervous eyes tracked toward the cabin. "But there's other dogs at the cabin." Their barking grew louder as they closed.

"They're coming up from the cabin!" Lakalo said.

"They sound like bad dogs."

"They're coming!"

Frightened, Katz grabbed Lakalo. "What're they going to do?"

Out of the dark came Joey's ominous voice. "They're going to eat us."

From down the hill, they heard the rustle of leaves as the dogs closed, then the slide of a shotgun.

"Pick up some rocks and get in a tight circle!" Stu commanded. Thinking quickly, he thrust his hand out toward Virgil. "Let me have that rabbit skin."

"I can't find any rocks." Katz was desperate. "It's too dark."

"Grab a branch . . . anything!" Stu instructed. "Let me go. I can stand." As Virgil let him go, Stu sucked up the pain and balanced on his good ankle. "You got the rabbit skin?" Virgil quickly put it in his hand.

The crashing of bush and barking intensified. Stu turned the rabbit skin inside out and put it tightly around his fist. They all rammed into a tight group. The ones with knives had them out, pointing toward the terrible cry of the rapidly closing dogs. Hearts pounded, waiting, waiting.

Out of the darkness charged two Dobermans, fiercely barking. They stopped three feet in front of the troop, snarling and barking. A bobbing flashlight illuminated the bush, then held on the ten young men, their eyes glowing. The light shone on Stu, who shakily lifted what looked like a bloodied fist.

Out of the darkness came a testy voice. "What are you doing here?"

"We're lost and looking for help."

"Lost? Lost folks around here aren't seen again."

The foreboding way the man spoke sent a chill down Stu's spine. Without thinking, he changed his story, blurting, "Mister . . . we're on the run."

The wiry guy slapped one barking dog across the back. The dog yelped. "Shut up, you!" The Doberman swung about, fearfully eyeing his master. The man stepped toward Stu.

Stu could barely make out an angular face behind the flashlight, but the man's movements reflected one who'd had too many doses of speed. A hint of light exposed a cold gray eye, skinny face, yellow teeth, and greasy black hair.

His worn nerves shook the flashlight. "Who you running from?"

Stu was desperate. "You hear them coming?" In the distance came the sound of a baying hound."

The wiry guy shone the light on Stu's bloodied fist. The backside of the rabbit skin made it look as if he was missing skin and had no fingers.

"Why they after you?"

"'Cause . . . Jim Bob's . . . dead." The last word hung in the air like a foul smell.

The shotgun began to vibrate. "What'd he do?"

With his eyes locked on the edgy man, Stu slowly thrust his bloody hand toward him. "They got my . . ." he lifted what looked like a stump of a hand. " . . . but my brother . . . " He angled his head toward Spencer. ". . . my brother, he got him."

There was a pause as the wiry man's drug-hazed reasoning caught up with Stu's fingerless hand and the dried blood marks on Spencer's face. His jaw dropped, and his breath came in a gasp. "Siiiick." He took a step away from Stu, staring at him as if he had the black plague.

Stu pointed backward toward the distant sound of the dogs. "Can you help us? They're coming."

The man's gaze was fixed on the amber goo around Stu's hand, his mind reeling a thousand miles an hour. *If they came for these crazy kids, they'd come for him.* Hearing the distant hounds baying, barking, closing, the man shook. A guttural moan came from him as he backed away from the beleaguered boys.

"Can you please help?"

The man turned. "You're on your own!" He ran for his cabin. The dogs bolted after him.

There was a tense stillness among the troop as they listened to the thrashing in the bush recede. Then, releasing their stress they suddenly patted the storyteller.

"You did good, Miami . . . you did real good."

"I was scared. That man was bad."

"Those dogs were killers."

"You hear what he said about people who are lost?" Katz asked.

"I was so nervous." Lakalo exclaimed.

"Shhh," Stu whispered. "Shhhh."

Through the darkness, they could faintly hear leaves crackling under the man's boots. It wasn't long before they heard him yell. "Get in there!" A truck door creaked open, an engine revvved. They heard it back up, brake, then roar off.

Stu broke the silence, "He's gone. Let's go get some water at that cabin." Nervous laughs melted out their stress. Stu leaned into Virgil and started down the hill toward the cabin.

"You see how Idaho talked to him?" Lakalo admired his new hero. "He'd make Montana Stu proud."

The troop carefully stepped through the dark, heading for the cabin.

"Wait! You hear those dogs?"

"Stop! said Stu, "Listen!"

The troop halted and listened. The baying of the hounds was getting closer.

"Those dogs sound like they're headed our way."

"And there's a bunch of them."

"Probably off on a coon hunt," said Virgil.

They listened.

"Who's to say they're not hunting us," said Lakalo.

"Yeah. You see how scared that guy was? Maybe he knows something we don't."

Virgil took the rabbit hide and slung it onto a tree branch, thinking it might slow the dogs down. They moved more quickly now, heading downhill, toward the light of the cabin.

CHAPTER 17

Gaining the cabin's back step, Stu hobbled up and cautiously pushed the door open. The kitchen was lit by a hanging lantern. Seeing some pots cooking from a Coleman, Stu asked, "Anybody here?"

The others pressed in behind, desperate to get water. They were met by a dreadful, putrid smell. So wretched was the urine-like stench that they would not have entered but for their desperate thirst. Wary and alert, Stu limped forward. The lantern illuminated the mess; garbage piled high in one corner. A flame atop a camping stove roared away under a pot of caustic brew. Beside it, another pot boiled.

"Pigs." Daniel winced as he looked at the miscellaneous garbage piled on the floor.

"This is gross," said Lakalo with a wrinkled face.

Joey's nostrils burned.

Covering his mouth, Stu reluctantly took a small breath.

Adam groaned when no water came out of the tap. He turned away, glancing about, and spotted a raggedy, skinny calico cat that was slowly backing toward the dark shadows of another room.

"There's no water here," Katz said, nearly to the point of tears.

Desperate for water, Rubin searched the area, wishing the lantern cast more light. "There's got to be water here."

"Every house has got water."

"This isn't a house; it's a dump," Katz said and headed for the back door, seeking fresh air.

"I bet they've been making drugs."

Israel headed for the front door to catch a breath.

Stu covered his nose, hobbled to the flaming Coleman and, closing one eye at the caustic brew, reached as far as he could to turn the on/off dial. He backed away, took a breath then stepped in again to shut off the other. The flame went out.

"I say these guys are druggies."

"Druggies?"

Rubin spotted a five-gallon blue jug and examined it to see if it held water.

Lakalo opened the refrigerator. A half-empty six-pack of beer sat atop a block of ice that dripped down the front of the refrigerator onto the floor. His eyes widened at the ice. He grabbed the plastic bag it was in, pulled it from the refrigerator and lifted it to the counter. It banged down on the Formica. "We got ice!" The boys gathered around him.

"I wouldn't put it there." Adam pointed at the ice. "That counter could have drug dust on it."

Most were so focused on getting a piece of ice that they didn't notice Rubin who was down on one knee, opening the lid on the blue five gallon jug. Rubin sniffed the opening. He couldn't smell anything, so he poured some onto his palm and looked suspiciously at the wet. He tasted it.

"See if there's an ice pick or hammer or something around."

Joey and Spencer quickly searched cabinet drawers while Daniel peered into boxes under the table. Virgil checked a closet door. Adam methodically went through the upper cabinets. Most were empty, but in the last cupboard he found three cans of pork and beans huddled in a corner.

"There's beans here," Adam exclaimed, grabbing them.

In the midst of all this, Israel came limping back from the front door, his arms flayling, making a long warning moan. "Ahhhhhh." He tried to speak but couldn't get his words out fast enough. He pincered Stu's arm. "Tttthaarrrse a"—his awkward arm swung toward the front door—"ahh man out derrr . . . ccccoming."

The words *man* and *coming* struck – there was an abrupt, wild scramble for the back door. Adam rushed down the back steps, carrying the cans of pork and beans. Lakalo was right on his tail, cradling the block of ice, while Rubin pushed in from behind, carrying the five-gallon blue jug. At the bottom of the steps, Adam stumbled and the other two went down with him. The five-gallon blue jug sloshed, chugging water out. In a flash the three scrambled to their feet. Stu hobbled painfully with Israel behind, loping, hunched, dragging his right foot at an odd angle.

On the back porch, Virgil grabbed Stu's arm to give support. They made it down the steps with Israel plowing into them knocking them over. Amazingly, Israel didn't lose his footing but kept on going, hastening past the others, and ended up at a garage which was within fifteen feet from the cabin. Breathing heavy, he stared at the garage door's small window, while listening to the baying of dogs up the hill. The rest had gathered around the end of the cabin. They too were listening. The dull thud of boots walking about the cabin's wood floor echoed into the night.

A hint of the cabin's light reflected off the whites of Rubin's fearful eyes. He tapped Stu then pointed in the direction of the baying hounds. The hounds sounded as if they were coming down the hill.

Stu nodded, acknowledging, then limped toward Israel. The troop followed. Reaching the garage, he nudged Israel through the side door. It was pitch dark inside, but the approaching dogs and the thought of the man inside the house pushed him on.

Behind him, Lakalo shifted the ice from hand to hand and stumbled as he walked through the door. Rubin followed him with the heavy water jug cradled in his arms. The darkened space smelled like old oil. Daniel was last and shut the garage door, muffling the cry of the baying hounds.

The clouds shifted, and the half-moon appeared, cresting the trees, exposing the backside of the house and garage. Moonbeams filtered through the glass in the door, revealing a truck and an old car. Stu limped over to the old car and opened the passenger door; the overhead light of a 1958 DeSoto dimly glowed. Spotting the key in the ignition, he crawled across the seat toward the steering wheel.

Inside the cabin, the druggie's partner suspiciously looked around his kitchen. *Why was water on the floor? And why was the refrigerator door hanging open?* Even though there was no shortage of trash, he knew where the trash should be and recognized things were out of place. He shot a glance toward the darkened room and saw the cat moving toward the pile of dirty clothes. He thought about killing the scraggly cat, which kept marking their clothes but again he studied the puddle. There was too much there to be cat urine. *Where was the blue water jug?* His gaze traveled over the cabinets, all the cabinet's doors were hanging open. *Why had his partner left so abruptly? And why was the back door open?* Moving toward it, he pulled out his Buck knife and snapped it open, then frowned at the sound of baying hounds. He stepped over the threshold, stopped, and looked up the dark hill toward the sound. A clang bounced over concrete in the garage. Quietly, he came off the landing, down the steps and crept along the back of the house. Light from the half-moon illuminated his knife.

Inside the garage, Joey tripped on an assortment of tools.

"SHHHHHH!" Rubin whispered.

Joey noisily snagged three wrenches off the concrete, desperate for their protection. In front of him Israel waited to get inside the DeSoto. While Lakalo struggled to haul the plastic bag of ice into the backseat, Rubin came behind with the five-gallon water jug.

In the front Katz pressed up against Stu, then Adam slid in next to him.

Stu glanced up at the dome light. "That light's a beacon . . . get in!"

In the backseat, Lakalo whispered to Rubin, "You're going to have to get rid of that water jug 'cause we're not going to make it. There's too many of us."

As if his life depended on it, Rubin snapped back, "No way!"

Stu's voice rose. "We need to get six in the back and four in the front." He thumbed at Joey. "Get in the back."

Joey whined, "I want to sit in the front. Why can't we have five in the front?"

"Shut up, Joey, and get back here," Lakalo snarled.

Joey reluctantly slid by Israel and crammed in the back beside Virgil.

"Shut the door."

Crammed in the backseat, Daniel, the smallest, pressed upward through Lakalo and Spencer toward the back window ledge. Using his elbows, and with a foot braced against Lakalo's back, he half-crawled to get up into the window well.

"Hurry!" Stu commanded, looking at the side door of the garage.

Israel hung at the open door, mechanically moving about, trying to get into position to enter the car.

Katz, squished next to Stu, urgently asked, "Do you know how to drive?"

Stu gave him a telling eye. "I've been driving all my life."

"I hope you're not related to Montana Stu."

Stu looked past him at Israel. "Get in!"

With a slow, odd movement to his left leg and a jerk to his hip, Israel flopped his rear end onto the front seat. He moved like a wild deer attempting to sit in a car and drew the other leg up.

"Com'on!" snarled Joey

"Shut the door!" said Rubin.

Israel's arm jerked about as he struggled against his uncooperative muscles to grab the door handle. Joey rolled his eyes, thinking it would be faster to climb over the backseat and shut the door himself.

The side door of the garage creaked, and everybody turned to look. They saw an open door, and Daniel thought he saw a dark form moving past.

"Hurry!" said Rubin.

Israel grabbed the handle and yanked. The door slammed. A pounding sound came from Rubin's palm beating along the top of the door to lock it. Stu found the lock on his side and pounded it down.

"Shhhhhhhh," Stu whispered, demanding silence.

In the backseat, they all craned their necks and peered into the blackness. Stu fingered the keys. The muffled baying of the hounds was the only sound.

Joey thought he saw a dark form move past.

Someone shook the door handle.

"Ahhhhhhhhhhhh." Israel jerked, flailing his arm into Adam's ribs. The rest of them jumped in terror. Panicked, their breathing grew hyper.

Stu turned the ignition key. Over and over the engine turned. He could hear someone tap the hood as if he were using it to guide himself around to the driver's side.

"Give me one of those wrenches," Virgil whispered to Joey.

Stu reached his foot toward the gas pedal, but as he extended it, a shot of pain went through his ankle. Desperate, he heaved himself forward on the seat and again pushed with his foot. His foot clumsily hit the gas pedal and slid off.

Holding the wrench, Virgil whispered, "If he comes through the window, I'll get him with this." No one could see what he held, but his confidence gave the others courage, and there was a flurry of movement as they dug for their pocketknives.

Stu thumped Katz next to him. "Get down there and work the gas pedal!" Katz quickly obeyed and Stu turned the key.

Directly to his left there was a sudden smack on the windshield. Everybody jumped.

Glimpsing a kid behind the wheel, the man yelled, "You're dead!" He yanked the door handle.

The engine came alive in a series of revs from Katz, who was laid out on the floorboard, pressing the gas pedal. "Let off the gas," Stu said and madly looked for the shifter on the column.

"Let's go!" Lakalo called.

"I can't find the shifter."

The man's fist banged the window next to Stu's ear.

"You don't know how to drive," moaned Joey.

"A light! Anybody got a light?" Stu's panicked hands roved over the dash, searching for some way to put it in drive. He felt a series of buttons on the left side of the steering wheel and pushed one, thinking it had something to do with the lights. But it was the automatic shifter that engaged the car in reverse. The DeSoto jolted backward, crashing into the workbench, knocking the back wall off of its foundation.

"Brake!" Stu demanded. "Brake!"

Hearing wood splintering and crushing as tires churned backward, Katz let off the gas.

"Brake!"

A sudden impact of a boot slamming into the car door jolted them all.

Spencer flicked on the overhead light, and Stu spotted a D button next to the R. Assuming it meant Drive, he jammed his finger into it and commanded, "Go! . . . Go!"

Katz floored it. Tires screeched. The headlights flashed on, exposing a silhouette of the man leaping to get across the front of the vehicle. A thump, and the man slid over the hood and hit the windshield. The front of the car ripped off the garage door as it powered out. The man's face, rammed into the windshield, glared at Israel.

"Brake!" Stu yelled.

Below, Katz slammed on the brakes. The tires skidded with a force so great that the man, along with any remains of the garage door, were swept off, and Israel banged his head on the glass.

Behind the DeSoto, the entire dilapidated garage leaned forward, then fell.

Stu attempted to turn, but the power steering was out. It was like turning the old tractor that needed to be on the move to work fluidly. "Go!" he hollered.

Again Katz floored it. Stu desperately tried to steer around the crawling man but couldn't—his legs were too close, and the car took off too fast. There was a thumping sound as the front tires ran over the garage boards—one back tire took out the man's boot. The steering was so wild that Israel slammed into Adam.

Staring out the back window, Daniel blurted, "I think you ran him over."

"It's not my fault!" Stu curved around a corner. "There's something wrong with the steering. Brake!" The car roared around the corner and down the narrow road. Stu was buzzing, perched up, trying to control the beast. "Slow down!"

Katz didn't hear him and the car sped toward another curve. It swung around it in a muddy slide, pressing dangerously into the side of the dirt road.

"Brake!" Stu shouted. Coming out of the turn, the DeSoto zoomed ahead and barreled down a straight stretch, roaring, gaining speed. Stu could see the looming turn and knew he wouldn't make it. Fearful, he yelled, "Brake!" and stuck his heel in Katz's back.

At last, Katz slammed on the brakes. Israel fell off the seat onto him, and Daniel tumbled out of his window perch. Mud spattered the car as it slid across the dirt road and finally hit a tree.

The impact was slight, but Stu was fuming. As Katz dug himself up, Stu gave him an angry frown. "If I tell you to slow down, you slow down!"

Frustrated, Katz tried to wrench his legs out from under Israel. "Get off me, Israel." He glared up at Stu. "I didn't even hear you say slow down."

"That's 'cause you're flooring it too much!"

"Somebody," Lakalo pleaded, "roll down the window. I'm dying."

"It stinks back here. Who farted?" Rubin said.

"Man, you got bad breath," Joey said to Daniel.

"What do you expect? I haven't eaten in two days." Daniel purposely blew on him.

Stu found the electric switch on his window, punched it, and down it came.

Angling himself toward the opening, Lakalo took a deep breath. "Whew! What a relief."

"I can do with a bath right about now," Joey said. "My pants are sticking on my rump."

Katz poked his head up from the floorboards. "Does anybody else want to do this?"

"Who keeps farting?" Lakalo gasped.

"I don't think anybody is. That's just the way we smell," Daniel said.

The headlights glowed on the trees in front of the car as laughter relieved their stress.

Israel snapped his head around and gazed at Rubin. "Wwwwater . . . you got wwwwwwater?"

"I got water," blurted Rubin but he couldn't lift the blue jug; it was wedged in by the many bodies.

"You sure that's water?" Spencer asked, suspicious of all the drug stuff.

"Let me out," Adam pushed toward the door, "let's drink some water."

Stu opened the door and was barely out when the ones in the backseat pushed his seat forward to leap out. On the other side, a long moment passed as Israel's fingers awkwardly pincered the door to open it. By the time he got himself out, the car was empty and a few had taken desperate drinks from the water jug.

"If that water is poisonous we are all going to die," Katz said as he waited his turn. He poked at Rubin who was taking a swig, "Hurry up, you're drinking everything." Rubin tried to steady the five gallon plastic jerry jug that sat on the car's hood but more water hit the ground than his mouth.

Lakalo placed the bag of ice on the hood, and he and Adam began banging away at it with the wrenches. A piece came off. "Hold it," Lakalo said and reached inside the plastic. He handed the ice to Israel, who gazed at it intently, then gave Lakalo a huge grin.

Israel aimed the ice toward his mouth, but when it touched his lips it slipped from his hand and fell to the dirt. He moaned.

Behind him, Katz was finally taking his turn at the water jug. Lakalo handed Israel another piece of ice. Sucking thankfully on it, he walked to the front of the car and looked down the embankment. The lights revealed a shallow ravine with long shadows stretched behind the many trees and another hill angled up beyond. Hunched over, he awkwardly turned to the troop and pointed back. "It's a good tttttthing that ttttttree was there. Thank GGGGGod for tttrees."

Rubin gazed over the edge, his eyes widening. "You know it!"

Behind him, Lakalo's stomach growled, "We should cook those pork and beans up."

"I think we should get farther away from this place before we go cooking up anything," Spencer suggested.

"Yeah," Rubin agreed, looking back from where they'd come.

"That's a good idea. What if that guy come after us?" Adam said.

"I don't think he'll be coming after us . . . not anymore." Virgil held the water jug for Israel as he awkwardly bent down for it. While Israel drank, water splashed down his shirt.

"You never know," said Daniel.

"I'm starving. Let's cook it up now," said Katz. Reaching in, he grabbed the cans of pork and beans.

Adam thought he heard a vehicle. Scratching the side of his cheek, he tilted his head to listen. "What's that sound?"

"What sound?"

"That sound."

All Joey could hear was the splashing of water coming off Israel's chin onto the ground.

Spencer listened. "Sounds like it's coming from the cabin." He apprehensively adjusted his glasses.

Joey blurted, "Stop pouring the water!"

A quiet covered the troop. They listened.

"Sounds like a motor."

"It's getting louder." Rubin's eyes widened.

"Closer!"

A mad scramble of boys hurled themselves at the car. They smashed into

each other, fighting to get in. In the calamity of this fearful rush, the cans of pork and beans fell out of Katz's grip and rolled under the car. In an instant, Katz was down and crawling after them, blocking half the driver's side doorway. Lakalo tripped over Katz's foot, lost his grip on the block of ice which hit Katz in the rump and landed on Virgil's foot. Virgil fell into Rubin, causing the blue jug to slosh water across Katz's back. It could've been much worse for Virgil, but he managed to catch himself on the seat's edge.

It couldn't have been worse for Katz. One person after another stumbled over him. When he finally rose, his shirt was soaked with footprints driven into it.

"Get in!"

Tossing the cans in the back, Katz attempted to follow them in. But Lakalo and Joey indignantly pointed toward the front and yelled, "You're up there! Hurry! Down on the floor!"

Stu hopped in behind Katz and shut the door. Israel was the only one left outside. Standing beside the passenger door, he tried to angle his contorted body to get in. The sound of the approaching vehicle rose.

"In, Israel! In!" the troop yelled.

But making all his muscles mechanically fold down to get in was no small feat. He sweated.

"Get in, Israel!"

Rubin panicked when he saw a hint of light shining through the trees. "He's coming!" he yelled.

Adam reached and pulled Israel toward him, flopping him onto the crowded bit of seat that remained. Stu didn't wait for the door to close. Putting the DeSoto in reverse, he looked down at Katz, "Give it some gas but only a little, only a little." Laid out across the floor, Katz attempted to restrain himself by giving the gas pedal a push. Even so, the car jerked backward. "Brake!"

The car slid to a stop, Israel's door slammed and Stu pressed his finger onto the drive button. The transmission engaged.

Anticipating the truck, the back-seaters turned to look behind.

"Go!" shouted Rubin, his eyes brightening as lights rounded the corner. The DeSoto's wheels caught, throwing gravel in a huge rooster tail. Everyone was rammed backward.

"Slow down!" Stu shouted, nudging Katz's shoulder with his left foot. Katz let off the gas and the car slowed. "Give it more than that!"

"Go!" shouted Rubin.

Headlights closed on their bumper.

Katz jammed down the pedal.

Ahead, the road snaked. The long DeSoto was moving so fast that Stu struggled to control the car as it went into the corner. "Brake!" he shouted. Katz braked. The DeSoto angled sideways, sliding with such force that Israel slid forward, his knees ramming into Katz's legs.

"Get off me!" Katz yelped.

Perched in the window ledge, Daniel watched a truck race up behind them. "Go!" he shouted.

Katz gave it gas and once again yelled, "Get off me!"

Crammed forward over the seat, Spencer saw Katz down on the floor. He grew concerned for him because he hadn't had his medication in two days.

Stu shouted, "Brake!" Israel flopped forward, his hands held the dash. Behind them, Daniel slid onto the backseat boys.

"Go!" Rubin shouted into Stu's ear then stared bug-eyed at the oncoming truck. The DeSoto threw mud and gravel, but the truck ate it, closing on the car's fender.

Katz' head angled painfully back. "Get off me, Israel!" The car swerved around yet another corner, its tires went past the road's edge, its fenders smacking tree limbs.

"Brake!" Stu shouted and winced in pain from his sore ankle, which was pressed into Katz's shoulder. Katz slammed on the brake.

"Go!" shouted Rubin from the backseat, the five-gallon jug crammed against his knees. Katz let off the brake and pushed down on the gas pedal. The car shot over a rise with such force that it lifted the backseat boys upward.

Down the car came in a bouncing series of up-and-down motions, cutting into bushes on the side of the road. Daniel was halfway out of his perch, his knee pressed into Spencer's neck, his palm over Lakalo's ear, and his foot against Virgil's back.

"Brake!" Stu hit Katz again with his foot. "Brake!"

Exasperated, and having his gut full of everybody telling him what to do, Katz leaned on the brake, then struggled to rise. From his cramped position on the floor, he glared at Stu. "You don't push me with your shoe!"

Intent on steering, Stu didn't appear as if he were paying any attention.

"Go!" shouted Rubin, nervously staring at the truck's closing headlights. "Go!"

Katz hollered from the floorboards, "Rubin, you shut your mouth! You don't tell me what to do!"

Rubin didn't pay any attention to Katz, his total focus was on the closing truck.

Stu moaned in pain as he pressed his foot into Katz's arm. "Goooo!"

The truck slammed the rear of the car, jolting Katz's body into Stu's bad leg.

Stu winced in pain. "Ahhhhh!"

"Go!" shouted Rubin, trembling. He felt the truck powering the car forward. "Go, go!"

Joey leaned over the seat and shouted, "Go!"

Angered, Katz swung around and rammed Stu's leg. "Don't push me like that."

Again, the truck slammed the back of the car.

"Ahhhhhhhh!"

Katz pressed the gas pedal down. The engine roared and the car pulled away.

Stu swung the steering wheel left and cut around the next corner. The DeSoto fishtailed. One back tire swept over the road's edge. Stu curved it back, praying the road would straighten out. But there was no straightening to it. The DeSoto swerved around the next corner with the truck right on its tail. Big eyed, Rubin stared at the headlights bearing down on them.

"Brake!" shouted Stu. "Brake!" Katz jammed on the brakes.

"Go!" shouted Rubin. The truck smashed the bumper.

In the crammed, dark floorboards, below everybody's feet, Katz pushed down on the gas pedal.

The car angled left and the truck tore up on the inside. Rubin could see the driver now. He was an angry white man with the devil in his eye. The driver gritted his teeth, and with a cruel sneer cut the steering wheel hard left to cut them off. The truck smashed into the side of the DeSoto.

"Go!" shouted everybody in the back seat. The truck slammed the car again and raced almost even with it, shoving it further left toward the road's outer edge.

The Montanan countered, yelling, "Brake!" He swung the steering wheel right and smashed into the truck's side. The DeSoto outweighed the truck, and being ahead of it, Stu muscled the steering wheel hard right. This, coupled with Katz slamming on the brakes, sealed the truck's fate. With one last thundering crunch, it bounced off the DeSoto, shot over the road's edge, plowed through brush, tore down a slope and crashed into a tree.

Inside the DeSoto, a deafening roar of cheers erupted. The troop could see the truck's motionless headlights filtering through the trees. The glow disappeared as they rounded yet another corner.

Squashed in the backseat, Lakalo worked his arm forward and patted Stu on the shoulder. "You got him, Miami! You got him good!"

"Where'd you learn to drive like that?" Rubin blurted.

"Not so fast!" Stu instructed Katz as he swung the car wide. The front tire edged off the road. He brought it back, but Israel went down again. "That's it . . ." Now in control of the big car, yet coming off an adrenaline rush, he took a deep breath.

Again, Rubin asked, "Where'd you learn to drive like that?"

"The ranch, mostly." He glanced down at Katz. "He did good, too." Stu's nerves bled out in a relieving grin.

With tension behind them the fun of the backseat crowd was topped off with Daniel falling out of his window perch into everybody.

"There ain't no ranches in Miami, least not in the city limits. But I think you've come up a notch. What say we knight him 'Idaho'?" said Lakalo, looking about the backseat boys. There was a thrill of excitement amongst the troop. Daniel again fell out of his perch to be a part of it, half-squashing Joey, Spencer, and Virgil in doing so.

"Hey, Miami, are you still nutty about being Montana Stu?"

Stu nodded. "'Fraid so."

Daniel reached over and patted Stu on the shoulder. "He got us this far. He's got my vote."

"He drives like Montana Stu." Lakalo chuckled as he stared at the fluorescent hair. "He wrecked the garage, then ran the truck off the road. That's what Montana Stu would do. He wrecks everything."

CHAPTER 18

A flurry of men and dogs were inside and outside the druggies' cabin. Two search and rescue dogs sniffed the kitchen floor. The black-and-tan wrinkled its nose and sneezed, then shook its head and stared at the floor. The hound sneezed again.

"Com'on, boy," the search and rescue worker said, grabbing the dog by the collar and escorting him past another rescuer toward the back door. The dog sneezed again.

"This dog will never figure out why people do drugs."

Released outside, the black-and-tan sneezed again, then shook its head as if it had a bumble bee stuck in its nose. Near a cedar, another hound dog shook the rabbit skin back and forth as if it were alive. As the rescue worker delivered another sneezing dog out the back door, a fourth dog carefully sniffed the ground near the fallen garage.

Red looked over the garage's roof which lay in a heap ten feet beyond the foundation, then he spoke into a walky-talky. "We've got drugs here. Over."

There was a long pause and some static, then a voice came over the radio. "From the sounds of it, these people aren't friendlies? Over."

Red pushed the tab on the walky-talky. "That's a Roger. It doesn't look good. We heard vehicles take off. There's a garage that's on the ground, and this cabin is definitely a drug lab. Over."

* * *

"Brake," Stu said as the Desoto's tires rolled toward a paved road perpendicular to them. "Not so much."

Israel fell off the seat into Katz.

Laid out on the floorboards, Katz moaned, "Get off me, Israel."

Israel struggled to sit up, pressing off the dash with his awkward hand. "Sorry, Kkkatz."

From the backseat, Spencer lifted his head from his compass and pointed right. "I think we have to go that way to get back to the trailhead."

Virgil watched him suspiciously, not at all trusting Spencer's compass abilities.

"Give it some gas," Stu said, looking down at Katz. Katz pressed down the gas pedal. "Not so much." Stu curved right; the DeSoto drove onto the pavement and headed north.

Katz cut the gas pedal and moaned, "Does anybody else want to do this?"

"We're almost there," Spencer said, with hope in his voice, watching the road with expectant eyes. "It won't be long before we get back to the van."

"Good, I got my money in the van," Katz said with renewed vigor, his hand pressed down on the gas pedal.

Israel pushed himself away from the dash. "I hope he's got some . . . 'ccccause I'mmmm . . . hungry." A broad grin broke across his face.

Rubin reached way across and patted Israel's shoulder, agreeing with his friend. "I'm hungry, too."

Lakalo's voice was definite. "I'm going to get me a double hamburger with cheese."

"I'm going to get two double hamburgers and if Commander Charles doesn't pay for the second one, then I'm buying it out of my own money."

"Commander Charles isn't going to pay."

"Why not?"

"Think about it." Joey said. "He's gone."

"It's going to be sad when they tell his wife."

Adam sighed, feeling sad for the loss of his Commander. "Ohhhh. It's too bad."

"Brake," Stu commanded. The long DeSoto came into another corner. As it rounded the curve, Stu saw trucks and vans along the road, one after another, until they culminated in a packed parking lot of vehicles crammed around a trailhead.

"Slow down," Stu said.

Katz let off the gas.

"Is this the place?" Stu looked toward the trailhead the boys had come in on.

Everybody looked around. The DeSoto's headlights illuminated the many vehicles used by the search and rescue workers, but a van blocked the trailhead sign.

"This isn't the place." Spencer added. "There's too many vehicles."

"This trailhead must be the one that goes to the lake or something," Joey said.

"Yeah, I don't remember this place," Virgil said, somewhat perplexed. "There should just be the van."

"I bet the other trailhead is down the road."

Stu yawned. "You can give it gas, Katz."

The car stretched around yet another corner, then another. Virgil looked back and felt oddly baffled by their new direction.

"Who farted?"

"Get the window down," Lakalo demanded. "Just keep the window down!"

Adam watched the darkened silhouette of trees that crowded the road. "Hurry up, I'm dying."

Laid out on the floor Katz felt his hand getting stiff. He shifted to the other and pushed the gas pedal down. Five minutes into it, he started to nod off.

"Go faster," Stu said.

Katz awakened and gave it gas but it wasn't long before his eye lids again got heavy.

"Go faster."

He did this a number of times. Each time he nodded off he let off the gas and the vehicle slowed, and Daniel happily fell into the backseat boys.

"Go faster," Stu directed.

Dead-tired, Katz opened his eyes and stared at the dark floor.

Back and forth, this scenario went, with sleep knocking Katz out, his hand relaxing against the gas pedal, and Stu waking him up, commanding, "Go faster."

After twenty minute of this Adam grew concerned with their turtle-like speed."You think we'll make Jamberama?"

"Commander Charles said it's an eight-hour trip from the trailhead, but that's if we go at least the speed limit, not fifteen miles an hour."

Stu was getting more and more frustrated with the slow speed.

Another five minutes went by, and their speed kept slowly dropping till they were going less than ten miles an hour.

A car came up behind, then sped past, its lights shining on the trees. The boys in the back watched the car's headlights curve around the next corner.

Katz woke up. He stared at the dark floor and didn't have a clue where he was. With a slow lift to his head, he tried to take in the darkened floor area, then his eyes grew heavy.

"Hey, can't we speed up, we're not getting anywhere."

"Speed up."

But this time, the command didn't register. Katz was asleep, and his head fell onto the floorboard. Once again, the car slowed.

All of the boys started to yell at him.

"Common Katz, speed up!"

"What's wrong with you?"

"Speed-up"

Stu shook him, then shook him again.

It scared Katz awake.

"What's wrong with you?"

"Speed-up!"

Katz was quick to sit up and his shoulder smacked into the steering column. "Ahhhhhh!" There was a wildness to his eyes, he thought he was locked in. He struggled like mad to get free, swinging his arms, hitting Stu in the legs as he rose. "Let me go!" he shouted, unaware of where he was, panicked by the caged nightmare he was in.

Stu shielded himself as the whirling, fighting blur rose and clambered over him. The door swung open. The car was slowly rolling when Katz jumped. Hitting the pavement, he fell, driving his chest into the asphalt. He struggled up and limped toward the headlights, then broke into a run as if something was chasing him.

Behind him the car stopped.

They watched Katz run away from them. Headlights illuminated his silhouette cutting across the white line.

"What's got in to him?"

"He's been off his medication for two days."

The darkened silhouette disappeared over the embankment.

Stu's ankle hurt as he strained and slowly pushed on the gas to bring the car to the side of the road. He set the brake but left the lights on, the engine running.

Virgil was the first out of the car. He took off after Katz, heading up the road. "Katz?" He gained the embankment and stared into the dark forest. "Katz?"

Stu watched the troop follow Virgil down the embankment with Israel trailing. He finally limped to the side of the road but didn't dare go down the embankment because of his swollen, sore ankle. Light from the half-moon revealed Israel awkwardly going down the embankment.

When Israel got to the bottom of the embankment he heard someone crying. "Katz?" Hunched over, he dragged his awkward leg past a firefly and around a tree, where he saw a dark form. "Katz?" His voice was full of sympathy. "What's wwwwrong?"

Katz whimpered. The concerto of locusts played on. "I was scared."

Israel came near and angled his hand over, mechanically placing it on Katz's shoulder. "You're my ffffriend."

Leaves scrunched as Virgil and Rubin approached. "Hey, Katz?"

Lakalo, Adam, and Spencer came in from different directions. "You okay, Katz?"

Embarrassed about his tears, Katz turned away and wiped his face. There was a long quiet.

At last Daniel gave Katz a friendly punch in the arm. "You're my buddy, Katz."

Katz slowly nodded. "It's okay. You guys go on. I'll wait here for Commander Charles."

"We're out in the middle of nowhere, Katz. You can't stay here," Joey said, staring into the bush. Then his eyes shifted back to him. "You can't stay here. That's stupid."

"Don't call him that," Lakalo growled.

"I didn't call him stupid. I just meant it would be stupid to stay here. Commander Charles isn't around anymore."

"It's okay." Katz stared down. "You go on."

"We're not leaving without you," Lakalo said with conviction.

A distant owl called.

Rubin looked about the dark woods, moonlight reflected off the whites of his eyes. "There's Sasquatch out here." The comment put apprehension in all.

"Awoooooo." The owl called.

The locust chirps halted. Everyone's ears perked.

"Something's out here."

The ominous cloud snapped Katz out of his misery. He straightened, peering into the dark; the forest suddenly seemed very creepy. "Maybe we should go."

There was an instant rush toward the road—nobody wanted to be the last one to the car. Ahead of the troop, Rubin burst through the bush and scrambled up the embankment. When he ran past Stu he exclaimed, "There's sasquatch down there!"

Virgil, the only civil one, helped Israel up the embankment. The rest made a mad dash for the DeSoto.

At the top of the embankment, Spencer glanced back at the unknown. Again, the long eerie call of the owl sifted through the dark. He felt a rush of fear—it pressed him on to the car.

Virgil and Israel crested the embankment and approached Stu.

"I'll work the gas and brake pedal," Virgil said.

"That'll be good," said Stu, limping quickly toward the car.

When Rubin opened the car door, Katz pushed by him to get into the backseat.

"Hurry! Get up!" Joey followed Daniel who crawled into the back window ledge.

Up front, Virgil jammed his legs across the narrow space. Stu slid behind the steering wheel.

"Shut the door!"

On the other side of the DeSoto, Israel pulled his legs in, and Spencer slammed the door.

"Lock it!"

Their relief was substantial when both locks smacked down.

Stu shoved the D button. "Okay, give it gas," he instructed.

Virgil slowly pushed the gas pedal down, but the DeSoto didn't move forward.

"Give it more gas."

The Kentuckian gave it more gas.

Stu wondered why the car was going so slow. He heard the engine whine, but still the car moved along at best twenty miles an hour. "Give it some more gas."

Sensing something was wrong, Adam asked, "Do you have it in the right gear?"

From over Stu's shoulder, came Lakalo's voice. "You got the brake on?"

"Oh," said the surprised Montanan, who bent over and released it. The car shot forward.

In the window well, Daniel grinned, feeling his body pressed into the rear glass.

"Slow down!" Stu commanded.

Virgil let off the gas.

"That's it, right there."

"The trailhead can't be much farther," Spencer observed.

Virgil's voice came up from the floor. "I'm surprised we haven't hit it already. We've driven quite a ways."

Spencer pulled out his compass and studied it. North was in a different position from what he figured, and for the first time he grew perplexed at where he thought they should be.

CHAPTER 19

The bus's headlights glowed, illuminating the security station at the entrance to Jamberama. Behind, one bus after another waited to enter the dark, heavily treed area.

In the middle of the bus, Johnny Revv triumphantly shook his fist in the air. "We're here! Jamberama!" The entire bus cheered.

Lonny, their official cameraman, caught the other Scouts' shouts, hoots, and hollers on video. The driver leaned out the window to hear directions from a burly security guard.

After the bus cleared security, it drove to the massive parking lot, its lights shining on row upon row of buses. Air brakes blasted, and Rangers and commanders piled out.

Stepping off the last step, Johnny Revv was greeted by a light sprinkle. He stepped aside and closed his eyes for a moment of bliss, taking in the moist air with a big breath, amazed that it was so damp. He treasured the moisture; he'd never experienced rain in the summertime in Lovelock, Nevada. Behind him, Scouts continued to pile out, their faces plastered with the same happy gaze, their eyes darting about, looking at the thick green undergrowth and the row of cabins. In the background, a sea of white tents fought the darkness to display their canvas tops.

Glancing at the license plate on the bus, a man from registration asked, "Are you from the Nevada district?

"Yep," replied Johnny, now a seventeen-year-old.

The man blinked, surprised at Johnny's low voice. "You check in over there." He pointed toward a large log cabin.

Johnny looked back at Lonny. "Can you believe it's raining in the summertime?"

Lonny put his arm out to feel the rain. "You ever ride a dirt bike in the rain?"

"No," Johnny replied as they headed to the log cabin with their troop.

"It slides all over the place."

Their Commander, Commander Bob, came alongside, carrying his briefcase, looking very robust for his sixty-year-old frame. "You know, we traveled nineteen hundred and seventy-six miles?"

Johnny opened the cabin door for him. "My rump feels like we traveled it."

"Hold up!" said Commander Monte, coming in after Commander Bob. "Gracias," he acknowledged Johnny who was holding the door.

The rest of the troop crammed into the packed check-in station. Lonny turned on the video and began filming. Although the room looked old, with logs chinked in masonry, it had a new feel to it as its back wall was lined with computers.

In front of them, one long line after another led up to a row of teenage girls who were checking-in the Scouts, giving each a pass.

"Are you from New Mexico?"

Down the line, the various towns and states could be heard: Newport Beach, Rhode Island, Mississauga, New Orleans, Illinois, Texas.

The group from Nevada finally made it to the front of one line. The girl behind the computer leaned forward, checking off each Scout from a list of names, then handed each his security clearance and food pass. It all went smoothly till she came to Johnny Revv.

"Johnny Revv?" she said.

Johnny stepped up, wide-eyed, nodding.

"Are you Johnny Revv?" she asked as it came to her that this could be the real Johnny Revv—the one she'd seen in the real Montana Stu movie, the Johnny Revv she'd fallen in love with, the Johnny Revv she wanted to marry, the Johnny Revv she wanted to have six kids with. Her eyes swooned over him. Losing herself in wonder, she covered her mouth. It was him! Her voice hit a high squeaky pitch as she gasped, "Johnny Revv?"

She was so loud and thrilled that the place went quiet. The entire line of girls' heads snapped toward him—along with everybody else's. They took in the star. Aiming the video camera, Lonny zoomed it right at Johnny's reddening face.

Commander Bob broke the spell. "I'm afraid it's him. And believe it or not, folks, he breathes, eats, and smells just like the rest of us."

There were chuckles.

"I do need a shower," Johnny said casually to the group, as if talking to his family.

A Scout in the line next to him asked, "Did you drive the Chevelle out?"

"No, but it's coming. We're going to use it in a skit." He nodded toward his troop. "I got to ride in the bus with the rest of these goof-balls."

"I hear Montana Stu's coming."

"Yeah, he's flying up in his uncle's plane." Johnny grinned, feeling instant goose bumps. "I'm really looking forward to seeing him."

"Com'on, girls. Let's get back to work," the office manager instructed, staring at the wanna-be bride in front of Johnny. "Ashley, these Scouts need to get to their tents for bed-ee-bye."

The chatter started up again, but many of the girls cast an envious eye at Ashley. She fluffed her hair and winked and blinked at poor Johnny till she finally blurted, "Would you marry me?"

The question fell on the carpet and just lay there. There were nervous chuckles from Scouts anticipating Johnny's response, and again Lonny aimed the camera up at him.

Johnny's eyes widened, looking tentative, deep in thought, somehow wanting to come to her rescue but without the marrying feature. "Uhhhhh, I'm a little young to be getting married."

In hearing this, the mortified young lady wanted to melt through her shoes, her lips gaped. She had exposed her innermost feelings in front the world's stage—certainly on Lonny's video. She looked like a raccoon under a riflescope. If only there was a way to vacuum up her spilled words and wifey desires.

"But," Johnny continued, "maybe we can have breakfast tomorrow." He grinned at the attractive redhead.

Beaming, she took a deep breath.

"Hey, what's holding up those lines?"

Ashley looked over at the other girls as if she'd just become the luckiest girl in the world.

* * *

The DeSoto's headlights glowed past a **Welcome to Huntsville** sign. Spencer adjusted his glasses, then gazed at it, perplexed.

Lakalo pointed at the sign. "We should've hit the trailhead long before we hit a town."

"We must've made a mistake somewhere."

"'Least we're going north," Adam said.

Ahead, the lights of the small town glowed. They passed a Dairy Queen billboard.

"We could eat there."

"You got any money?"

"Commander Charles has got my money."

"I got some money," Lakalo said, anxious to get his hands on a cheeseburger.

"Can you buy me a hamburger with cheese?" Adam asked. "I'll pay you back."

"I don't have that much money. I think I only have three bucks."

"Anybody else have any money?"

"I got some," Stu said.

"Goody. Miami's got some money." Adam grinned excitedly, moving his hands like a praying mantis, then slapped Katz to wake him. Katz opened one eye. "Miami's going to buy us some burgers." The eye fell shut.

"I hate to tell 'ya, but I'm using the money for gas." Stu glanced over at Adam. "If we're going to Missouri, we're going to need a lot of gas. And all I got is six dollars."

Joey moaned, "We're going to die of starvation. I know it. We're going to die of starvation."

Adam lifted the cans. "I got three cans of pork and beans. We can heat them up."

Virgil's voice came up from the floor. "I can start a fire."

"But let's not start it in town." Daniel joked.

Joey whined, "Roll down the window. It stinks back here."

"It's because everybody hasn't eaten. You get bad breath when you haven't eaten. It's the acid," Spencer explained.

"Thank you, Spencer," Daniel said, theatrically, "for your scientific explanation."

Stu glanced down at Virgil. "Slow down, Virgil. We're coming to a town." Virgil overreacted by slamming on the brake. The tires caught, screeching, and the shift was so abrupt that Israel hit the dash.

Down the road at a rundown store, an old man sat, his fingers picking at his banjo as he watched the DeSoto come to a stop outside the town. It was a odd to stop because there were no stop signs. At last, the car began to move again. He wondered why the car's actions were so jerky, so sudden. At best the DeSoto was going twenty miles an hour.

"Hold it right there," Stu said as he looked over the town, which was no longer than a block. There were no buildings on the left-hand side, and the glowing lights of an old gas station marked its far boundary.

Lakalo pointed at the Dairy Queen which was a hundred yards before the gas station. "You got to stop there."

Stu asked him, "Are you going to share your hamburger with the rest of us?"

Lakalo frowned at all the expectant faces staring at him. Finally, he nodded. "I can share it." Smiles were easy, Israel's was the broadest.

"Shut that grin down," Joey said teasingly to Israel. "That thing's going to envelope your head." Israel couldn't stop grinning; he was tickled that food was coming his way.

The car passed the old grocery store, where the old-timer sat picking his banjo, a lazy hound resting at his feet. Daniel pushed Katz, who was asleep, then leaned out the window. "Mr. Bojangles?" he yelled. "Can you DANCE?"

To his surprise, the old-timer rose to his feet; his old dog merely found enough strength give a tired howl. As the howl died away, the old-timer did a soft shoe, ending with his fingers pointing at Daniel.

Loving it, Daniel pulled his head back, asking, "You see that? You see him dance?"

"Slow down," the Montanan said.

Virgil let up on the gas, and Stu steered the car across the shoulder toward the Dairy Queen.

"Put on the brake," Stu commanded. The car headed toward a pole that supported an overhang five feet in front of the building. "Brake more . . ." he fearfully said, "More! Brake!" The brakes locked up.

Israel hit the dash.

Inside the Dairy Queen, the wide-eyed owner watched the car slide through the gravel toward the metal pole. The DeSoto stopped one inch in front of the structural support.

"Bunch of hillbillies!" the put-out Dairy Queen owner exclaimed.

The passenger door bolted opened and a mass exodus ensued. Daniel had a leap in his step and angled back toward the road to wave at the old-timer.

Most of the troop had found their way to the Dairy Queen counter. Virgil pulled up the rear, ready to help Stu, who limped along holding the car for balance. At the front bumper, they stopped and looked down at the pole. Virgil was surprised to see how close they'd come to hitting it.

Stu caught Virgil's eye and angled his head toward the owner. "I think you took a year or two off that fellow."

"I couldn't see what was going on."

Stu grinned, then broke away from him and hopped over to a round table in front of the order window. The light from the order window extended its glow in that direction.

Daniel took off toward the store, wanting to talk to the old man.

"I'll go with you." Virgil called and hustled after Daniel.

The others pressed up against the counter, where the owner begrudgingly waited for their order.

Lakalo addressed him, "How much are your cheeseburgers?"

"Two fifty."

"What can I buy for fifty cents?"

"Nothing," the man said coldly, still hot over the car almost hitting his pole.

"Can I get another piece of meat on it?"

"Nope. You'll have to buy another cheeseburger."

"I only have three dollars." Lakalo lifted the dollars up for display.

The man shrugged. "That's your problem."

"Can I buy an extra patty?"

The man shook his head.

Katz blurted, "We need to get some plastic spoons for the beans and some cups too for the water. Can we get those?"

Looking ornery, the man chewed his lower lip and shook his head.

"How about . . ." Katz continued.

Lakalo elbowed him.

"What'd you do that for?" Katz asked.

Lakalo responded, "Why do you have to be so pushy?"

The man's wife walked up behind him, cheerfully looking over the excited troop, and recalled her own poverty-stricken past. "Sure, you can buy an extra piece."

Everybody cheered.

This disturbed the owner, who tossed the order pad down and walked away from the counter, mumbling, "Here they nearly destroyed the place, and you want to give the farm away?"

His wife turned to address him. "Oh, Teddy, it's just one patty."

He took off his cook's apron, tossed it in a hamper, then walked out the back door.

She looked back at the troop to see Israel's revealing grin and couldn't help but smile.

Lakalo handed over the three dollars. "Could you cut the hamburger up into ten pieces?"

She stared at him for as the thought of cutting a hamburger into ten slices sunk in. "Be happy to."

"Do you know how far Missouri is?"

"It's a ways."

"We're going to Jamberama," Rubin said proudly.

"Oh . . . what's that?"

"It's the biggest campout ever. Everybody from all over the world goes there."

"Where're you boys from?"

"We're from Los Angeles."

"Except Hillbilly. He's from Kentucky. And Idaho is from Miami." Joey thumbed toward Stu, who sat on the bench, leaning over his foot.

Katz added, "He hurt his foot jumping out an airplane."

Unsure of his airplane story, she raised a brow. "You can't be too careful when you jump out an airplane. Give me a minute on your order." She turned to go.

"I'll wait forever. We haven't eaten in two days."

Astonished, she spun about. "Where've you been?"

"We've been lost in the forest 'cause the Sasquatch came and got the Commanders."

"Then we nearly got run over by a guy who makes illegal drugs," Rubin added.

"My word! Have you told the Sheriff?"

"No, can we use your phone?"

"Last night's storm knocked down lines. The phones are out all over the place," she said.

"Do you know where the police are?"

"I heard on the radio that the Sheriff and half the deputies are out looking for some kidnappers who are involved with drugs, somewhere up in the wilderness."

CHAPTER 20

The Sheriff, Commander Charles and Commander Rex stood inside the kitchen of the cabin, looking over the stove used to cook the caustic brew.

"I don't know how I'm ever going to explain this drug lab to their parents." Totally at a loss, Commander Charles shook his head.

"This place smells horrid."

A deputy appeared at the back doorway, holding his walky-talky. "Good news. We've caught the driver of the truck, and he says the kids were in the car." He stared directly at Commander Charles. "Maybe your boys will show up back at the trailhead."

A rush of excitement and hope took hold of the Commanders.

"I wonder who was driving?" said Commander Charles. "I bet it was Lakalo or Adam."

The Sheriff joked, "Just tell the boys' parents that they broke up the biggest drug lab in Texarkana. There should be a merit for that."

Commander Charles let off his stress with a big chuckle. Very pleased his boys were alive, he stepped through the doorway. Outside, he looked up toward the dark heavens. The half-moon reflected a thankful tear in his eye.

* * *

With great care, the Dairy Queen lady finished cutting the double cheeseburger into ten pieces, then took it to the front counter. A candled birthday cake couldn't have been more thrilling to the hungry, expectant boys. They stared at the many pieces. Lakalo closed his eyes and took a whiff. It was heavenly. Everybody waited for him to take the first pick. Pulling out what he thought was the biggest piece; he looked back at the lady who was watching. "Thank you."

A flurry of hands reached in to grab their portions. Four small pieces were left. The lady watched as Israel mechanically moved his awkward hand around, his mouth hanging open while he eyed the pieces like a scientist eyeing his first moon rock. He finally took two pieces, carefully carried them to the table, and angled them down in front of Stu.

"Go ahead, Idaho . . . yyyyou take it."

"Thanks, Israel." Stu took his piece.

"Boys?" The lady placed a stack of empty plastic cups and a handful of spoons on the counter. "Here's some cups and spoons."

Adam went to get them. "Thank you very much."

"Can we get some ice?" Katz asked.

Lakalo elbowed him.

"What you do that for?" Katz frowned.

Lakalo said to the lady, "We don't need no ice, and thanks for the cups and spoons." Then he gave Katz a stern glare. "Here she gives us the extra stuff and all you want is more?"

"It's just ice."

"You don't have no timing."

"I don't know about that. I got my piece right after you got your piece." Katz leaned over the tasty remnants of his small piece.

Lakalo stared at the scratches on Katz's chin, from when he had hit the asphalt after jumping out of the DeSoto, then the swollen bruise on his forehead. He figured Katz was a lost cause, and went back to the grand task of devouring his precious little piece.

"This is gooooood," Rubin said, rapturously. "I don't think I ever had a hamburger that was this good."

Lakalo finished his piece by picking the tiniest bits off the napkin. He enjoyed every morsel.

Israel's eating habits were a novelty to watch. The most common task for most, putting something into their mouths, was a total chore for the boy with cerebral palsy. He angled his head and eyed the hamburger as if it were a bird readying for flight. Pincering it up, he held it with four fingers and lowered his head. He grinned at his accomplishment as his hand mechanically came toward his very open mouth.

Beyond him, Lakalo focused in on the two remaining pieces, sitting atop the counter. "If those guys don't get back soon I'm going to eat theirs."

Adam caught his attention by hitting Lakalo's shoe with the end of his foot. Lakalo nodded, knowing he wanted a piece, too. But just as they rose, Virgil and Daniel came into view.

Behind the Dairy Queen window, the lady watched the boys in admiration. They reminded her of the only time she'd ever been treated to a drive-in when she was their age; it had been a special moment that she'd always treasured. She watched Stu hop to the Formica counter and give her a nod.

"Howdy, ma'am."

She noticed him eyeing the fries that sat waiting in their stainless steel bin.

Stu eyed it like a magpie looking over scraps. "We'll sing you a song if you give up those fries."

"A song? What kind of a song?" Her voice was playful.

"It'd be a good song. One that you'd like."

She teased, "What if I don't like it?"

"Then hang onto the fries." He shrugged. "I'll understand."

Her palm opened, offering him the chance. "Everybody will have to sing, though."

Stu nodded and hopped back to the table. Nearing the troop, he leaned forward. "Hey . . . we can get some fries if we sing her a song. But we all got to sing."

"What song?"

"I know *I've Been Working on the Railroad,*" Virgil said.

"I know *Three Blind Mice,*" Katz said.

"It should be ten blind mice, the way we've been going," Joey commented. "That's a stupid song."

"Shut up, Joey."

"I know *The Old Rugged Cross,*" said Rubin.

"She says it's got to be a good one."

"I know that camp song, *Throw Her out the Window,*" Adam said.

"We'll never get the fries by singing that to a lady."

Stu perked up. "Anybody know *My Home's in Montana*?"

They shook their heads. Lakalo looked at Stu's strange fluorescent hair, then said, "Miami, you must've watched Montana Stu one too many times." He nodded. "You need to get over trying to be like him. We like you the way you are."

Stu gave a lopsided grin. "I thought I'd been elevated to 'Idaho?'"

"'Miami' suits you better."

Stu rolled his eyes, knowing he'd never convince them otherwise.

Lakalo thumbed back at Daniel, who was just finishing his hamburger. "Daniel knows how to sing. His dad plays in some clubs. Do you know any songs we could sing?"

Everybody's eyes fell on Daniel.

Enjoying the last bits and crumbs, Daniel seemed oblivious to their stares and their quest. At last he toyed with them, "Sing whatever you think is good." He picked up the remains of the burger.

"Do you know a good song we can sing?"

Daniel absently pulled his harmonica from his pocket and glanced at Stu, "Are there many fries?"

"There's enough."

"Does anybody know *Five Hundred Miles*?" Everybody shook their heads. Daniel brought the harmonica up to his lips and gave a slight blow. The tone was pleasant. "It's easy. You just sing the chorus."

He went over the tune, explaining when they would come in. Katz and Joey looked dead in the water, but Daniel's confidence, and their hunger, carried them forward. "Com'on. We can do it."

"Wouldn't it be something if we could get them fries?" Rubin said, with rising hope.

Again Daniel put his harmonica to his mouth for a small blow, then pulled it out and said, "Let's go." They rose from the table and headed toward the window opening. The Dairy Queen lady curiously watched the one with a red hair organize the rest in front of the counter, four in the front row and five in the back. Gaining the front, he faced the troop, lifted his hand like a wand, and instructed, "Just sing the words to the chorus, and when I squeeze my fist, you stop."

She clarified, "It's got to be good."

Realizing the fullness of her statement, Daniel became serious and glanced back at her. "Can you give us a minute?" She nodded. He thumbed toward the other side of the car. "We got to practice." The troop followed him to the far side of the car, and as they passed the window front, everyone looked in at the coveted fries.

Out of earshot of the lady, Daniel lined them up again and instructed, "It goes like this. I sing *'If you miss the . . . '"*

After going through the chorus a number of times, Daniel thought the troop was ready, so he guided them toward the Dairy Queen counter. In passing, they again stared at the fries. He lined them up six feet from the order window in front of the amused Dairy Queen lady. Taking a deep breath, he looked back at her, giving a nod. She returned the nod, enjoying this ragtag troop.

The strains of Daniel's harmonica filtered out in a mournful prelude that took hold of the woman. He pulled the harmonica from his lips, then softly sang, "If you miss . . ."

On the chorus, the troop joined in like a pack of hungry wolves, hard and strong. ""A hundred miles, a hundred miles, a hundred miles, you can hear the whistle blow'en a hundred miles."

The melody rose, filling the night air with such a sweet sound, it gave the woman a distant, lonesome feeling. She felt like she'd never had a home, like she'd never belonged anywhere. She watched in wonder as memories of her childhood flooded back. Her dad had been in the military, and she'd moved from place to place. Now, this kid with his harmonica was touching those fifty-plus moves.

Down the dark road the old hound dog bayed.

In finishing, Daniel's lone voice softly rose. There was a quiet stillness; even the crickets had stopped their chirping. Daniel had not turned, but the rest of the troop fixed expectant eyes on the sole member of the audience, awaiting her approval. The stillness was broken by her sudden claps. Then, Daniel turned and peered in the window, hoping she'd enjoyed it, but when he stepped closer, all he noticed were her moist eyes.

"Are you all right?"

* * *

A misty rain covered the rows and rows of tents at Jamberama. Under the night sky, Johnny Revv and Lonny walked the dark path between tents.

Johnny touched one white canvas flap in admiration and quietly said, "Doesn't this remind you of the Civil War and what the soldiers would have slept in?"

Lonny nodded.

Johnny took two more steps, then stopped when he heard snoring coming from the large tent before him. He pointed at the Outfitter tent and whispered, "Got another tree frog."

Lonny aimed his video camera at Johnny.

Johnny looked as if he was readying for an interview, straightening, he adjusted his shirt collar. Lonny engaged the camera.

Johnny began, "We've got a contest going here. We're going to find out who's the world's best snorer." He grinned into the camera. "You ready?" He slowly opened the tent's canvas and looked inside. It was dark, but Johnny held his palm over the end of a flashlight to keep it from illuminating too much. He was just able to view two Commanders and five Scouts.

They entered stealthily, low, like two spies on a mission. Lonny brought up the rear, his video camera running. They approached the snorer. The noise coming from the Commander sounded like an out-of-tune chainsaw. Lonny zoomed in on his lips. His whiskers rattled when he snored. They twitched like bug's legs, vibrating on the intake. Johnny cleared his throat to catch Lonny's attention. Lonny brought the camera up to take in Johnny, who held the flashlight just under his own chin and whispered, "Tonight, we have our tenth contestant in the snorers' contest. You can," he swirled the flashlight about, searching for the words, "sense that this Commander has burned out a few valves and blown a muffler."

Lonny swung the camera back to the Commander.

The Commander ran his hand across his face, his lips staggered for a moment then the snorer rumbled on. "Haaazzz"—increasing in speed— "Zuuuuuuu"—waiting for a breath—"Ha . . ."—backfiring—"Aaa-Zuuuuuu. Haaaazuuuuuu, Haaaaazuuuuuu, Haaaaazuuuuuu."

Johnny tapped Lonny and said into the camera, "I think he should chew more before swallowing."

Lonny covered his mouth to silence his laugh. The snorer's timing was perfect, stutter-stepping—"Ha, Haaa, Haaaa"—rude enough to make a potbellied pig blush.

Lifting an eyebrow, Johnny leaned toward the noisemaker and asked, "What do you like best about Jamberama?"

"Shleeeep," the Commander answered subconsciously, rolling away from him, pulling the blankets. "Haaaazuuuuuu."

Behind him, an awakened Scout said, "Hey, you're Johnny Revv. Aren't you Johnny Revv?" In the distance, an outhouse door banged.

Johnny glanced at him. "Shhhh."

* * *

The DeSoto screeched away from the Dairy Queen.

"Slow down! Slow down!" Stu nudged his foot against Virgil. The big car rolled down the dark road.

"We need to call the police and tell them about the druggies," Spencer said.

"Yeah, and we need to tell them about Commander Charles and Commander Rex and Junior Commander Alan," Adam added.

"You think they'll let us go to Jamberama if we tell them all that?" Rubin asked, scratching his cheek.

"I don't think so," Lakalo said. "They'll probably send us back home."

Virgil's voice came up from the floor. "Nobody knows we're lost. Can't we just call the police after we get to Jamberama?"

Katz asked, "But what if Commander Charles is getting hammered by the Sasquatch and is nearly dead?"

"It would take a while to find him in that forest. Anyway, who's to say they'd even find him," said Joey, deadly serious. "'Least we'd get to see Jamberama."

"That's not right. We should call the police right away," Spencer adjusted his glasses as if putting an exclamation point to it.

"Spence is right," said Stu. "And we should call in on the druggies right away, too, so they can get 'em."

Up from the floor came Virgil's voice again. "Why couldn't we just call in, tell them what happened, then keep on going to Jamberama?"

As the boys considered this, Adam turned on the radio but no sound came out. Hoping to get a station, he spun the tuning dial all the way to the end then back again. The radio appeared dead, but he heard static as he reached for the on/off knob. Adam turned up the radio and leaned closer.

A homesick feeling came over Katz. "I wouldn't mind heading back home." He looked out the window into the darkness. "I miss my mom."

Lakalo said determinedly, "I want to go to Jamberama. I didn't come all this way *not* to go to Jamberama. I've been waiting and saving to go to Jamberama for months."

"Jamberama's going to be great," Stu remarked. He glanced down at Virgil. "Slow down, Virgil. We're coming to a gas station."

More static crackled on the radio, then the voice of Elvis Presley leaped out, singing something about a hound dog. It abruptly fuzzed out. Stu glanced at the gas gauge and looked ahead to the gas station that sat at the outskirts of a tiny town.

More static came from the radio, then the voice of a local news broadcaster said, "Broward County Police are on the look out for a blue DeSoto, license plate number AFW913, in connection with a drug-related kidnapping."

"You hear that?" Adam blurted.

"Turn it up. Turn it up!" Adam turned the dial up, but it fuzzed out.

"Kidnapping? Who are they talking about when they say 'drug-related kidnapping'?"

"They must think Miami kidnapped us," said Joey.

Daniel fell off his window perch, wiggled between Lakalo and Spencer, leaned over the seat like a jester and said, "You can go to jail for life if you kidnap somebody."

"The Dairy Queen lady said the Sheriff was out at the druggies' place." Katz looked at Stu as it dawned on him. "They must think you're the druggie kidnapper!"

Joey tapped Katz on the shoulder. "That would make you an accomplice 'cause you were down there giving it gas."

Katz's grin evaporated. "I didn't kidnap nobody!"

Full of himself, Daniel wig-wagged his head about playfully. "But that's what the radio said and . . . that goes along with what my dad says."

The statement hung in the air till Spencer asked, "What's that?"

"That right is wrong and wrong is right." He rubbed the top of the vinyl seat, then thumped his palm down on Stu's shoulder. "So, Miami would go to prison."

"We can tell them that he didn't kidnap us."

"Yeah, but by that time he'd be in prison, and they'd have cut his gizzard out."

"I don't care," said Stu, his worries on the gas station, "as long as they don't put me on an airplane."

"What's wrong with planes?"

"It's the worst torture there is . . . Brake!" Stu's voice rose as he turned the DeSoto toward the gas station.

Virgil squashed down to brake. The headlights glowed, aiming at the gas station fuel pumps. With a loud skid, the DeSoto slid up to the fuel pump and finally stopped.

"That's enough . . . Hooooee," said Stu, letting out a relieved breath.

"What are you hoooee'n about?" Daniel asked, leaning over the seat, goofy as ever, patting his shoulder. To his right Israel opened the door to get out.

"It's a big adventure just to stop this rig." Stu glanced back at him. "But if my foot was working . . . there'd be nothing to it." He watched Joey squeeze around Israel to get out the door.

"Why don't you just use your left foot?"

The most perplexed look crossed Stu's face. He blinked as the question sunk in. "I never thought of it."

Katz leaned over the seat and questioned, "You mean to tell me I didn't need to be down there?"

Stu chuckled and gave him a sheepish grin. "I guess so."

"You're bad, Miami . . . you're really bad." Daniel glanced at Katz, who was getting out. "Here you're stomping on Katz and Virgil . . ." He rolled his head, grinning at the thought. "I might like to do that myself."

A skinny seventeen-year-old came out to pump the gas. Recognizing the vehicle, he slowed as he drew near. Taken aback at Stu and the pack of boys piling out, he asked, "Isn't this Jimmy's?"

"Ahhh . . . Yeah." Stu noted suspicion in his eyes.

"Does he know you got it?"

"Ahhh, yeah. He sure does." Stu reasoned that they'd almost been murdered by somebody trying to get the car back. It had to be Jimmy.

Katz brushed by the attendant, asking in a loud voice, "You got a bathroom?"

The teen thumbed toward the glowing office. "You got a driver's license?" He gave Stu a condescending glare.

"Six dollars worth," Stu said, dodging the question. Then he yelled at Katz, who was about to enter the office, "Hey, Katz? Find out how far it is to Missouri."

Katz nodded and followed Israel through the door.

Inside the station, a mechanic gave Israel a second look. He'd never seen such an awkward kid. *And what was with all these boys filing in and out of the bathroom?*

Joey came out holding his nose, "Poooeee!"

"Can you tell me how far it is to Missouri?" Katz asked.

Wiping his greasy hands on a rag, the mechanic angled his head toward a map. "Well, let's see on the map here." The mechanic spent some time going over the miles index and crossed over and down. "Best I can make out . . . it's a little over three hundred and fifty miles."

"Do you know how long that'll take?"

"It all depends on how fast you're going. Say you had a car like Dale Earnhart's that goes a hundred seventy miles per hour. It would take you a little over two hours to get there."

Katz glanced back at Rubin. "We'll be there in no time."

"That's if you had a car that went that fast." The mechanic pointed at the DeSoto. "That DeSoto won't do a hundred and seventy. But say it was able to go a hundred miles an hour . . . It's got a hemi. That would take you a little over three and a half hours."

Katz's eyes flashed wide. "We'd still be there by morning."

Spencer's face was grim. "At the rate we're going, we'll be lucky to average forty miles an hour. So, it will take us at least nine hours. Then add to that the bathroom and gas fill-ups, and that's going to be at least an hour. And that's if we drove straight without any sleep, and that doesn't even take into account . . ."

Virgil interrupted, "Cooking up the beans."

"That's right," Spencer said. "That's going to take some time."

The mechanic headed to the garage to work on a tire.

Virgil asked him, "Can I use your phone?"

The mechanic glanced at him, perplexed. "The phone lines are out. The storm knocked them out."

Katz was still in the bathroom when the rest of them headed back to the car.

Walking toward the gas pumps, Spencer commented, "We can speed it up if we don't stop every time somebody has to go to the bathroom. And we don't have to eat those beans."

"We're going to eat those pork and beans." Lakalo's nod was definite. "That's going to happen. We're going to. I'm starving."

"Me, too," moaned Adam.

They piled back in. With a yank Israel slammed the DeSoto's door. Stu started the car, then pushed his left foot on the brake pedal and put it in gear.

Outside Stu's window, the suspicious gas station attendant asked, "Are you a friend of Jimmy's?"

The Montanan stared at him blankly, then gave it gas, pressing down with his left foot. The DeSoto's tires screeched out, its back bumper nearly hitting the gas pump as it curved past. Taken aback, the attendant watched the vehicle's one brake light glow when it neared the street. With the tires screeching out again, it zoomed onto the two-lane road and headed north. A moment later, the headlights flashed on to illuminate the dark road.

Inside the DeSoto, Stu's confidence grew, for his left foot wasn't having any problem holding down the gas pedal. "Katz, how far is it to Missouri?"

Spencer answered, "He said it's just over three hundred and fifty miles." He looked over the eight heads, searching for Katz. "And if we can go fifty-five without stopping for fuel and bathroom stops, we'll be there in about six and a half hours."

Daniel gave him a playful thump on the back. "Very good, genius."

Spencer frowned, realizing Katz wasn't there. "Katz?" There was no answer. "Katz isn't here!"

Stu hit the brakes. The abruptness of the stop was great enough to send Daniel off his window perch and Israel into the dash.

The gas station attendant frowned, watching the vehicle screech to the side of the road. His eye caught movement on his right. Katz bolted past, tearing toward the road. Desperate, he shot one hand in the air and cried out, "Wait! Wait for meeee!"

CHAPTER 21

Forty-eight miles fell under the DeSoto's tires. Headlights beamed the corners as the car took the curves. In the distance, Stu could see faint lights of another small town. He gave it gas, but the DeSoto hesitated, sputtered, then engaged, then sputtered, then died. Stu looked at the gas gauge—empty.

Lakalo leaned over the seat, "Are you going to pull over, Miami, so we can cook up the pork and beans?"

Stu sadly advised, "I'm going to pull over 'cause we're out of gas."

"Out of gas! How are we going to get to Jamberama?" There were moans from the back.

"'Least we can eat the beans," said Lakalo.

The DeSoto slowed and Stu looked for a place to park. Headlights revealed a pull-out ahead. But the car was slowing and Stu didn't think it would be able to coast into it. It stopped halfway into the pullout.

As the backseat boys filed out, there was more moaning and complaining about how they were stranded until Lakalo said, "I don't care, I'm going to eat some beans." His statement seemed to inspire an ember of hope in them.

Virgil squeezed by Stu. "I'll get a fire going."

Stu shut off the headlights, leaned back in the seat, and stared at the town's lights in the distance. The town looked to be no more than a train stop and a few outbuildings.

Outside the car, Virgil scrounged around the roadside searching for dry grass, twigs, cardboard and paper.

Stu struggled out the driver's side. He didn't realize how tender his swollen ankle had become until he put weight on it. Wincing in pain, he stood next to the door.

Lakalo saw him. "Hey, Miami. What's the word?"

Stu gave a tired shrug.

"Can I give you a hand?" Lakalo came alongside and helped Stu over the edge of the road into the ditch. They followed Daniel down a dark path that led to where Virgil was getting ready to making a fire.

Thirty yards from the car, the path ended at railroad tracks. Just off the path, Virgil put the tinder he scrounged in a small stack. Adam set down the three cans of pork and beans next to it.

"There's not a whole lot of wood around, but I found a bit of tinder under the bushes."   Katz, Joey, Daniel, and Rubin stood looking about. Spencer was busy picking up anything that could burn. It was dark, and Adam could just see the end of a train on the outskirts of the town and the silhouette of a railroad man walking beside it.

Wary, Rubin stared into the darkness across the tracks. "This is spooky." He shifted his weight from one tired foot to the other. "I don't like it here. Something doesn't feel right."

Not far from him, Virgil readied his tinder. But his pile of wood was small, and he grew impatient with the others, who were just standing around. He admonished them, "Are you guys going to stand around all night, or help find some wood?"

"This is bad. This whole thing's bad." Joey flopped down. "I'm tired."

"What are you talking about?" Virgil responded. "'Least it's not raining. We're doing good. Look how far we've come. Heck, we got pork and beans, we got water, just had some hamburger, some fries—what else do you want?"

"Some gas," complained Joey.

"I want to go home," complained Katz, fatigued.

"How can you say that?" Lakalo asked, coming in with some dried grass. "We're almost to Jamberama. If we make it to Jamberama, it's all good."

Rubin looked across the tracks. "It's awful dark." He gazed at the forest,

"This is spooky."

Using his magnesium strip, Virgil started the fire. The rest of the troop

drew near the tiny light, watching it grow.

"This is going out if you don't get me some more wood," Virgil said.

The small light gave Rubin new hope. He joined the wood pickers in their search for fuel for the fire, but he still felt uneasy and cast a wary eye about, still worried about some ominous creature.

Behind him, Spencer used his Swiss Army knife to open the lid on one of the cans. He placed the can on the fire's edge.

"You shouldn't take off the top. Just open it halfway so if it falls over, it won't spill out," Virgil said. "That's what we do when we go camping. And no ashes get in it."

Spencer nodded, adjusted his glasses, looking at Virgil in the firelight. "Good idea." He reflected on the fight they'd had earlier and felt strangely closer to the Kentuckian. Bending over, he opened the next can only halfway and placed it near the fire.

The flames grew with the addition of more wood. The mesmerizing glow drew the boys nearer. Katz put his hands out to feel the warmth.

Watching the flames dancing upward, Daniel began humming an old folk song, then pulled out his harmonica and blew into it. As the tune drifted out, many an eye looked down the tracks at the train.

"I bet it's taking off soon."

"Could be."

"The tracks are heading north."

"Jamberama's north."

Confident the fire was going well, Virgil drew away, and walked up the embankment that led to the train tracks.

"Where're you going?"

Virgil glanced back then pointed at the train. "I'm going to see if there's a place we can ride it or something."

"I'll go with you if you give me a hand." Stu struggled to get up, and then hopped toward him, favoring his sore ankle.

Virgil came back to help him.

"I want to see, too," said Israel, awkwardly rising.

With Virgil helping Stu, the three looked like the walking-wounded as they went down the track.

At the edge of the fire, Joey began to nod off. In the distance there was a klaxon of train cars as the locomotive engaged, its wheels creaking as they rolled forward.

Daniel's harmonica tune brought back memories for Lakalo of the beginning of the trip and the troop's excitement. He grinned, thinking how far they'd come, then thought of Commander Charles, Commander Rex, and Junior Commander Alan and grew sad. He missed them.

"The beans smell good." Adam took a long whiff.

"I like beans," said big Lakalo, thinking of honey-baked beans.

"Beans are good," Rubin added. "My uncle makes good ham-hocks and beans."

"These beans are about ready." Adam's stomach growled and he moved in closer, admiring the juice from the pork and beans oozing out. "They smell so good."

"I got the spoons." Katz excitedly lifted the Dairy Queen spoons.

"I wonder if the Commanders are getting any food."

"It's sad . . . it's sad."

The firelight showed the whites of Rubin's eyes. "I bet Junior Commander Alan has a lot of bruises on him." He nodded. "'Cause he hops around too much, and no Sasquatch is going to put up with that."

"I wonder if they're dead."

"Don't say that! Don't say that! Jesus will save 'em."

"But what if Jesus don't save 'em—I mean, from dying?"

"Don't say that! Don't say that! Jesus will always save 'em."

"It's sad . . . it's sad," said Katz. "Who's going to look after the Scout meetings with Commander Rex and Commander Charles gone?"

"I betcha there'll be no more Scouts." Adam shook his head in disappointment.

"It's too bad we didn't make Jamberama. That would've been so much fun."

As the realization of not making Jamberama sank in, a somber air fell on the troop.

Minutes passed slowly, then Joey, who had nodded off, suddenly awoke on hearing gravel crunching and saw the dark silhouette of someone running toward him. Panicked, he scuffled backward. "Ohhh!" He didn't recognize the figure coming down the tracks, nor his surroundings.

They heard Virgil yell, "Com'on! We can catch this train . . . " He waved at them. "It's going north . . . Jamberama's north!"

In a rush of excitement, Lakalo pulled Joey up. "Let's go."

Rubin and Daniel hustled up the embankment and ran down the middle of the tracks, heading for Virgil.

The others could see the train beginning to chug away from them; in seconds a throng of boys hurled themselves after it with no thought of where the train was actually going. The fact that it was heading north, toward Jamberama, and that the others were part of the wild dash was good enough.

As Rubin and Spencer passed Virgil, he said, "Go to the right, Stu and Israel are in the second boxcar."

Halfway down the tracks, Lakalo turned and yelled at Daniel, "Daniel . . . go back and get the beans!"

Daniel swung off, jumping over the track and ran back. With no light to assist him, it was slow going. He hopped back over the rail, seeing the tiny glow in the distance.

When he reached the embers, he quickly bent and touched a can to see how hot it was.

Lakalo's distant voice called out, "Hurry, Daniel."

Daniel whipped off his T-shirt and gathered the three cans together within the fabric. Taking care to balance the beans so they wouldn't drop, he rose and jerkily found his way to the tracks. He leaped into the middle and trotted between the rails. As he ran along, he lifted his head to see the outlines of four boys nearing the back of the moving train. Farther down the line, he glimpsed a body disappearing into an open boxcar. The fear of being left behind gripped him, and sweat poured down his face as he ran. Rocks smacked under his feet. Bits of warm sauce splattered out of one open can and hit him in his bare chest. Ahead, the mechanical pounding of the train grew louder. He could see a flurry of hands coming out of the boxcar to pull in Adam.

Lakalo had fallen back, but it didn't take long for him to gain the edge of the boxcar opening, his arms reaching for the troops' arms. Inside the doorway, the others bumped into each other, trying for a chance to grab him. They grabbed anything they could get their hands on: arm, shirt, hair, torso, and pulled him halfway in. Rubin, Katz, and Stu grabbed his pants and dragged what was left of Lakalo across the planked floor.

Running in the middle of the tracks, Daniel curved right, leaped the rail and tore along the side of the track. Nearing the back of the train, he could feel the wind coming up from the boxcar. He sprinted alongside it. His shoes pounded the gravel, smacking it as he tore for the opening in the next boxcar. But the train's speed gained. He was ten feet behind the boxcar, but it might as well have been a mile, his chest felt like it was going to burst.

Inside the boxcar, everybody yelled, "Come on Daniel!"

Down the track, the power and noise of the locomotive grew.

The words, "You can do it!" echoed in his skull.

Spencer noted how fast the train was going and didn't think Daniel would make it.

Virgil bent over and yelled, "Forget the beans! Forget the beans!"

The shouting intensified. Virgil and Spencer laid flat, reaching out so far that Stu thought they'd fall. Fearing they'd go over, he grabbed hold of Virgil's leg and big Lakalo flopped on Spencer's legs.

Daniel wasn't about to give up the beans. With his eyes riveted to the corner of the open door and his legs burning, he pushed himself as hard as he could. Little by little, he gained the open door until he was close enough to thrust his hands forward and offer up the pork and beans to the many fingers that stretched for him. The cans were snatched, along with the shirt. One can tipped over on the way, but Katz was quick to pick it up and lick off his fingers.

The train's speed had increased and Daniel had dropped three feet back. Their encouraging shouts poured out the opening. "Come on, Daniel!"

Daniel's arms shifted into a higher gear, pumping as if his life depended. Gaining the door, a number of hands grabbed him, madly pulling his arms, wrists, and hair. His feet slipped but the hands held him firm.

"Heave!" Stu shouted.

Daniel's bare chest swept over the cold steel as he was dragged inside the boxcar. Rolling over, he lay flat on his back, his lungs bursting. While everybody patted him, he heard their joy, and praises.

"You're my hero, Daniel."

"You did good, Daniel. You did really good!"

Spent, Daniel flopped his arms out above his head and tried to find his wind.

Everybody talked at the same time, while Katz marched about singing, "Pork and beans is getting it tonight. Getting it tonight!"

Still unable to speak, Daniel took in deep breaths. The rolling rhythm of the train worked over his bare back. *Clickety-clack, clickety-clack.* The wind cooled his sweaty sides.

Stu couldn't see everybody. It was too dark. He grew concerned. "Hey! Wait a minute! Is everybody here?"

"I'm here," said Rubin, who stepped forward and thumbed his chest.

"I'm here, tttttto." With an awkward step, Israel came into the hint of light between the two open boxcar doors.

"There should be ten of us," Spencer calculated, counting. He pointed at Joey, Adam, and Lakalo, mumbling, "Seven, eight, nine"—then, aimed his finger down at Daniel—"ten. There's ten."

"We'd have to get off the train if Daniel didn't make it." Adam grinned. "I don't know how we would've done that 'cause Israel and Stu can't jump."

Lakalo added, "Unless we had pillows or something. Otherwise, we'd have to wait till it stopped."

"We're lucky we made it."

Still panting, Daniel rose onto his knees.

"Israel, don't step on them pork and beans." Adam pointed at the cans in the middle of the box car. "If you knock them over, you're not getting any."

Rubin stared at the opposite end of the box car but was unable to see anything. "It sure is dark back there."

"Go check it out."

"I'm not going back there. The bogey man's back there."

"You think the bogey man's everywhere."

Israel slurred, "You gggggib me a shotgun and a bbbbbig fffflashlight and I'll go back and ccccccheck."

Lakalo chuckled.

"Daniel, here's your shirt back." Daniel didn't take it. He was still trying to catch his breath, so Katz used it to fan air down on him.

Stu looked around the dark boxcar, but even with the other door open, it was too dark to see either end. Outside, the outline of trees flashed by.

Inside, Katz stomped about swinging the shirt and sang, "I got a lot, a lot of beans to do."

Spencer held his compass near the door, angling it toward the hint of moonlight, "We're going north." He faced Virgil and excitedly repeated, "We're going north!"

Stu sat down and leaned against the side wall.

"Good," said Katz, goofy as ever. "Jamberama's north." He swung Daniel's shirt about.

Israel bent down to prop himself up against the wall next to Stu. He liked the sound of the clickety-clack of the wheels on the railroad tracks.

At last, Daniel felt he could stand. He got up, rubbing his ear which someone had pulled in their rough efforts to get him on board.

Katz stopped stomping about, knelt down on one knee, and stared into the open can of pork and beans, then bent lower and took a heavenly sniff. He grinned, then became serious. "Some of this got out."

Daniel felt bad, "I couldn't help it. It was the jiggling when I was running."

Lakalo encouraged him with a pat on the shoulder. "Don't worry about it. You did great!" Lakalo sat down next to the beans. Others followed.

Katz gave Daniel his shirt. Daniel could feel the dampness in spots, but it was too dark to see the brown sauce from the pork and beans. He held it out so the wind from the doorway could dry it.

"Are we going to eat those beans or what?" asked Lakalo, rubbing his hands together.

"How are we going to split it up?" asked Adam.

"It'd be easiest if we did it by spoon. Like each take three spoonfuls, then go like that, till we get down to the end. Then each just get one spoon."

Katz handed out the spoons.

"That's as good an idea as any."

Spencer took the lids off the other cans. He could feel warmth

coming up at him. Pork and beans had never smelled so good. Everybody scooted over, encircling the three cans.

"This is the most I've ever looked forward to pork and beans in all my life!" Lakalo said.

"We should say a prayer," Rubin added.

"Go ahead," said Lakalo.

"Be careful," Joey joked, "the last time he prayed Idaho showed up,"

There were chuckles.

"Idaho should pray, then," Katz stated.

A long pause followed as Stu readied to pray for the food. The clickety-clack of the wheels on the tracks beat a mesmerizing rhythm. Stu began, "Dear Lord . . ."

Out of the darkness, came a deep, husky, menacing voice, "Where's my portion?"

Stunned, shocked, nobody moved as they realized there was someone else in the boxcar. Then, there was a mad scramble to get away. They bumped into each other to get to the opposite end. All that remained exposed in the wide door's shallow light were the three cans of pork and beans.

Lakalo was so starved that he dashed forward, snatched them, and tore back, banging into Joey.

Joey moaned, holding his head. "You bashed my head."

"Sorry."

There was whispering, then silence. Ten pairs of eyes stared into the coal-black void.

"Get your knives out," Virgil advised.

Lakalo, Spencer, Katz, and Adam pulled out their pocketknives and hastily opened them.

Virgil took comfort in knowing that whoever was down there couldn't see them, but he felt naked without his knife and whispered, "Katz, can I use your knife?"

"No way, I'm keeping my knife," Katz said aloud.

Again, there was quiet. Outside the boxcar, trees gave way to a small meadow, allowing more moonlight to spread across the interior. Virgil leaned forward to see if he could make out the being behind the voice. All was darkness.

A deep, cunning chuckle came from the opposite wall.

Creepy shivers crawled down Rubin's spine. Israel's breath caught in his throat, and Joey's palms felt cold and clammy.

"I just want some food." The ominous voice was so deep that Katz envisioned someone seven feet tall and weighing four hundred pounds.

After a long pause, Lakalo ventured, "How much you want?"

"I'm a big man." His growl was so low, it could have been peeled off the floor. "I need it all."

On hearing this, Stu boldly asked, "Who are you?"

"I'm an all-star wrestler . . . Ever hear of Bomb-Blast?"

This comment stunned them.

Rubin gasped, "That's the devil."

The darkness rumbled with another low chuckle. "So, you do believe in the one who makes things flashy and brings 'em home in a driving beat?" His mocking chuckle rumbled.

Israel struggled to ask, "Hhhhhhow'd you kkkknow?"

"Be quiet! Don't talk to him."

Over the continuing rumble of the clacking boxcar, Katz blurted, "I want you to know that my uncle's neighbor is a police officer!"

A harsh chuckle rolled eerily out of the dark, pervading the boxcar.

"Give him the small can," Katz whispered to Lakalo. "The one that's half-full."

Again the chuckle flowed across the boxcar. "You boys are playing with me?"

Lakalo scurried out and placed the can in the middle of the box car, saying, "There it is." He scrambled back into the shadowy dark.

The train rolled on through the forest. The boys with knifes still had them out. All eyes watched the can of pork and beans, the shadows flashing over it. The clickety-clack, clickety-clack of the wheels rolled on. Out of the darkness came a dark hand. The can vanished.

Seconds passed, a minute, five minutes, then the deep voice startled them. "I'm a big man . . . I need those other cans."

Israel moaned, "I need . . . a gggggun."

"Listen, mister." Joey's voice quivered. "We haven't eaten in three days, and I'm going to die if I don't get some pork and beans."

The deep voice rolled, "Everybody's got to die. . . Why the last fella I had in the ring couldn't even crawl out. I broke his back."

There was a gasp from Israel and Rubin.

"Give him the pork and beans," insisted Rubin.

"He's not getting my pork and beans," Daniel retorted. "I didn't bust my rump so he could eat them all."

"He's got his; he ain't getting mine," Lakalo protested.

Rubin blurted, "Mister, I just want you to know that I ain't eating none."

The low voice rumbled, "You'll be the only one left alive."

There was a long pause, then the empty can of pork and beans bounced near the door. The boy's eyes followed it as it rolled toward the edge then disappeared out the opening.

Katz called out, "I'm not eating none, either,"

"I won't hurt you none, but if those beans come your way, you bring them down to me."

"He's working us one against another," said Spencer. "Don't give the cans to Katz or Rubin. Don't do that."

"You, boy, listen here," the voice threatened. "You're going to be the first one I throw off this here train."

Spencer felt doomed, there was nowhere to run; even the air around him seemed thin. He quietly moaned.

Virgil felt for him and called out, "Mister, you go after him, then I'm going after you!" His comment brought a rush of hope that flowed through the troop.

"You touch him, and I'm fighting you, too," Stu said, matter-of-factly. "And I can rope a bull and bring him down!"

"It's *dddddda,* same with me. And I ggggggggot a big kkkknife." Israel struggled to get his words out while hanging onto his small pocketknife. Then, he awkwardly dropped it. It was so pitch dark that when he fumbled for it, he knocked it forward, then gasped and groped around in a panic, his hands patting the rough floor.

Lakalo handed one can to Stu then took three spoonfuls from his can. Though Virgil sat next he couldn't see through the dark to hand him the beans. "Sound off, or you won't get any . . . Everybody sound off."

"It's me," Virgil said.

"Here." Lakalo thrust the can out. "Don't give it to Katz or Rubin and only take three spoonfuls."

Virgil dug in. In no time he finished his three spoonfuls and moved the can toward Joey. "Joey?"

"I'm here."

"Only take three spoonfuls."

There was some fumbling, and Joey took the can. He held it near his nose, enjoying the smell, then indulged in a few quick bites. Chomping, he dug in for one last spoonful.

"Hey? It's me . . . Adam."

When Joey passed the warm can, it hit Adam in the chest. Without hesitation, Adam took his three spoonfuls, downing them like a mulching machine, and sent the can back to Joey.

Joey handed it to Virgil, who groped about, then gave it to Lakalo, who dug in again.

The deep voice commanded, "You boys bring me them beans!"

Stu and Israel had crawled around Rubin and Katz and ended up squatted next to Daniel and Spencer. "Here Israel." Stu shoved the can into Israel's chest.

Israel worked on his three spoonfuls. It was good that no one could see him, for he was a drooler.

Beside him, Rubin smelled the pork and beans. He leaned into Israel and whispered, "Give me some beans. I got to eat, too."

Chewing on a mouthful of beans, Israel moaned, "Noooo." He swallowed, gasped, then jerked the can toward the opposite end of the boxcar. "You have to tttttttell . . . him." He groped around then mechanically handed the can back to Stu.

Rubin swallowed, feeling his growling stomach. "Mister, I'm the kid that said I'm not eating the beans."

"You got the beans?" growled the intimidating voice. "Bring em down."

"No!" Rubin blurted. He considered the consequences. *Were the beans worth dying for?*

A moment passed, then the accusing voice continued, "Why haven't you brought them?"

Rubin heard a spoon clicking off the side of the can and knew his portion was being eaten by others. Hunger drove his response. "Because . . . because I'm going to eat them." The statement was so profound, so weighty, uttered in such a serious manner, that Israel moaned as he tried to stifle his laughter. He almost choked as his stress bled out in hilarity. The sought-after, near-empty can of pork and beans was immediately handed to Rubin.

"You're one kid that I'm not going to throw off the train," the deep voice rumbled.

Surprised, Rubin relaxed and let out a sigh. Then, he heard the man continue: "No, no. I'm going to torture you first, then throw you out."

Katz had been determined not to eat a thing, but his heart started to pound when he heard Rubin's spoon bounce off the can's walls. His tongue came out to touch his upper lip, then he swallowed, wanting the beans, yet not wanting to die. But something greater drove him. Gritting his teeth, he stared into the darkness toward the other end of the boxcar and loudly declared, "They're my buddies, and I'm sticking with them!"

There was a threatening silence.

Out of the blackness came a hiss. "I'llllllll have to kill you alllll."

The hair on Virgil's scalp rose. "Quick, hand this can to Katz," he said. The near-empty can went down the dark line to Katz. Though disappointed by its weight, Katz wasted no time and dug in with the spoon.

"Give him the other can," Stu said. "There's not much in that one."

"You're trapped, like chickens in a hen house. You can't run," the voice jeered. "And I'm the fox . . . the crafty fox. I'm going to wait till you go to sleep, then I'll be coming.

One by one I'm going to fling you out. You're going to fly through the air, just a-screaming."

"If you touch me, mister, you're going to burn in hell." Katz stared into the darkness toward the foreboding voice.

The rocking of the boxcar had made Stu's bottom numb. He shifted his weight but kept his focus on the blackness at the opposite end of the car.

Joey held his knife out.

"Too bad we can't get this thing over with," whispered Virgil.

"It's better to wait than fight."

"I'd rather fight than sit here waiting for him." Virgil wished he had some water to wash the salty bean residue down.

With the mechanical rhythm of the wheels against the rails echoing up, the train rolled on and on through forest, farmland, and trees. Katz intently watched for movement coming out of the darkness just beyond the shadows of the open doors. He leaned forward and thought he could see a foot stepping toward him, but the flickering shadows cast by the trees were illusionary. They flashed over and over, dark and light, appearing at different angles, different patterns.

At the opposite end of the boxcar, the man's mind mulled over what the boy had said about burning in hell. He didn't believe there was such a place. The train rolled rhythmically on and his eyes grew heavy.

At the troop's end of the boxcar, Katz was mesmerized by a small beam of moonlight shining on the boxcar floor. Shadows of passing trees flashed over the wood planking.

His eyes widened when he saw something darker. *Is it a shoe?* He grew perplexed, for suddenly, it wasn't there. He leaned forward, staring hard. *Is it real?* His head jerked. *Did another shoe appear?* But it was gone. As soon as it disappeared, another shoe appeared. The shoes kept appearing, disappearing, then reappearing to the rhythmic beat of the wheels on the tracks and the motion of the boxcar, over and over, till the black shoes began taking on the beat of the train, flashing in and out of the shadows as if they were dancing on the edge of light and dark—touch and tap, touch and tap, touch and tap, *clickety-clack*, touch and tap, *clickety-clack,* tapping to a hot, humid rhythm.

They were startled when the man's deep voice sang to the rhythm, "There's no such-a-thing as hell, son. There's no such-a-thing as hell."

His song continued till Stu found his voice, "You keep telling yourself that, mister!"

A hollow chuckle rolled across the boxcar, embracing them with scorn.

Stu commanded the troop, "Keep your eyes peeled!"

On and on, the train rolled, and thirty minutes passed, but the calming, *clickety-clack* of the boxcar had no calming effect on the troop. Transfixed with fear, Katz gazed toward the dark, wondering at what moment the man would appear. He jumped when he heard something hit the floor. The boy had no clue that sleep had overcome the man and his foot was jerking about as a nightmare gripped him.

In the man's dark dream, weeping, ripping sounds engulfed him as hands came through the boxcar floorboards to grab him. He struggled, gritting his teeth, gnashing them together, madly attempting to free himself from the nightmare's grip. He blurted, "Nooo!"

This desperate, gut-wrenching plea jerked everybody to attention. The troop sat wide-eyed, ready.

The eerie nightmare played over the man's mind, with larger hands coming up from the floorboards to grip him. "Noooo!"

The shriek brought Katz to his knees. He expected the man to burst out of the darkness any second.

"Noooo!"

Panicked, Virgil felt around the floor, searching. "Anybody got any paper?" Lakalo's left hand moved to the floorboard, his fingers also searching, while his right hand pointed the knife toward the darkness.

"Virgil!" Joey gasped, thrusting a piece of paper in his direction. Virgil grabbed it, wrinkled it, and having readied his char cloth, hurriedly struck his aluminum stick against the magnesium. Green sparks flew off and burned into the char cloth. Lightly blowing into the spark, he lifted it along with the paper. The ember grew.

"Nooo!" cried the tortured voice.

"What're you doing?" Katz asked.

Virgil had turned the works upside down and was blowing into it.

"You got your knife out?"

"Yeah," Lakalo whispered.

It wasn't long before a flame took hold, and Virgil carefully righted the paper to slow it down. The light revealed their faces. All eyes watched as the flame quickly climbed up the edge of the paper and lit the area like a small torch in a cave.

Virgil rose. "Com'on," he said. Katz and Rubin stared in surprise at the fire that was heading away from them.

Stu winced in pain as he struggled up. "Let's go."

His words had a releasing effect on the ones who were fighting their fears. Gripping what weapons they had, they rose to their feet.

Lakalo leaned into Israel. "Israel, you stay here."

Following Lakalo, Stu, and Virgil, the rest held their blades out and moved away from the end of the boxcar.

"Grab that piece of paper, there." Virgil pointed to a crumpled paper. With the flame rapidly disappearing, the troop passed the doorways. A breeze came in the doors and shook what remained of the flame, causing weird shadows to stretch and yawn. Spencer hastily handed Virgil the paper. The Kentuckian fed it into the fire while half looking ahead into the dark. As the flame spread into the newspaper, he dropped what was left of the first bit of paper, which was nearly eating his fingers, and took a cautious step forward, holding his new flickering torch in front to light the area.

"Nooo!" The man's gut-wrenching cry sent chills down their spines.

Virgil halted and lifted the flame. A shoe was exposed, then a leg. It perplexed him. He'd expected a giant shoe, a huge leg. Gaining courage, he stepped forward. The light exposed the man's torso, an arm. Even in the shadows, he could see the arm shaking, trembling, reacting to the nightmare.

"Nooo!"

Virgil set his jaw and pushed himself forward. His paper was burning down. He lifted the light, and the flame moved across the torso to reveal a deep brown face, its forehead damp and wrinkled. Virgil was stunned. This was no huge wrestler but an old, short, skinny man. Lakalo was just as surprised.

"Mister?" Virgil's mouth was dry. He felt the warmth of the flame as it burned toward his fingers. "Mister?" He tapped the sole of the man's shoe with his boot.

The man's eyes flashed open—wild, crazed eyes. His gaze riveted on what he saw: a small flame and just above it, a shadowed face, a strange young face that was difficult to make out, a ghost-like face. If the abyss wasn't real before, it was now. The weakened flame seemed to vaporize the young man's face, holding him, drawing him where he didn't want to go. Then, the flame fell to the floor, where its glow rocked back and forth, back and forth to the boxcar's motion.

"Mister?"

"Get away!" It was the gut-wrenching growl of a crazed man who scrambled to escape the hellish face, the nightmarish hands. He bolted and smashed into the boxcar wall, his forehead hitting with such force that his teeth were driven into his tongue.

Katz gasped, terrified.

Everybody stepped back.

Though the impact had knocked the man down, he quickly rose. Off-balance and woozy, he staggered toward the troop. Their dark silhouettes melted back through the hint of light from the boxcar's doorways. The disoriented man emerged from the darkness, having no thought of the real world, no thought of the speed of the train or the gravel below the tracks, only the hellish nightmare. The *clickety-clack, clickety-clack* sound rocked him.

A small voice gasped, "He's coming."

The man glanced sideways toward the voice and stumbled into Katz. Both went down in terrified shrieks. There was a mad shuffling as others attempted to get away. The man could feel hands, Katz's hands, hands that wildly pushed him, hit him. This drove a greater terror into the stricken man. The hands!

He rolled to get away from the hands, only to hit the side wall near the opening. Breathing hard, he rose, swaying on the edge of the boxcar doorway, then took a staggering step back. The wind blew against his shirt in a vain attempt to stop him from falling. His arms swept up past the iron opening into nothing but air.

Shock was reflected in the eyes that had witnessed his disappearance. They could see the shadow of trees flash by and felt the rocking rhythm of the train, but nothing seemed to register.

Numbed by the man's tragic fall, Lakalo finally spoke, "You see that?" He slowly got up and approached the open doorway. "You see that?" He stopped and took firm hold of the doorframe. The wind caught his hair as he cautiously leaned out and looked back along the side of the tracks. "He's gone!" Darkness and the speed of the train covered the gravel.

Katz joined him, but was too afraid to look down the tracks for fear of falling out. In shock, he put his hand on Lakalo's arm to steady himself.

"He's gone!" said Lakalo again. He blankly stared at the shadows from the trees playing on Katz's face.

"He ran right into me!" Katz wiped his damp eyes. "He just ran into me!"

"It's not your fault."

"He was crazy!"

"He 'bout scared me to death!" said Rubin, coming up from behind. "That man was bad."

"He had to be crazy!"

The hint of light coming in from the doorway illuminated tears flowing down Katz's cheeks.

* * *

Seven hours later the train came to a halt under a rusted water tower that spoke of a time when trains were run on coal and wood and required an abundance of water.

A railroad man walked alongside the boxcars. He aimed his flashlight over each one.

Lying inside the boxcar, Virgil watched the bright light moving across the opposite wall, then heard the crunch of rocks as the man approached. A bird chirped, but its warning couldn't keep Virgil's eyes from growing heavy with sleep, they closed.

The railroad man shone his light on the empty end of the boxcar but wasn't thorough enough to check the other end. He continued down the track.

Little by little the morning sun began to edge the night sky.

The train's engine engaged, sending an abrupt jolt from boxcar to boxcar.

The sound jarred Virgil awake. He sat up and gazed at the open boxcar door. Confused and unaware of where he was, he felt an odd apprehension. To his right Katz came up on his knees, said a line of gibberish and crawled about on all fours. Below him, the train's wheels slowly rolled down the track.

Virgil grew concerned over Katz's sleepwalking abilities. "Katz?"

Katz turned toward Virgil, repeated his gibberish then rose and stumbled toward the light of the open doorway.

"Katz?" Virgil scrambled after him.

At the opening, Katz turned, his body swaying with the train's motion; another step and he'd be gone.

Virgil came on with such intensity that when he yanked Katz away from the doorway his momentum carried him out. He hit the gravel with force, stumbled and fell, his palm scraping the sharp rocks.

The train had just cleared the station, slowly gaining speed as it headed east toward the rising sun.

Inside the boxcar, Katz laid face-up, staring at the top of the metal roof—the blue sky beyond. He was awake now, yet unsure of his surroundings. He could faintly hear a rooster crow. Below him the gaining *clickety-clack* of the boxcar vibrated his back.

Spencer's eyes blinked open. He gazed about the rolling train then saw Katz, laid out near the door. Fearing for him, he got up and walked over.

"Grab hold, Katz."

Hands joined and Spencer pulled him up. He studied the bruise on Katz's forehead which he'd received from the oak tree the night before, then gazed upon the scratches on his chin which he'd received from jumping out of the DeSoto. "You okay?"

"Hey!" Virgil's yell startled them.

Looking out the boxcar, they saw Virgil, tearing along, just about up to the doorway.

Quick to size-up Virgil's plight, Spencer called to the sleepers, "Give a hand here!" He moved to the corner of the doorway, took hold of the door with one hand, knelt, and stretched for Virgil with the other.

Behind him Katz grabbed hold of Spencer's shirt and braced himself.

Daniel put a hand on Spencer's shoulder and bent to his knees to give a hand.

Spencer's hair blew back as he leaned out. "Virgil! You can do it!"

The train's speed had increased and Daniel found it weird to be on the opposite side of the scenario played out the night before.

Half sleepy eyed, Lakalo got up to the opening and was stunned to see Virgil running toward them. In no time he was leaning over the side, yelling, "Com'on, Virgil!"

Breathing hard, legs churning, Virgil achieved the boxcar door. Inside, hands reached, and grabbed him, powering him upward. As they pulled him in, his sweaty face passed Spencer's. Though Spencer had fought with him the day prior he was overjoyed. While Virgil lay there breathing, he grinned at him.

CHAPTER 22

Inside a tent, a junior commander licked his lips and glanced down at Johnny Revv who was fast asleep. As he lifted his trumpet and gathered a large breath, readying to blow, a finger tapped him on the shoulder. He frowned and saw an excited Scout pointing at Commander Bob. The Commander held a video camera. Beside the Commander, the rest of the excited troop, all sporting expectant grins, awaited the horn's blast. Across from Johnny, Lonny, snoozed away on his cot. The Commander gave the trumpeter a thumbs-up, and the trumpeter bent over Johnny's face. He puckered then blew.

BLUUUUUUUUUUR

Johnny's arms bolted outward as if hit with high voltage.

BLUUUUUUR

Johnny's body jerked upward, his face hit the rim of the trumpet. Falling backward, his eyes rolled.

The trumpeter would've kept blowing, but the expression on Johnny's face was so slurred, so hopeless that he couldn't keep it up and burst out laughing. Lonny, who also had been raised from the dead, rolled sideways and punched the trumpeter in the leg. The trumpeter couldn't stop laughing and limped back toward the others.

In unison, they yelled, "Good morning, Johnny Revv!"

Johnny slowly sat up and cast a tired gaze at them. Then bending his head to scratch his ear, he mumbled, "That was cruel."

With a chuckle Commander Bob said, "Your bride was waiting for you at breakfast."

In the distance, an outhouse door banged.

Johnny quickly looked at his watch—8:30. His eyes widened because he'd agreed to meet Ashley at 7:30.

"You're going to have to kiss-up now. She's hurting."

A Scout behind added, "They're always hurting."

Johnny lay back in bed, rubbing his eyes, then quickly glanced at the trumpeter, fearing he would do it again.

* * *

Having missed his morning date with Ashley, Johnny Revv paced toward the food service area. Lonny trailed with his video camera. Dressed in a frontiersman costume, Johnny carried a bear hide. The leather fringes on his buckskin coat danced about as he hurriedly looked for Ashley amongst the food servers. He stopped to tuck his satchel into his colorful red sash.

Off to the side a number of Scouts admired Johnny's voyageur hat, knee-high moccasins, buckskin pants and coat, calico shirt, red suspenders, and bear claw necklace.

One scout pointed toward the intricate red and black beadwork on Johnny's knife sheath. "That looks cool."

Another kid said to Johnny, "You look like one of those guys who used to trap beaver."

"That's what I'm supposed to look like." Johnny half glanced his way then back to the food service area. In the distance, an outhouse door slammed, then another.

Carrying his black bearskin, Johnny approached the back of the service area and scanned the girls who were serving food to the eight lines of men and boys that funneled into the tent. It was lunchtime, and they were dishing out mashed potatoes, corn, fried chicken, salad, and buns. He was searching for Ashley. His eyes brightened when he finally spotted her. He turned toward Lonny, then pointed in Ashley's direction. "What do you think I should tell her?"

"Tell her the truth. Tell her that you're a no-good-for-nothing dog that ain't worthy of her time."

Johnny repeated, "Ashley, I'm a no-good-for-nothing dog that ain't worthy of your time."

"That'll do. She'll get all teary-eyed and say a bunch of lally-goo, stupid stuff like my sister says to her boyfriend. Then it'll be all better."

Johnny repeated, "Ashley, I'm a no-good-for-nothing dog that ain't worthy of your time."

"Girls like it when guys say they're sorry. They're silly like that." He chuckled, then sang, *"I'm sorry . . . sooo sorry . . . "* He lifted the video camera. "I'll catch it on film . . . it'll be good."

Johnny gave the camera a goofy grin, then headed for Ashley. There was an opening at one end of the serving area, and as Johnny went through, a kid on the inside handed him a white serving apron along with a hair net. Cocking an eyebrow at the camera, Johnny dropped the apron while lifting the hair net, then with a shrug spread it over his thick hair. Ready, he theatrically displayed his palms and proceeded down a line of servers.

The servers moved like robots, their arms mechanical, quickly shoving food forward to the hungry Scouts.

Johnny stopped and mouthed his line one more time. "Ashley, I'm a no-good-for-nothing dog that's not worthy of your time."

Lonny went around the other way to get a better shot of him, cutting in front of the line on the opposite side. This interrupted the flow of the line as Scouts had to walk around him to get their food, causing many a curious eye to follow the camera's direction.

Coming up behind Ashley, Johnny threw the bearskin over his shoulders and bent down. He capped his face with its black muzzle, looked through the vacant holes that once were the bear's eyes and pressed his fingers into its claws.

Lonny grinned as he filmed the black furry beast that was on all fours approaching Ashley. The slow and cumbersome movement of the beast looked real.

Ashley was intent on feeding the line. Quick and efficient, she scooped up a scoop of scramble eggs and extended the spatula out, aiming it at a Commander's plate, all the while unaware of the many eyes that watched the threatening black bear that approached her from the rear.

Beneath the black fur came a low growl. "RuuuuuuuuuuGgggHhhhh."

Ashley glanced back. "Ahhhhhhhhhhhhhhhhh!" The scramble went flying. She went flying, jumping, skirting, scrambling wildly, anything to get away from the menacing beast. There was nothing ladylike in her retreat. She bolted twenty feet in a tenth of a second, leaving a trail of scrambled eggs spewed across the grass. Hilarious laughter followed the poor redhead. Totally embarrassed, she stood red-faced and panting, yet somehow still holding the spatula.

Johnny rose and came out of the bearskin, sporting a bearish grin. The black fur along with the hairnet fell behind him. He walked toward her with hands extended.

She dropped her head but smiled lopsidedly.

He came close to her, tenderly taking her elbow. "I'm sorry, Ashley."

"No . . . you're not!" She smacked his shoulder with the spatula.

CHAPTER 23

With a slow stretch and wide yawn, Israel awoke to a view of the boxcar's metal roof. He rolled and turned one hand at an awkward forty-five-degree angle to press his knuckles into the floor, then pushed himself up to look about the boxcar. Everybody else was awake, some lying down, some sitting.

Stu had his sore leg stretched out in front of him. He fanned his face but soon found it was a waste of energy against the oppressive heat.

Daniel was bent over. His red hair didn't sway much, even with the *clickety-clack* movement of the boxcar. It was too dirty.

Virgil and Spencer, the only ones standing, were near the door, and from the way they spoke to each other, one would never know that they'd fought the day before. The Kentuckian was pointing toward the long shadows that extended from the trees.

Spencer asked Virgil, "Do you know how long we've been going east?"

Virgil ran his palm over his sweaty forehead. "Ever since I got up, and who knows before that."

"It's too bad," Spencer said sadly. "We'll never make it to Jamberama going east."

"Are we heading east?" Joey asked, loud enough so everyone could hear.

Virgil's discouraged countenance spoke for itself as he pressed his hand into his dirty, sweat soaked T-shirt.

"We got to get off at the next stop and get back on the right tracks," Stu said.

Tired of sitting on his rump, Joey rose and walked toward the opposite door to look out. Rubin and Katz joined him, gazing at a field of okra. In the distance was an irrigation ditch, and beyond that, another field of okra.

Joey moaned, "I'm going to die if I don't get some water."

Spencer tiredly retorted. "You can live three days without water and you had water last night."

"You see how dry my lips are?" Joey pressed them out for display. "My mouth feels like dirt. If I don't get water soon, I'm going to die."

Lakalo shrugged his shoulders, "You'll have to die, then." He wandered toward the other end of the boxcar and began searching the floor for anything the man might have left behind. A worn reddish shoelace lay six feet or so in front of the back wall. Reaching down, he picked it up. "Hey, guys. Look at this!" Lakalo displayed the shoelace. "That's all that's left of that man."

"That's sad," Stu said, limping toward him, his shoulders rolling.

"That man was crazier than a peach orchard boar," said Virgil.

Lakalo dangled the string. "I hope he made it."

Heavy-hearted, Katz shot a glance at the string, then leaned into the door. His damp eyes stared blankly at the passing landscape which hastened backward with such speed it appeared one long blur. But nothing could blur the memory of his desperate struggle to get free of the man. It was etched in his mind. A rush of emotions flooded over him. His eyes welled, and a lump filled his throat.

Rubin broke his meditation. "That man scared me bad." He ran the back of his hand across his sweaty forehead.

Stu examined the shoelace. "From his low voice, I thought he weighed five hundred pounds."

Israel's right foot angled badly as he walked hunched over to the group. "You think he mmmmmmade it?

Rubin looked troubled. "Last night, after the man went out the train, all I could dream about was that guy getting back on the train."

Stu limped toward the open door. "I don't think he'll be getting back on any trains." The wind blew his hair as he glanced over at Katz, who was rubbing his eye, pushing back tears. "You all right, Katz?"

Katz slowly nodded, but he didn't look up.

"It's so hot. Boy howdy, it's so hot." Stu puffed his shirt out from his chest and glanced up at the boxcar's metal roof.

Joey fanned his damp shirt. "It's a good thing the wind's coming in. I'd burn up if it didn't. This is the hottest place there is!"

"Hell's hotter," Rubin stated.

"I meant on this planet. This is way hotter than Death Valley. I've been there in the summertime," Joey said.

"No, it's not," Spencer objected. "Death Valley is a good twenty degrees hotter. It's the humidity here that makes it so extreme."

"The humidity makes you feel dirty." Adam ran his index finger across his damp forearm. "It's like I got a hot layer of grease all over me."

Stu took hold of the door frame and stared out at the passing farmland. "This sure is hotter than Montana. A black cow would roast on her hooves in this."

Daniel gazed at Stu's dyed hair. "You think it's hotter than Miami?"

Stu rolled his eyes, figuring he'd never shuck that name. He glanced over at Katz, whose head was tilted down with his hand over his forehead to shield his face. "Are you all right, Katz?"

Katz nodded and tried to gain his composure. He wiped an eye, then pulled his hand away and stared down. A teardrop hit the floor. Below him the rocks and rails seem to disappear in a blurred kaleidoscope.

* * *

It wasn't quite noon when Commander Charles and Commander Rex peered into the abandoned DeSoto while an Arkansas patrolman swung the car's door open.

With little sleep in the last forty-eight hours, Commander Charles was running on nerves. "What are we going to tell their parents?"

Rex mumbled, "Let's try to stay positive."

Commander Charles's voice pitched. "Yes." Overwhelmed, he simply nodded, but his thoughts drifted to the boys' parents. He'd already explained to them about

Junior Commander Alan, the drug lab, and the missing DeSoto. Now he wondered how he was going to tell them about the abandoned vehicle.

Sitting in the DeSoto's driver's seat the Arkansas patrolman turned on the key and checked the gas gauge. "Looks like they ran out of gas."

Near the railroad tracks another officer came across the remnants of a campfire. "I've got a fire here," he called. He spotted some beans on the ground and bent to pick one up. Feeling it between his fingers, he crushed it then smelled it. "This smells like pork and beans, and it's fresh." He expectantly looked about for more beans. He spotted one on the gravel that led up to the railroad tracks, then saw a few more on a railroad tie.

The two Commanders and the other patrolman headed toward him.

"I've got a trail of pork and beans," yelled the officer, holding one bean in the air.

The other patrolman glanced at Charles. He noticed his face was twitching and tried to encourage him. "Least it's not a blood trail . . . That's the good news."

"That's good news," Rex reiterated in a dull voice. He tapped Charles with his knuckles, offering him some Gummy Bears.

Terribly distraught and ignoring the Gummy Bears, Charles nodded. "That's what I'll tell them. They'll understand that. That's the shred of goodness that'll hold them together." His words were hopeless, to the point of being comical. "I'll just tell them that they found the car but not to worry, there was no blood."

The patrolman walked down the track following a bean here and a bean there. He looked up toward the railroad station, then glanced back and said, "I wonder if they got on a train."

Commander Charles took a few deep breaths, and his eyes fastened vacantly on the train station as he tried to grasp all of this. Frazzled, his mind mulled. *How can I tell the boys' parents that their sons might be on a train*? He looked as if the information were too great to comprehend. His heavy face began to twitch then he mumbled something.

Rex could see his plight and encouraged, "I think he was joking."

CHAPTER 24

A US Army Huey helicopter swept over the tree tops of Jamberama. In the back of the chopper, Johnny Revv's hair blew wildly as he held the microphone to his lips. He grinned at Lonny, who was across from him, aiming the camera. The rotor blades were deafening. Johnny shouted, "Lonny, I'm up here above Jamberama." He motioned with his hand. "Look at this!"

The camera caught Johnny's disheveled hair, his safety cable, and the vast blue sky beyond the open door. Lonny aimed the camera down at rows and rows of white tents. In the distance were five sparkling swimming pools with hundreds of kids leaping about. To the right was the outdoor stage.

Johnny pointed down. "Those tents are Ohio. There's Michigan and Illinois. That's Eagle Rock store, and there's the Johnny Barns Lodge. Over there is the Pioneer log fort, and there's Frontier Village. I'm going there next."

As the camera took all this in, Johnny lay down on the metal floor and playfully pedaled his shoes up in the air. "Lonny, check it out. Bicycling bears . . . bicycling bears."

Lonny chuckled.

A second later, the copilot looked back to see Johnny lying on his back, giving an arm flex back at the camera while leaning out the opening. "Hey!" the copilot yelled, pointing back to the seat, "Sit down!"

The horseplay ended. Johnny and Lonny scrambled to their respective seats.

* * *

The boxcar's *clickety-clac, clickety-clack* rhythm had no settling effect on Stu. He was desperate for water and tried to swallow but his mouth was too parched. Propped against the boxcar, he gazed out the large doorway at the fields of farmland. Sweat flowed off his brow, dampening his collar. He mumbled, "It's so hot."

"Whhhhat?" Israel asked beside him.

"There's no cattle out there. It's too hot." The Montanan moved his heated head toward Israel. His weary eyes fell over the rest of the troop who were haphazardly laid out on the floor of the boxcar. Most were lying flat with their arms out wide to catch any breeze that came through the boxcar door.

Staring up at the metal ceiling, Lakalo wondered if Joey could be right about dying from heat and lack of water. The shadow of a tree splashed past. He rolled his head sideways in despair and saw other trees come into view, then the odd house. The train began to slow.

Though the stifling heat had drained their energy, the troop responded with a rising sense of excitement as they felt the brakes take hold. Virgil and Daniel sat up; the rest followed. Lakalo stiffly rose and walked near the door. He gazed up the line. A railroad station was up ahead.

"We're coming to a station!" Lakalo looked over the troop then approached Israel, his hand extended. "We're coming to a station, Israel! We're going to get off here!"

"I kkkkknow." Israel awkwardly rose. Weak, he stumbled.

Behind him, Adam offered Stu his arm. "Here you go, Miami." Stu's swollen ankle pained him as he rose. He limped toward the door, then leaned into Adam to steady himself as the brakes took hold. Stu saw an old-timer who was sitting under the shade of a tree and gave him a respectful nod.

The old-timer waved back, then his face wrinkled more as he wondered why there were so many boys a-hoboing.

As the station came into view, they could see a small town that worked its way backward into farm fields. Stu heard the brakes pressing on the steel wheels; he gripped the door and tiredly mouthed the name of the town: "Middleton, Georgia."

"Can you believe we're in Georgia!?" Adam exclaimed, staring dumbfounded at the sign.

Along the rail, a switchman watched the boxcar roll toward him. He pointed at the troop. "You boys better get." The boxcar rolled four cars past him, then stopped. When it stopped, there was a resounding jolt that reverberated down the entire length of the train as each car came to a halt.

"We'd better get out the other door, otherwise, that guy is going to get us," Katz said.

"I don't care if he does," Rubin said, "as long as he's got some water." He dangled his legs over the doorway, hopped down then looked up at Katz. "What's it matter anymore? We're not going to make it to Jamberama."

His statement was a killer—if their faces weren't long enough already they got even longer.

While the rest of the troop hopped down, the switchman walked toward them and called, "You boys are going to be charged with murder if you don't get."

Katz stared at him, wondering how he knew about the crazy guy. "I didn't kill him! He just jumped."

The switchman frowned at the young man. He'd been joking, yet this kid was serious.

Fear swept over the dehydrated kid. "How's he know?" Katz whispered to Lakalo as the switchman came nearer.

Lakalo pulled at Katz to change his direction, aiming him in the opposite direction, to avoid the man. The rest wearily followed. So, instead of going into the station to get water, they headed back from where they'd come.

They walked along the fence like a pack of beaten, dirty, starving dogs.

Stu hobbled along with Adam's help.

Katz kept looking back at the switchman, then ran his hand across his eyes as they teared up.

"What's wrong, Katz?" Adam asked.

Feeling guilty, Katz didn't answer, but kept his eyes on the tracks.

Stu took a firmer grip on Adam's arm for support. Adam asked, "How bad's your foot?"

The Montanan hopped forward, sucking up the pain. "I'm finnne." He drew the statement out the way his grandfather had taught him, but his ankle wasn't fine. It was swollen. Limping past the last fence, he gave Lakalo a sad grin. "I just wish we could've made Jamberama."

The same old-timer who had seen the troop of hobos earlier, watched them trailing past the fence. He thought the troop a terribly sad lot. Daniel, Joey, Virgil, and Spencer were in the lead. Lakalo and Rubin were behind them with Katz, walking beside Israel, who was hunched over, pigeon-toed, dragging his leg. Stu held Adam and limped along at the back of the troop.

The old-timer slowly rose and went to his hose that was watering his garden. He lifted it, aiming it at the young men. "You boys want some water?"

"Yes . . . please," Joey said, in a begging manner.

Like sheep, they headed into the old man's large yard, walking across the tilled soil to a row of corn. They watched as Joey took the first drink, water spilling off his lips into the damp soil beside the corn stocks. The others moved in thirstily.

"You boys been traveling long?"

"We've been going for eleven days," Spencer said, taking off his smudged glasses then searched for a clean area on his shirt to clean them, but there was none.

"On the train?" the old-timer asked.

"No. The van mostly. Then we were lost in the wilderness, then we got a car at the cabin and then we got on the train."

"Where you headed?"

"We were going to Jamberama."

"Where's that?"

"It's up in Missouri."

"Missouri? You boys are a long way off." He could see the sadness in Rubin's eyes.

"And tonight's the closing ceremony." Adam's shoulders slumped even more.

"Where you from?"

"We're from Los Angeles," said Lakalo, then glanced over at Stu. "What state you say you were from, Miami?"

"I came out from California, too."

"Here we been calling you 'Miami.'"

"What's this Jamberama?"

"Why it's the biggest campout ever. Scouts from all over the world go." Katz gasped as he drank in the water, then glanced over at a cornhusk and swallowed. "That corn looks real good."

"You want one?"

"You bet!"

Adam thirstily grabbed the hose away from Katz.

"When did you last eat?" The old-timer hadn't seen such a ragtag group of dirty boys since WWII.

"Last night I had a bit of pork and beans, and we had enough to buy one hamburger that we split between all of us and some fries, too."

"Before that, we didn't have nothing for days," said Rubin. "We would've died if we didn't get the pork and beans, and then the guy on the train, he wanted to take it from us." To his side, Adam gave the hose to Lakalo.

The old man teased, "You boys hungry?"

There was a chorus of, "I'm starving."

Terribly thirsty, Daniel's eyes were fixed on the hose.

"I can eat that corn without cooking it," Katz said. The old man broke off a cornhusk and handed it to him.

"Thank you," Katz said, very pleased, and started ripping off the husk.

"I can fix you up a meal if you like." The old man stared at the bruise on Katz's forehead and the scratches on his chin, and wondered if he'd got in a fight.

"That'd be real nice of you," big Lakalo said appreciatively, his eyes brightening.

"Hurry up on that water," Rubin said, half pulling the hose away from Virgil.

The old man broke off cornhusks and handed them out. "Just put the husks on the ground there," he instructed, pointing to a pile of shriveled leaves. Then, he shuffled around to the next row, where he cut a number of beefy tomatoes from their vines. Handing some to Virgil, he glanced over at Rubin, who was getting another drink. "Going without food is no fun."

Rubin lifted his head and water dripped off his chin. "Nearly died."

Daniel pulled the hose away from him and couldn't get the water in his mouth fast enough.

"But you made it . . . right?"

Stu tugged at the hose, eagerly anticipating his turn.

"I'll wait till you all have a good drink." The old man gazed at the line-up of young men. "Then we'll go cook these up."

There were cheers from the hungry troop.

After they finally finished drinking the old timer instructed,

"Follow me, boys."

The troop followed, traipsing across the park-like grass.

Daniel came up on the old man's side. "You ever go without food?"

The old-timer glanced over at him. "Went eight days once but that was a long time ago."

"When was it?"

"Italy, during the war."

"What happened?"

"Our plane got shot down."

"Where did it happen?" Katz asked, coming up from behind. "During the Vietnam War?"

The old man grinned at him. "No. No. I was too old for that. It was during World War II."

"Against Japan?"

"Well I fought against Japan with Doolittle's Raiders but that wasn't when I went without food."

"What'd you do over there?"

"Not much. After a bomb run we ran out of fuel and had to parachute out."

The path the bedraggled troop followed led under the welcoming shade of fruit trees. Above, a squirrel chippered down at them. To their left was a red barn.

Katz point at it, "That's the biggest barn I ever did see."

Walking out of the shade, they crossed the dirt road, and Spencer noted how long and straight it was. It faded into green fields of okra that went on and on. They came upon the back door of a modest farmhouse.

The old man opened the screen door. "You boys come in, if you like. I'm thankful to have some company." He handed the door to Katz who didn't feel comfortable about entering. "Just give me a minute to get the corn on." The old man stepped into the kitchen and placed some corn on the counter.

"Can we hear the rest of your story?" Katz asked.

The old-timer said, "That was the war to end all wars. But the way it's going you may face a bigger war yet." Reaching under the counter, he pulled out a large pot.

The troop jammed up at his door and stared curiously in. Lakalo studied the frailty of the old man's arm, then looked about the kitchen. He thought the yellow chairs and the gray Formica table were old-fashioned.

"Are you a farmer?" Rubin asked.

The old man nodded. "This was my dad's place and his papa's before him." He went to the refrigerator and opened the freezer. "You boys like hot dogs?"

There was a jubilant round of approval. The troop vied for room, poking their heads in the door to see him pull a package of wieners out of the refrigerator.

Joey grinned from ear to ear. "I eat a hot dog every time we go see the Dodgers. It's my favorite."

Adam added, "I've eaten four hot dogs at one setting, at this place in Chicago. They were so good. I like mine with mustard and relish."

Curious about the plane story, Stu painfully stepped up into the jammed doorway and stood on the threshold. "What happened after you parachuted out?"

"At night we ran out of fuel over China and I had to parachute out." His eyes widened. "I spent the night atop a cliff. It's a good thing I didn't move till morning. Otherwise, you wouldn't be getting any corn right now." He grinned.

"Or hot dogs," added Joey, glowing in anticipation.

The old man's mouth hung as he looked over the troop, then suddenly the realization of the hot dogs came back to him, so he turned and got out a frying pan. "You know, sometimes I find myself bent over looking for something . . ." he grinned at them. ". . . when I forget what I was looking for."

The boys chuckled.

"Then what happened?"

"I got out of China and ended up flying bombing runs over Italy. It went fine for about six missions. But on the seventh . . ." He glanced toward the light of the window. The memories flooded back, and he thought of his friend Tony, the one who cheered them all up with his corny jokes, the one who'd gone into the German prison camp with him but never returned. He looked around the kitchen walls, sadly mourning for him, and took hold of the counter for balance.

Glancing back to the young men at the doorway, his eyes fastened on Virgil, who had features similar to his buddy. He nodded to himself, remembering his friend's sacrifice.

Virgil felt uncomfortably odd with the lone, quiet stare of the old man.

Finally, Katz asked, "What happened on the seventh trip?"

"We got shot down. I had to parachute out. We ended up in a prison

Camp." He turned on the grill. "I escaped from there and was on the run for six months before I was recaptured."

"I bet you never flew again," Stu said, the thought of his uncle's plane was fresh.

The old-timer shook his head. "No, I started flying again as soon as I got my strength back." He set his jaw, proudly adding, "In life, you have to face your fears." Running a knife through the plastic he opened the package of wieners.

Stu's idea of facing another plane ride disturbed him – there was no way. If a vehicle was not available, he'd take the bus, go by rail or on horseback, or walk.

"A lot of good fellas died so Europe could enjoy freedom." The old-timer set the wieners one by one on the grill then glanced back at the troop. "How many of you are there?"

"There's ten of us, including Miami."

"Will any of you want more than one hot dog?"

He was encompassed by a roar: "Yessssssssss!"

"I can eat ten of them myself," Katz said.

"I'll tell you what. . . If you sing me a song, I'll fry you up two hot dogs each."

"You serious?"

"You bet. But it's got to be a good song and well sung."

"You mind if only one of us sings?"

"A solo's fine."

Lakalo asked, "Can you give us a minute?"

The old-timer nodded with a slight grin on his face.

They turned away from him and huddled outside the door, talking with each other while constantly glancing back at him.

Joey chided, "These Southerners must think we sing like a bunch of meadowlarks."

"Everybody down here must sing for their supper."

"What song does anybody know?" Lakalo asked, looking straight at Daniel.

All eyes were on Daniel, but Stu lifted his hand. "I know *My Home's in Montana*." His face was hopeful.

"Oh, com'on, Miami." The big Hawaiian again gazed directly at Daniel, hoping for another knockout song.

Daniel thought of all the songs he'd sung with his dad. The clubs hired his dad's small band because they liked his rendition of all the '60s folk songs. As he stared through the open doorway at the old flier, one song came to mind.

The troop was relieved to see Daniel finally nod and say, "I know a song. It's a folk song."

Lakalo theatrically opened his palm toward the kitchen to usher Daniel forward. The others moved aside, and Daniel stepped up to the kitchen threshold. Katz and Rubin patted him on the back, both thankful this task didn't rest with them.

Lakalo spoke up, "Excuse me, mister, but Daniel's about to sing you a song. He's the best we got."

The old-timer turned to face the kid with red hair.

Daniel asked, "Is now a good time?"

"Now's as good a time as ever, I sure wish my wife was here to see this, but she's been gone for a while."

"I'm sorry to hear that," Daniel said.

"That's okay; she would've enjoyed this." He waved. "Go ahead then."

Daniel silently tapped his toe to gain the rhythm. Lifting his harmonica, he gave it a slight blow, then rubbed his lips to moisten them, and grinned as he attempted to relax. After a long pause, the strains of the harmonica slowly drifted out. It was a sad memorial tune, true enough to give them all goose bumps.

Daniel's clear voice drew them in. *"Anyone heeere . . ."* The words to the song spoke of the ones that fought for freedom. The tone, the theme, of how friends die young, captured the old man. He gripped the chair as memories of his fallen buddies flooded back. When the song ended, the old timer pressed his hand into his eyes to mask his emotions. There was a hallowedness about the kitchen. The old-timer stood for a long moment staring at the vinyl floor.

"You like it, mister?" Katz asked, anxious to get two hotdogs.

Seeing the old-timer was moved by the tune, Lakalo gave Katz a shove.

"What?" Katz whined as if he'd been slugged.

The kitchen was dead silent with all the boys expectantly watching the old-timer.

At last he shuffled to the freezer, and oh the grins and slaps on Daniel's back when the old timer pulled out another pack of wieners.

"Where you fellas say you're going, again?"

Katz was thrilled to see the icy vapors coming off the pack.

"We were going to Jamberama," Lakalo replied.

"But today is the last day and we're not going to make it," Adam said sadly.

The mood among the troop suddenly changed.

"Tell me again what's so special about this place?"

"It's the largest campout ever. People come from all over the world, and it only happens once every four years," Lakalo said.

"Where in Missouri did you say?"

"It's called Eagle Rock."

"I know where that is." The old-timer glanced at his watch, then rolled the sizzling meat. "It's a long way off. I'd say at least six hundred miles. You say it ends tonight?"

CHAPTER 25

Johnny couldn't believe they had placed his Chevelle SS on display between Nascar's Jim Marlin's Dodge and Blade Earnhart's Ford.

What a thrill to rub shoulders with men who raced 180 miles an hour. Even the way they stood showed confidence—all costumed in their team racing gear. They were a selfless bunch; if they weren't signing autographs, they were getting their picture taken with Scouts. Sponsors' decals entirely covered their cars. The hoods were open, and it was a good thing the front area was roped off, because some of the numerous car buffs packing the front would've loved to crawl inside the pipes.

"This is over-the-top," Johnny said to Lonny. "I can't believe they let a kid from Lovelock, Nevada in with the big daddies."

"You wouldn't feel it if I pinched 'ya, would you?"

"Nope." He was grinning so constantly that his jaw began to ache. Feeling as if he could float, Johnny looked past Mike Mears' Chevrolet at Marty Shotenburg's Ford. "The only sad thing is Jamberama will be over in five more hours . . . maaaan," he said, disappointed as he looked toward the field of booths and all the events. "Three days is just too short. If this could just go on and on and on and on. I haven't had any time to spend with the professional baseball players and they're just right there," he inclined his head toward the next booth, "nor the professional football players or the basketball players." Lineups spilled out beyond each booth, with Scouts eager to meet the athletes and get their autographs.

In the midst of this all-male camp, a teenage girl looked out of place as she walked toward the roped-off area. Spotting her coming from the Pinewood Derby entrance, Johnny broke off his conversation with Lonny and hurried over to greet her.

"Hey, Ashley," he said, beaming. He lifted the rope so she could come under. "Welcome to my house."

For a moment, she hesitated, appearing apprehensive. Then, fixing her eyes on him, she ducked under the rope. "Johnny . . . I've come to say good-bye."

Johnny looked surprised. "You leaving? Already?"

"Yes." She angled her head up the hill toward a waiting bus. "The bus is," her countenance dropped, "going to be leaving."

"Bus? What bus?"

"The one that takes the food service crew back to Tulsa."

Johnny tried to think of something spectacular to say while glancing up the hill at the buses then back at her. Nothing came. "Maybe we could write."

She nodded, handing him a piece a paper. He opened it and perused the Oklahoma address, then glanced at her small, slender hand and wanted to take it. "Boy, I wish we had more time. Can I walk you to the bus?"

As he turned to go, he saw her eyes look beyond him, then felt a tap on his shoulder. A hand came round his side, grabbing him, locking him in. It was Marty Shotenburg. Right behind him, Earnhart was quick to get a grip. Skinner and Marlin pushed in close to prevent Johnny's escape.

Marty's eyes twinkled. His soft Southern drawl addressed Ashley, "I hear this guy's been giving you a little trouble?" He stretched Johnny's arm out. "Giving you a hard time."

Ashley shrugged her shoulder, not sure how to respond, then gasped when she saw the grabbing gang sweep Johnny off his feet and stretch him out lengthwise. Johnny laughed hilariously and struggled to pull his foot or arm in. There was no way he was getting away from the power of these wiry NASCAR men.

Marty chuckled. "Girl, now's the time to get him back."

Behind Ashley, Scouts leaned over the ropes cheering her on. Johnny jerked about like a stuck frog.

"Go for it."

She pianoed her fingers across his jerky tummy, then dug her knuckles into vulnerable ticklish spots on his ribs. Lonny's camera swept in, catching Johnny wildly squirming, laughing so hard it was a wonder he didn't choke.

CHAPTER 26

B eside the railroad tracks an ambulance driver and his partner lifted the black man onto a gurney. From the bloody, torn pants and shirt, it was obvious he had hit the gravel hard. A white sheet was placed over the body, then tucked in around the gurney's edges. The driver straightened and sadly glanced down the railroad tracks, wondering how the man had fallen from a train.

A patrol car approached. It pulled to the side of the road and stopped.

An officer, along with Commander Charles and Commander Rex stepped out and headed toward the two ambulance personnel.

Commander Charles solemnly rubbed his fingers as they neared the gurney.

The officer gave a nod to the ambulance driver and the driver pulled the sheet away from the dead man's face.

Commander Charles shook his head. *Can this glazed-eyed man somehow be connected to my troop?* Taking a deep breath, he walked past the body onto the gravel of the railroad tracks and stared down the iron rails. They stretched smooth and straight in a long line that disappeared into the horizon. The parallel tracks were running just the opposite of his scattered mind, which was strung out, going in a thousand different directions. *Where are my Scouts? Are they alive? Are any of them hurt? Will I have to explain this dead man to their parents?*

* * *

The old-timer hung on the phone while gazing out the kitchen window at the boys who were scarfing down on corn and hot dogs. He had a rising expectancy about him—his plan was coming together and might become reality, if this one last buddy was available.

"Yes, I'll be there," said his friend on the other end of the phone.

Returning the receiver to its cradle, he stepped over the threshold onto the porch like he'd been given new life.

Proudly overlooking the eaters, he announced, "You boys sing me another song, and if it's good, I'll take you to Jamberama."

The bun stuck out of Katz's mouth as he gave the old-timer a long steady stare. Rubin nearly choked on his hot dog.

* * *

Perched on a chair at a Jamberama's hamburger stand, Johnny chewed a corn dog and watched a Scout, costumed as a Liberty soldier, walk past. He so admired the soldier's three-sided hat that he didn't notice Commander Bob's approach.

"Hey, Johnny Revv." Commander Bob gave Johnny a forearm shake.

Johnny grinned, "Commander Bob."

"I got some bad news about Stu."

Johnny frowned, waiting.

"The plane he was on had some engine trouble. Stu had to bail out."

"My little buddy?"

"They found the parachute, but there's no sign of him."

Johnny put his corn dog on the counter, considering. "I should get down there and search for him."

"I think Stu would want you to stay and finish tonight's performance."

Johnny nodded and unconsciously stared at the rows of Scouts lined up at the water dunk tank and balloon fight area. Then it struck him. "How are we going to do cowboys and Indians without Stu?"

"It's just going to have to be Indian and Indian night, unless you can find a kid who knows how to ride."

Johnny looked toward Grizzly Lodge and the hundreds of young men, dads, and Commanders who were either going into it or heading past it, migrating toward the Frontier Village. "They're all expecting to see Montana Stu."

"Well, his horse is here."

"But they want to see Montana Stu."

"What's our motto?"

"*Ready.*"

"I suggest you get ready."

Johnny rose. "I'll see if I can find a kid who can ride, and I mean ride."

* * *

With a twist of the doorknob, the old-timer opened his closet door and surveyed the few suits that hung there. Reaching in, he took out the one draped in plastic and removed the covering. He set it on the bed and took a long look at his WWII uniform. Even though it was more than sixty years old, it still looked crisp and professional. Admiringly, he ran his hand over the fabric. A flood of memories returned as he looked over the medals and his Air wings. He could almost hear the hum of the plane's engines—like a loud swarm of bees on safari. He bent and touched his Air wings. The memories came stronger—the early morning flight over the Pacific, the coast of Japan, looking down on the city of Tokyo and thinking it strange the people were so unaware of an attack, then seeing enemy aircraft, the Zeros with their formidable firepower. He ran his finger across a medal – he knew he had one last mission.

* * *

Near the trees of Jamberama's park like setting, Stu's grandfather, Pops, held the Montanan's famous horse. Gray looked tired, and Pops wondered if the animal was having a difficult time adjusting to the heat and humidity of the Missouri sun.

Beside Gray stood Johnny, who grew frustrated as he tried to explain to a lineup of potential riders, "This is not, I repeat not, a horsy-riding event." Johnny was upset with the ones who had tried out; so far, none had a clue about riding a horse. Exasperated, he stared down the long line. "This is a tryout. In other words, if you don't know how to ride, and ride well, then get," he shot an aggravated thumb to his left, "out of this line."

"I know how to ride," the next Scout said.

Johnny pointed toward Gray.

The kid appeared promising in his leap to get up on Gray's back. But unable to hold on, he slid right over the saddle, fell and hit the grass. Gray nonchalantly looked back at him.

At a loss, Johnny gazed at Lonny with a long, discouraged stare.

CHAPTER 27

The old-timer, who was dressed in his World War II uniform, flipped his hand toward the towering barn doors. "Young men! Open those doors."

Lakalo and Adam grabbed one rope, Spencer and Virgil took the other. With squeaks and rumbles, the huge barn doors slowly slid open.

"Whooee!" Katz exclaimed. "That's huge!" His eyes were fixed on an immense B-25 aircraft. Its nose was so large it seemed alive, looking as if it wanted to poke out the doors.

"That's the plane I was telling you about."

The troop was awestruck, gazing up at the massive Army green aircraft, with its sixty-seven-foot wing span. In a tree just off the road, a squirrel leaned over a branch and gawked as well.

Stu was the only one gripped by fear. Queasiness instantly pulled at his stomach, tension spread up his back. He knew what was forthcoming and broke away from the troop, limping and hopping toward the train tracks.

Just then, a 1950 Chrysler Windsor came into view as it drove down the lane.

The old-timer glanced toward it and recognized his friend. Though his friend looked ancient, he too wore his Army uniform.

"Looks like my navigator's here. All I need now is my copilot and gunner."

"What do you need a gunner for?"

The old-timer grinned and patted Katz on the shoulder. "Just in case things get out of hand."

Beside them, Lakalo noticed Stu limping toward the tracks. "Hey, Miami. Where you going?"

Stu didn't answer.

Lakalo took a few steps toward Stu then yelled at the gawkers. "Hey, you guys, something's wrong with Miami."

The troop saw Lakalo waving for them to follow.

"Com'on." Lakalo hustled across the road while looking back. "Com'on!"

Snapping out of the plane's magnetic hold, the troop dashed across the road, and hustled to catch up with Lakalo.

Israel attempted to move quickly, his shoulders going up and down like a hunchback with his right foot twisted in. He fell and struggled to get up, then carried forward in his erratic gait.

Ten feet behind Stu, Lakalo called out, "Hey, Miami. What's the word?"

Stu sadly shook his head, not wanting to talk, and continued to limp toward the train.

Lakalo came up on him. "Com'on, Miami. You can talk to me."

Virgil, Rubin, and Katz ran up.

Katz patted Stu on the back. "Hey, Idaho. How's it going?"

Stu slowed.

"You want to hold onto my arm?" Virgil asked, offering him his elbow.

The Montanan wouldn't stop. "You guys go ahead." He limped toward the tracks. "Planes and me don't get along."

"What?"

"I'm going to catch the next train."

"No way, Miami." Virgil reached for Stu and kindly took hold of his arm. Stu stopped.

The rest of the troop caught up and surrounded him. Each gave his two bits on why Stu shouldn't get back on that train. It ended with Rubin's explanation of bad guys – "They eat your beans and suck your blood."

"Com'on, Miami," Lakalo said, "you say you're a Scout. We're all going to Jamberama. You're one of us, we got to stick together."

In the distance, one big engine of the B-25 came to life, coughing, rattling, then roaring.

"I'm not going to Jamberama if Miami's not going," Adam said sternly.

Lakalo moaned, "Then we're all not going." He jerked upon hearing the plane's other engine come to life.

"I'll go tell them not to take it out," Adam said, breaking away from the crumbling, dejected troop.

Everybody watched Adam as he walked toward the plane.

Then Lakalo looked at Stu. *What a pathetic dream-breaker.* "If Montana Stu was here, he'd go."

"He'd go for sure," Katz piped in.

"'Cause he's not afraid of nothing," Rubin added .

"Everybody's afraid of something," Daniel said, defending Stu.

"Yeah, but Montana Stu's not afraid." Lakalo gave Stu a condescending eye. "He'd go on a plane even if he got the wind knocked out of him and broke both legs. He'd still go."

"I don't know about that," Katz said, perplexed. "How could he go if he couldn't walk?"

"Montana Stu would figure out a way. Yeah, the real Montana Stu would go," said Lakalo, then sneered at him. "It's not right to impersonate someone else."

Stu swallowed, wishing he wasn't related to himself.

Katz dumbly added, "Montana Stu could jump out of a plane riding his pony."

Exasperated, Joey twisted his palm toward the plane and said in a whiny manner, "Miami, it's only a plaaane."

"Leave him be," Spencer said. "We need to see if we can borrow a phone and call home."

"Yea . . ." said Lakalo, casting his disappointment at Stu, ". . . tell them we almost made Jamberama,"

His statement angered the Montanan. Stu drew back, clenching his fist, and glared at Lakalo. "I'm not stopping you from going on that plane. If you want to go, go!"

"That's easy for you to say, but we're a troop! And a troop doesn't leave the other guy"—Lakalo angled his chin toward the iron rails—"by himself, at the railroad tracks . . . and call himself a Scout!"

CHAPTER 28

Dust settled on Johnny's boots as he and Lonny stood by a roadway to the main Jamberama stage. They expectantly watched ten thousand-plus Scouts march by. The massive troop hastily marched forward while its lead man called out, "We are the Rangers!"

"WE ARE THE RANGERS!" thundered the troop. Stragglers hustled to keep up.

"Mighty, mighty Rangers!"

"MIGHTY, MIGHTY RANGERS!" Their voices were so loud it was a wonder they didn't cause a wind.

Johnny ran his hand along the back of his neck. "Man, my neck hairs stood up on that." He glanced at Lonny and mouthed the word, "Wow," then turned toward the troop and gave a military salute.

* * *

With both engines roaring, the big B-25 taxied out of the barn. In a tree across the road, a squirrel dashed through the branches, tearing away from the howling beast. The old-timer looked out of the pilot's window at his buddy, who directed him using a small flag, while keeping a keen eye on the end of the wing tips to avoid the trees.

The navigator, gunner and the rest of the troop stood on the grass, waiting to get on board. Except for the Montana cowboy, an intense excitement gripped everyone. From the cockpit, the pilot grinned out the window at Stu. But his joy no calming effects on the kid from Montana.

The B-25 rolled to a stop. The plane's engines were cut back, a hatch door opened, and a metal ladder was let down. Wind from the propeller blades blew back, disheveling everybody's hair.

Stu panted as he tried to somehow contain his fears of entering the casket.

The navigator guided the troop toward the rear of the plane, yelling, "You don't want to go near those blades!" He pointed at the propellers.

One by one, the Scouts went up the ladder. Stu was last.

In front of him, Lakalo stepped aside and palmed his hand toward the rungs in a gracious offering manner. "Hey, Montana."

Stu took hold of the Army green ladder, then released it and stepped away. His legs had gone weak, his breath came in pants.

Lakalo could see the stress in his eyes and encouraged, "Montana Stu would do a backflip into that door."

Stu somehow grabbed hold of the bar, and took the longest climb of his life, one tentative step after another. He was sickly white when the gunner helped him through the hatch.

Inside, the other Scouts looked about the long empty metal tube. Light poured in the two windows, illuminating the green aluminum sheeting that was riveted to the metal framework.

The eighty-nine-year-old navigator had to speak over the hum of the engine. "Gentlemen, your seating is there." His wrinkled hand pointed toward a long seat that ran against the side wall.

"Where're the seat belts?" Katz asked.

The engines powered, and the B-25 moved forward, jolting the navigator, who grinned, enjoying its force. After gaining his balance, he responded to Katz, "Have you ever heard the term 'flying by the seat of your pants'?"

Katz shook his head. "No."

"That's what we do every time we take off," the ninety-one-year-old gunner interjected, then shot a nod at the navigator.

The gunner's comment had an ill effect on Stu. He felt a lump in his gut as he watched the old airman pull up the ladder, then batten down the door. He was locked in now and the only Scout standing. The gunner slowly righted himself and leaned into the Montanan to steady himself. Stu held his arm and hoped the old-timer wouldn't fall over.

"That's good. I can get it from here." The old gunner stumbled forward and angled toward the seat.

Watching him, Stu grew even more afraid—each one of these old men looked as if he would fall over any second. The old gunner sank down beside the navigator, who was sitting in front of a map behind the cockpit firewall.

Even though Stu could feel the plane moving beneath his feet, he figured there was still time to open a door or hatch or anything and jump. His eyes locked onto the hatch in the floor.

Joey was bragging to Katz about how many times he'd flown, while the rest of the troop watched Stu. Stu suddenly melted to his knees and started toward the hatch. Daniel, Lakalo, and Adam bolted out of their seats. Lakalo and Adam positioned next to the hatch, making it impossible to open, while Daniel bent and placed his palm on Stu's arm.

"Hey, Miami. What do you say we head on over to the bench . . ." Daniel pointed to it, ". . . and sit down?"

Spencer, Virgil, Katz, Israel, and Rubin surrounded Stu.

Rubin patted his shoulder. "Hey, Miami." Stu reached for the hatch.

Israel's head oddly angled, "Hhhhhow you dddddoing?" His forehead leaned toward Stu's face. "Idddddaho?"

Feeling like he was in a cage that was compressing the air out of his heart, Stu gasped for breath. His eyes had a watery, crazy look to them. Daniel showered him with pats. "It's going to be all right."

"You don't need to worry about nothing." Lakalo also patted him.

Stu remained on all fours.

"Yea, everything's going to work out."

Katz noted Stu's fluorescent hair. "Montana Stu could jump over buildings and could crawl through hatches."

Lakalo pushed Katz and hissed, "Do you have to say that?"

"Come-on, Miami." Adam's voice was soothing. He bent down, placed his hand on Stu's shoulder and stared into his frantic eyes. "It's not good to be down here."

"You boys find yourselves a seat on the bench," called the old gunner.

Eight hands helped Stu up. Virgil compassionately took him. "Com'on, Miami."

Stu was guided toward the seat. A mournful, forlorn look covered the Montanan who stared back at the hatch.

Outside the plane, heat waves danced across green fields of okra which were spread out on both sides of the long dirt road. The plane taxied amidst them. At a crossing, it turned left, causing wind from the propeller to blow okra leaves back along the runway.

Inside, the pilot glanced at his control board then turned to look through the doorway at the navigator who gave him a thumbs-up. The old-timer returned it with glee.

Engines revved as the throttles were pressed down. The plane, being without insulation, sounded as if it was going to rattle apart.

Stu gripped the seat and prayed while staring directly at an old bullet hole in the metal. The plane tore down the runway, its deck bouncing. Stu's thoughts jumped to Old Custer barreling down the runway, the shifting wind, the noise, the parachute, and the terrible leap into empty sky. *What's happened to Uncle Hawthorne?* Stu's eyes watered, for he was sure his uncle had crashed.

The B-25 lifted into the air.

Again, Stu started to pant. He felt the lack of air, the squeeze. Sweat beaded across his forehead and flowed down his neck into his T-shirt.

Powering upward, the plane banked, turning toward its northern heading, and Stu felt his stomach churn then roll.

* * *

It was evening at Jamberama when a big band blasted its horns out over thousands of Scouts whose eyes were glued on the stage. They took in the dance-off between the Navy boys and Army boys. *Da, Da, Da, Dat, Da, Da, Da, Dat, Da, Da, Da, Dat. . .* Spotlights illuminated the white glow of five Navy sailors, who were jitter-bugging against five Army boys dressed in clean, pressed khakis. The dancers' bodies swung back and forth to the huge rumbling beat of pounding drums. Trumpets broke in, with the power of ten armies recalling the never ending strength of a generation gone by. Above the stage hung a huge USO banner. On the grass below, a Scout intently watched a Navy dancer slide dramatically across the dance floor. The wide-eyed Scout thought the Navy boys were getting the best of the Army until an Army kid gave a bicep flex and jitter-bugged as though his life depended on it.

* * *

In a cloudless sky, the B-25 leveled out at 8,000 feet.

Lakalo rose and walked to the end of the bench to address Stu. "That ain't half-bad, now, is it, Miami?"

Still fighting phantoms, Stu didn't look up at him.

"He looks like he's going to puke," Katz blurted.

On hearing this, Stu took a deep breath, attempting to hold down the queasies, and stared in the direction of the navigator.

Katz followed his eyes. "You think they got anything to throw-up in?"

Spotting a garbage pail, Lakalo broke away, quickly snagged it, then set the green pail at Stu's feet. "Just in case you need it."

Stu stared at the bucket's circular rim and water bled off his brow.

"What's the word, Stu?"

Stu was able to get one painful word out: "Parachute?" Then, he heaved, throwing-up into the garbage pail.

"Woorf," Lakalo barked, covering his own mouth, and abruptly headed for the navigator.

"Oh, man. Oh, my . . . man," said Adam, totally taken aback at the sight of vomit.

"That's soooo gross," Rubin moaned, squinting his eyes. "Poeee."

Katz was the only one who found the contents of the pail curious and stared into the green garbage can.

The smell was drifting down the line, and hands went up to cover mouths and noses. Each face told a story, from revulsion and disgust, to pity for the white-haired, white-faced kid.

Lakalo returned, holding a Kleenex, but he couldn't stand the smell, and the sight of his buddy heaving again. It made his skin crawl. He turned away from this agonizing scene, and felt his sweaty pants sticking to his legs. The Hawaiian felt dirty, very dirty. The days in the humid forest had taken their toll.

Noting droplets of sweat on Stu's brow, the old gunner remembered paratroopers during World War II and recalled the anxiety they'd faced before jumping into battle. He slowly walked toward the sick looking kid. "Are you all right, son?"

Stu's eyes rolled in pain as he took a short breath. "I'm doing finnne," he said, like his grandfather had taught him. His fluorescent hair, coupled with his pale skin, made the ghostly kid look anything but fine.

"We rigged up a bathroom down there on the left." The gunner pointed toward the back of the plane. Everybody watched Stu get up. He held his legs tightly together as he headed hastily for the bathroom.

With his hand still over his nose, Lakalo suggested, "We should get that bucket out of here, 'cause if it fell over, it'd be bad. We should put the bucket in the bathroom."

"I'll take it," Katz said, rising, grabbing the green pail by the edge, and looking directly into it as he headed for the bathroom.

With great relief the troop watched him haul it away.

Katz set the pail outside the bathroom door, then knocked. "I left the bucket outside, so don't trip over it . . . You hear me, Miami?" He knocked again on the door. "You hear me, Miami?"

"What?"

"I left the bucket of puke outside the door, so don't trip on it."

Ten minutes passed before Stu staggered out of the plane's bathroom. His foot smacked into the green bucket of slop. The bucket slid back and leaned, angling to fall. Wavering, the Montanan grabbed the rim just as it went over.

The wide-eyed troop gasped, then let out their breath, relieved to see nothing dribble out.

As Stu righted himself, he blinked, turning his nose away from the caustic stench. Swaying and weak from dehydration, he cleared his throat several times to hold his stomach down, then bent over and dry-heaved into it.

At last, he set the can on the floor and gave it a one-eyed stare.

Lakalo called out, "Flush it down the toilet!"

The listless one complied and dry-heaved again and again in doing so. The door to the tiny room was open, and the boys could hear his retches.

Feeling bad for him, Lakalo and Israel got up and walked back to check on him.

Lakalo ended up four feet from the door staring in at his buddy. Israel gained the door and peered in. It hurt to even look at Stu. His retching was so severe.

"You . . . okkkkkkay?" Israel awkwardly thrust his hand out to pat him.

The old gunner shuffled up and peered in. He saw a wasted young man wiping sweat from his brow. "How you doing, son?"

Stu's eyes rolled as he painfully said, "I'm fine."

Israel stepped aside as the old gunner grabbed hold of the door frame. "You don't look too fine to me," the old gunner said. "What can I get you?"

"A parachute."

"I'll get some water too." The gunner broke away and headed toward the front.

Stu dropped his head and panted as he exited the bathroom. Feeling terribly weak and sore the Montanan shuffled over the bomb bay doors toward the bench seat.

With an oddly contorted face, Israel asked, "How you ffffeel?"

The Montanan gave a weak nod and jadedly replied, "Lighter."

Chuckles broke out amongst the troop, and Daniel rubbed him on the shoulder. "You're going to get better now."

"Yeah," Lakalo agreed, feeling for Stu. "You're going to get a lot better."

Stu slumped onto the wood seat, just as the old gunner appeared, holding a bottled water and a parachute. "Here you go, son." He handed Stu the water bottle.

"Thanks," Stu whispered. Opening it, he took a sip to clear the acidic taste in his mouth while he stared across at the parachute the old gunner held. A kaleidoscope of memories flashed before him. He recalled the parachute sitting on the floor of Old Custer, the baling wire, his hand opening the plane's door, and the breathtaking vastness of the space beyond. His eyes widened when he spotted the pull cord.

"Son, do you want to put the parachute on?"

Stu nodded, coming to his feet. Everybody watched the old gunner help him put the parachute on and explain how to use it.

Katz rose, moved closer, then kindly patted Stu. "You'll be all right now, Miami. Even if this thing goes down, you still got a parachute."

Lakalo shoved Katz's shoulder. "Would you shut up?"

Katz couldn't figure out why Lakalo kept shaking his head at him, so he asked, "You think I need a parachute?"

The old gunner answered, "It depends. If you're jumping out, then you do." His grin was friendly.

* * *

As one performance ended on the Jamberama stage, a spotlight flashed to the opposite circular stage that revolved upward in a slow spiral. Lights magically illuminated Johnny Revv, costumed as Tom Sawyer, with a beat-up straw hat and knee-high worn, torn overalls that gave him the look of a carefree farm kid. Bent over, he concentrated on baiting his fishing hook with a two foot long rubbery snake. When he finally looked up, he acted as if he was surprised to see the hundred thousand plus. "WHOA!" He spat out the straw that he'd been chewing, and yelled, "HEY Ranger Scouts!"

They yelled back at him, "HEY, JOHNNY REVV!"

The Tom Sawyer lookalike took hold of his fishing pole. "What do you think of Jamberama?"

There was a mighty roar from the crowd.

"Tonight, we're going to do something a little different, give you guys a chance to spread your wings and shout. I'm going to separate you into a few groups to see who can out-shout their neighbors . . . I mean, sing!"

The lively crowd responded with whistles and hoots.

"This, by the way, is a snake." He lifted this two foot long rubbery snake that was hooked to his fishing line. And you . . ." he looked over the crowd. ". . . are nothing but a bunch of farm animals to me." Johnny heaved his fishing line toward them. A spotlight followed the rubbery snake wiggling through the air and exposed boys jumping away from it. "Why, you see this here group?" He pointed at the boys who had run from the phony snake. "You guys are definitely the chickens." Chuckling, he pointed at a towering, feathery, yellow chicken that had jumped out on the middle stage. Underneath the costume was Spree Chi, the tallest basketball player in the NBA. "Go get 'em, Spree!"

There was a wild roar from the crowd. Spree tucked his hands under his arms like a hen, and while playfully flapping his yellow feathered elbows, dashed across the stage, leaped off and ran down the aisle. Spree reached his group and hopped about like a goofy chicken.

Johnny yelled, "Chickkkkkkkens! Be proud of who you are!"

Nutty about his chicken part, the tall NBA player put his all into it, circling, jumping, and flapping his feathery wings.

"When it comes your turn to chick then be the men God wants you to be and chick with all your MIGHT!" Johnny's hand came up as he recalled, "Did I tell you we're going to sing Old McDonald?"

"NOOOOOO!" the excited crowd yelled in response.

Tom Sawyer suddenly pointed toward the Rangers in the far back. "HEY!" he shouted. "You look like a bunch of dogs!" He chuckled, turning back toward the stage, searching for their doggy mascot. "Sooooo! Where our big dog?"

Somebody pointed toward the backfield behind the crowd where a row of outhouses resided.

Johnny looked intently toward the outhouses, and as the crowd turned, a spotlight flashed on one of the Johnny-on-the-spots. Out of it came what looked like a six-foot-tall, three-foot-wide bull dog, who in fact was Cliff Buck, a huge linebacker from the Browns.

The outhouse door slammed behind the huge dog. Cliff cocked his head back and howled, "HOOOARRR, HOARRR."

"Who let that dog out?" shouted Tom Sawyer.

Cliff Buck's trot was that of a bull dog, proud and strong. He looked as if he'd bowl anybody over.

His group was so charged to have him as a mascot that men and boys in that area broke into uncontrollable barking. "HOARR! HOOOOARRR! HOOOOARRR!"

CHAPTER 29

D usk had settled across the landscape. Little light came through the airplane's small windows, and the cabin lights did not reflect off the green Army paint.

Joey whined, "My rump's sore." He stood up and rubbed it. "It feels like a board."

Lakalo nudged Spencer. "What time is it?"

Spencer checked his watch, his eyes widened. "It's getting late. It's almost seven o'clock."

"If we don't get there soon, we're going to miss the closing ceremonies."

They glanced toward the cockpit. The ever present noise of the plane's Wright R2600 Double Cyclone engines droned on.

Virgil noticed sweat steaming down Stu's forehead. "You thirsty?"

Stu shook his head. A few drops of his sweat fell and hit Joey's shoe.

"Ueeeeugh, drool," Joey whined, drawing his shoe back as if Stu had vomited on it. "You're a sissy, Miami." He glared at the culprit.

Stu felt so bad his shoulders slumped.

"What'd you say to him?" The big Hawaiian rose, tightening his fist, and stepped toward Joey.

"Miami's a sissy."

"You don't call Miami that!"

"Anybody who's got to wear a parachute on a plane is a sissy." Joey sent a disgusted look toward Stu.

"You take that back," Lakalo demanded and gave Joey a shove.

The old gunner happened to see the aggression. "Hey!" he called out. "No horseplay here."

Lakalo nodded at him, giving him a friendly look, then stared back at Joey, dead serious. "You take that back."

Unthreatened, Joey shook his head.

The old gunner waved his hand to catch Lakalo's attention. "Young man, I want you to find your seat."

Lakalo found his seat but wasn't done with Joey. "You think he's a sissy just because he's wearing a parachute?"

Joey nodded.

Lakalo looked over at the kid with fluorescent hair. The heavy parachute hung from Stu's shoulders. Turning, he asked Joey, "When was the last time you jumped out of a plane?"

Joey shrugged. "That's different."

"I say you're a whiner, Joey, and always been a whiner. Here, he jumps out of a plane and nearly broke his leg, hobbles across country, helps us escape two druggies, and you call him a sissy?"

Joey pointed at Stu's parachute. "Who wears a parachute when they're flying?"

Lakalo held a hard eye on Joey. "I'm going to." Determined, he headed for the old gunner to see if he could also get a parachute.

"I am, too," said Rubin, rising and trailing after Lakalo.

"Me, ttttttoo," Katz said, walking by Joey and staring down on him as if he were a pathetic nothing.

"Me, three," said Spencer.

"Me, four," said Virgil, looking Joey over, while following Spencer.

"Me, five," said Adam, grinning at Joey.

"Me, seven," said Daniel, theatrically. "And I'm going to wear that parachute with gusto."

"Me . . . too," said Israel, awkwardly scuffling past. His face contorted as he stared at Joey, then he thumbed back toward Stu. "He's tough."

All that remained on the bench were Stu and Joey. Joey swallowed, feeling ill at ease. He wished he'd never made the comment.

Stu gave him a mournful look, wishing he wasn't afraid to fly, wishing he didn't need a parachute. Near the rear of the plane the others were lined up, waiting on the navigator to get their parachutes. At the other end of the plane, Stu noticed the back of the pilot in the cockpit. Studying the old pilot, the Montanan wondered why the man would ever get back on a plane after having jumped out of one in China and another in Italy.

* * *

Lakalo leaned backward into his parachute and stretched his neck muscles. He yawned and gazed about the dark green walls of the plane. Shadows cast off the framework. As he rose, rubbing his sore rump, he felt the weight of the parachute and hunched his shoulders, hitching it to a more comfortable position. Then, he headed toward the gunner and navigator. Nearing them Lakalo gave a quick nod and ventured cautiously toward the cockpit doorway. He looked in and was awed by all of the dials and controls. It felt like he was back in time. Both the pilot and copilot were wearing their original uniforms.

At first, the two old-timers didn't notice him. The copilot was chuckling, laughing at the pilot's description of the boys when they'd first come off the train car. Then the copilot noticed Lakalo standing in the doorway. Adam and Katz appeared behind him, staring through the opening. Rubin pushed in.

The copilot welcomed them with a grin. "I hear you fellas been doing a bit of traveling?"

The plane hit headwinds and jerked upward, causing Lakalo and Adam to cling to the door opening. Katz and Rubin were pulled back by their heavy parachutes and fell over. The copilot chuckled.

"This headwind is putting a damper on our speed," said the pilot. Turning, he said to Lakalo, "How long does this Jamberama go for?"

"Tonight's the closing ceremony."

* * *

Below the night sky a banjo picker waited for the Jamberama audience to quell their laughter, he glanced off-stage at the cause of their hilarity, an Uncle Sam look-a-like who was picking himself off the grass after being shot out of a cannon.

Like a rumble from lightning a massive sound came from above. This thundering roar grew and grew. Everyone turned toward the Eastern sky. A great plane appeared over the tops of the trees. The banjo picker was awestruck by the dark silhouette of the B-25 bomber. It flew over the stage with a mighty roar. Everybody below was vibrated by the power of this World War II machine.

The banjo picker exclaimed, "Wow!" A half a moment passed before he regained his wit and joked, "You do a little spoof on taxes, and the Army shows up."

The hundred-thousand plus crowd were in awe, watching the dark, lone silhouette of the plane gain in altitude, heading higher into the night.

"I'm going to slow it down a bit and talk to you about those candles you received as you came in tonight," the banjo player told the crowd. "Can you get those out? We're going to light them shortly." He watched Uncle Sam stagger off, then pointed toward the packed hillside, proclaiming, "When you light those candles, I want you to consider your God-given talents, and what you are doing with those talents."

He plucked at his banjo while he crossed the stage. "In all the nations represented here, certain men have used their talents well. When you light those candles, consider what purpose God has for you on this planet. In other words . . . why are you here?"

* * *

The plane banked and rose higher, giving the old pilot an excellent view of the glow of the Jamberama stages. He glanced back at a few of the boys that were hanging around the cabin door, "I'm sorry, fellas."

"What?" Katz asked. He hung onto the doorframe and peered into the cockpit while others poked their heads into the opening.

"I'm sorry to say but that's the closest you're going to get to Jamberama." The old fellow pointed toward the window. "The local airport is some forty miles away. It'll be a good hour and a half by the time we land and drive back."

"Jamberama will be over by then," Katz said sadly.

"It was the headwinds," said the disappointed pilot.

Upset, Lakalo pushed away from the doorframe and positioned himself to look out the circular window. But not having enough height to peer down on the stage, he was quick to return to the cockpit door. "Can you maybe fly back over so we can just see what Jamberama looks like?"

The pilot nodded. "You bet. If you like, I can open the bomb bay doors. That way you can get a real good view."

"That'd be great."

"But you have to do one thing."

"What's that?" Lakalo asked.

"Set the protective line across there." The pilot pointed to a line hanging from the side wall, halfway down the aircraft. "You see that there? . . . Hook it to the opposite wall. Tell the others, they are not to go past that."

"I'll tell them."

"I don't want any of you falling out, parachute or not, it's a long way down."

Lakalo's fingers dug into the straps that held his parachute as he went back down the aircraft and took the rope off the wall to clasp it into a metal ring on the opposite wall.

The old pilot watched Lakalo talking to the others, pointing out the line, instructing them. The boys nodded to the warnings. Lakalo turned, caught his eye and gave a thumbs-up. With a push of a button the hydraulics engaged and the bomb bay doors began to open.

Wind swept in the opening, thrilling the troop. Those nearest the opening, Joey, Virgil, and Spencer, leaped from their seats to get away from the yawning gaping black void. Parachute or not, the opening created fear. The breeze swirled their hair as they made it back to the ones nervously milling about the cockpit door. Stu was the only one left sitting on the bench seat. The bomb bay doors locked fully open.

Katz exclaimed, "There's the stage!" He pointed out the opening.

In the distance, they could see tiny lights spread up the hillside, as thousands of flickering candles conquered the darkness.

"Look at all the little lights!" Rubin pointed in awe.

"That's so cool."

"They look like Christmas."

"It's like they're calling out to us."

"Oh, my gosh!"

"What do you think they're saying?" Virgil asked.

"Jump," Daniel said, chuckling.

Nobody else even grinned.

"I don't know how Army guys jump out of planes at night. That's a long way down." Lakalo could feel the plane angle upward as the pilot took it higher.

"You don't just jump out a plane without practicing a thousand times." Katz thumbed toward Stu. "Otherwise, you could end up like Miami."

"Miami must've really bonked his head to think he's Montana Stu."

They all looked over at the fluorescent-haired kid, who sat by himself on the bench seat with his parachute bulking over his shoulders.

Daniel shook his head, not fully understanding the Montanan. "It's odd, though. He seems to have purpose. It's not like he's lost his mind."

"I don't know. Who was the last guy you know who said he was Montana Stu?"

"Without him we wouldn't have made it this far," Lakalo commented.

Joey chuckled. "Yeah, but something's wrong with him." He pitched his chin toward Stu and smirked. "'Cause he's not Montana Stu."

Daniel studied the odd kid who called himself Montana Stu and wondered what made him tick. The whirling air kept the rest of the boys on edge. It drew their eyes back to the black hole.

Rubin blurted, "I'd never jump at night. Only in the daytime."

"You've never jumped, so shut up!" said Joey, and then he jokingly pushed Katz forward. "Jump!"

Jolted, unnerved to the core, Katz spun and pushed him back. "Don't

you . . . don't you ever touch me!"

Daniel looked over the thousands of lights. "Wouldn't it be something if we could just jump?"

Lakalo examined the borders of the opening. "Anybody's got to be nuts to jump out that hole. I don't know if I'd jump even if the plane was on fire." He glanced over at Stu, "I don't know how Miami ever jumped from the other plane."

Sitting motionless, Stu stared out the large opening at the distant glow of the stage. Beyond the glow, a mass of tiny twinkling lights covered the hillside. A whirlwind of emotions swirled about the Montanan. Gray would be down there. He was supposed to ride Gray in the Grand Finale to carry the American flag into the Ranger Scouts. That would've been so big, to charge up the aisle atop Gray. But it wouldn't happen now, without the plane landing.

Glancing toward the front, Stu saw the frame of the old pilot inside the cockpit, and wondered how the man could jump out of a plane in China, then get back on a plane just to get shot down in Italy. And now he owned this Army plane!

The Montanan wished he had the same courage, but one look through the dark opening told him that was a crazy wish. The twinkling lights were captivating, yet that black gaping void was not just sobering—it evoked fear. Even so, he couldn't help but imagine floating down and landing among the Scouts. A nervous grin crossed his lips. His dad and granddad would be there and Johnny Revv, too. He felt the thousands of lights calling to him, beckoning him, enticing him – but the dark chasm was too vast, too breathtaking. It was a hopeful dream, yet a fearsome one.

Seconds passed, he still felt the magnetic lights tug at him. He leaned toward the opening and stared down at the glow. There was such a pull on him that he didn't realize he had risen and stepped toward the bomb bay doors, like one who unconsciously draws near a fire. Abruptly, the wide-eyed Montanan caught himself, gasped, and took three steps back. His heart quickened, and he took another step back, yet something in his gut began to take hold, to grip him, to pull him. But his other side revolted—there was no way he was going to jump! Looking back at the lights, he limped away from the opening toward the others who hung about the cockpit door.

Lakalo patted him on the shoulder. "We almost made it, didn't we, Miami?" He grinned. "It would've been awesome."

Stu nodded and tried to swallow, but there was a lump in his throat.

"We made it through that storm, didn't we?" Daniel said.

"We made it out of the woods." Adam nodded several times with a sense of accomplishment.

"Those druggies' dogs didn't get us," said Rubin.

"That druggie driver didn't get us, either."

"And that Sasquatch didn't get us," Katz added.

"That crazy guy on the train didn't get us, either."

Rubin sadly shook his head. "That man scared me bad."

"That man didn't have a purpose," said Daniel. Drawing near Stu, he teased, "Hey, Miami, you got a purpose?"

Stu was hesitant to respond. Daniel's question had hit home. Gray was down there, a flag was waiting, but that night he wouldn't be riding Gray. Discouraged, Stu dropped his head.

"What's your purpose?"

Again the question hit Stu head on. He knew was supposed to be part of Jamberama's closing ceremony.

The pilot banked the plane to head back over the glowing lights of Jamberama. He announced, "Last flyover, fellas. Take a good look."

Lakalo stuck his head in the cockpit doorway. "I wish I had a camera." The copilot glanced at him. Lakalo leaned toward the old man. "How far are we above ground?"

"We've been climbing a bit." The copilot checked his altimeter. "About fifty-five hundred feet."

Lakalo caught Stu's eye. "We're just fifty-five hundred feet away from Jamberama." There was sadness in his voice. "That's just a mile from our destination."

The copilot leaned to look out the window. "We'll be overhead shortly."

Upon hearing this, the Montanan's mind sped up.

The pilot swung his face toward the back of the plane. "Take your last look at your Jamberama, fellas."

Daniel and Lakalo turned and took a few steps toward the bomb bay opening.

Stu abruptly stuck his hand forward to shake the old-pilot's. "Thanks for the ride."

Sporting a warm grin, the old-timer grasped it and gave it a hardy shake. "You're very welcome. It's what I do." He squeezed Stu's hand. "Glad you're doing better. If you don't mind the up and downs, flying can be fun."

Stu nodded, then glanced appreciatively at the copilot, pushed off the doorway, and taking a deep breath, turned. His eyes widened—there, twelve feet away, was the large opening with the yawning dark void beyond. His stiff legs limped forward. Beside him, the others were chattering away.

Lakalo glimpsed the glow of Stu's fluorescent hair as he went by. "Where you going, Miami?"

Disconnected from them, Stu fought his fearful memories. Daniel noticed his pale face and wondered if he was heading back to the bathroom. The old gunner and the navigator didn't notice for they were engaged in a heated political debate.

Daniel called out, "You okay, Miami?"

Stu didn't acknowledge him, his total focus now on the dark opening.

The attention of the entire troop was fixed on Stu who was limping toward the hole.

Adam whispered to Joey, "He really must've hurt his leg bad when he parachuted down. It doesn't seem to be getting any better."

Lakalo called out, "What's the word, Miami?"

There was no response from Stu. The only thing he heard was the thud of his own heart. It rang in his ears. He stared into the vast, dark void with a distant, glazed look in his eye. Though he was nearing the opening, nobody anticipated his mission.

"What's the word, Miami?" Lakalo saw the Montanan place his hand on the parachute's pull cord and step over the protective rope.

It struck Daniel and Lakalo at the same time. They bolted toward him, and despite their bulky chutes, moved quickly.

"Hey, Miami?" Daniel called out.

Even Katz noticed the anxiousness in Daniel's voice.

"You okay?" Lakalo cautiously stepped over the rope and extended his palm toward Stu.

A step behind, Daniel nervously watched the Montanan move closer to the opening. "Miami, maybe you should come . . ." he said, extending his hand toward Stu, ". . . maybe you should come over here." His eyes locked on Stu's, "Why don't you give me your hand?"

One step sideways, and Stu would be gone. An edgy tenseness hung over the troop. Their movements seemed surreal, and the wind swirled about their hair.

"Did I ever tell 'ya that you did good on the driving?" Lakalo's voice was low and cautious. Stu looked detached. "Why don't you give me your hand?" Lakalo angled his head toward the others. "It's better over here . . ." He knew Miami wasn't Montana Stu but, desperate to get him away from the opening, added, ". . . Montana."

Heedful of the danger, the others came slowly up from behind. Katz was so afraid of falling out that he bent low to be close to the floor, where he'd flop if things got out of hand. Daniel cautiously drew even with Lakalo.

Struggling through his fear, sweat trickled down Lakalo's brow. "Take my hand, Montana."

Stu's eyes focused on Lakalo, then on Daniel. He glanced at the rest, who were behind them. Daniel could sense he was about to do something and feared if Stu jumped and he was holding on, they'd both go, parachute or not. It was a frightening thought. His head jerked back at Virgil. "Grab hold of me," he said.

Virgil grabbed him by the belt. Other hands reached out, anchoring onto Virgil, and one by one, the rest grabbed hold of each other, locking arms, bending lower, and leaning back. Adam latched onto Lakalo's other arm while holding onto Spencer. They intertwined like one big spider web. Daniel slowly reached for Stu. "What's the word, Montana?"

The Montanan half-turned from the gaping bomb bay opening with his gaze locked onto Daniel. "Gray's waiting." He shifted his weight and the wind whipped his hair. Then he took a step over the bomb bay opening into –nothing.

Lakalo and Daniel lunged. Both grabbed him by the parachute straps, but Stu's legs swung sideways in a mid-air arc. His weight threatened to pull Lakalo and Daniel through the opening. Behind them the troop awkwardly shifted, hanging on for dear life.

Terrified, Daniel's heart raced. Below him, darkness. He could feel others pulling on him but the Montana anchor, coupled with the plane's speed, was severe.

The wind blasted Stu's face and plastered his pants tight against his shins.

Above him, Lakalo and Daniel were down on their knees, leaned way over, struggling against the G-forces and Stu's weight. It was a mad struggle, with Stu's body captured by the wind. Daniel glimpsed the stage lights of Jamberama almost directly underneath. His face strained as he attempted to hang on to Stu. Behind him, Virgil released Daniel's belt to grab Stu's parachute, but his action had the opposite effect, causing Daniel to be pulled forward by Stu's weight. Daniel's head pitched over the bomb bay opening. The troop pulled back on them with Virgil re-gripping, pressing his leg against the metal opening.

Stretched in both directions, Daniel knew he could save himself if he let go of Stu. He wouldn't. Behind him the intertwined troop were of the same mindset. Even though they were deathly close to the gaping hole, cantilevered near the edge of the bomb bay opening, they would not let go of a member of the troop. Each pulled on the one in front, so much so that when Joey's hand slipped off the rope, a chain reaction instantly occurred. The whole intertwined bunch slid.

Daniel and Lakalo followed Stu out the opening. Katz grabbed Joey as he slid past him. But Joey, being without a parachute, frantically kicked himself free and lay spread-eagled, hugging the deck. Before him the rest of the troop vanished.

In a rush of warm air the night sky welcomed their bodies.

Wind whistled past Stu's ears. Staring up at the heavens, he felt as if his heart would pound through his chest. Finally, he pulled the parachute cord. The strings from the parachute flew past his face, toward Katz. Abruptly, the chute caught and gave Stu a wild jerk. He hung like a breathless damp-eyed doll, staring blankly into the dark vastness. After a long moment, he gasped, attempting to catch his breath. Finally, he chanced a downward glance.

Past his dangling feet, he saw the stage lights, beyond glowed thousands of twinkling candle lights, lights that exhilarated him, beckoned him.

One by one, other white chutes popped open—two on his right, three on his left, and one directly ahead. He took a deep breath and stared upward at the stars, praying everybody's chute would open. Then, looking down, he saw two more white puffs appear.

* * *

On the grass in front of the stage, a Scout who'd fallen asleep suddenly awoke. He gazed up to see everybody holding candles then his eyes were drawn beyond to what looked like white puffs in the night sky. Curious, he wondered what the puffs were.

On the stage, the singer's deep voice rang, *"America, America, God shed his grace on thee!"*

Coming down an aisle, Stu's dad, Wes, led Gray. Atop the horse sat a kid who was thrilled to take Montana Stu's place. Gray whinnied nervously. Pops brought up the rear, his glass eye staring at Gray's tail while his good eye gazed at a number of Scouts holding up their candle lights.

The song ended, followed by a loud, cracking pop. Cheers erupted, then more blasts as a high-pitched whistling sound wound upward. With a burst, fireworks sprayed the night sky, spewing white sparkles in a circular array. As the sparkles sizzled and fizzled away, another red spray of fireworks burst and a blue glow splashed across the darkness.

Amidst this spectacular display came the white parachute of the wide-eyed Montanan whose only thought was to somehow touch down on his good foot, then roll so he wouldn't damage his swollen ankle. "Get out of the way!" he called.

Below him, a few in the unsuspecting crowd looked about for the warning voice, but with all the fireworks and the movement of a particular horse, no one got out of the way. Two Pioneer boys had no idea what hit them when Stu landed. Both fell. One scrambled up, but was dumbfounded by the silk of a white parachute that soon blanketed him. Smoke rose from someone's candle burning into the fabric. Two alert fathers quickly moved to put the flames out.

Three hundred feet above, another parachute floated down. When Rubin called, "Look out!" Rangers scrambled in all directions. A twenty-foot area emptied of all but chairs. Rubin knocked over five chairs, his chute settling beyond. When he staggered up, he was swarmed by awestruck Scouts.

Up the hill, Katz landed, crumpling to the ground. Several Pioneer kids near him clapped, thinking it was all part of the show. Katz awkwardly ripped up a clump of grass and rose, triumphantly holding it in the air, yelling, "Yeah, baby!"

Off to the side, thirty feet above, Virgil anxiously looked over the waiting crowd and yelled, "Give room!" A gap opened as boys backed away. Virgil hit the ground rolling. He was immediately surrounded and helped up by the excited crowd.

Spencer pushed into this throng with his arm over his balled-up parachute and stopped in front of Virgil. So many exhilarated thoughts were flowing through his scientific mind but they all seemed to freeze when Virgil stepped forward and hugged him. Spencer's eyes welled as a rush of emotions hit. Virgil leaned back and gazed at the one who he'd fought with. Their desperate journey had galvanized a strange bond of friendship.

Sixty feet down the hill, Israel lay on the ground, staring up at a group of Pioneers who were bent over, gawking at him. Israel jokingly snarled, "Whhhhat are you llllooking atttttt?" The comment, along with Israel's awkward facial expression, caused some to step back. Someone offered Israel a hand. He grabbed the hand and rose, his odd frame angled in a series of off balanced steps. Grinning, he kindly tapped a Pioneer and teased, "Whhhhen you become a Sccccout you get to jjjjjjump out of pppplanes."

With his hands pincered close to his chest, Israel looked over the kid's head at the field of boys and men, the stage, and the fireworks in the background. In the midst of this exciting Americana, his eyes caught the movement of a gray horse and the glow of fluorescent hair bobbing toward it. He was so ready to leap out of his skin that he plowed forward, moving like a short-legged scarecrow with parachute strings flowing off him.

In the distance, fireworks continued to paint the night sky, screaming up, bursting outward in a colorful display.

A Pioneer next to Katz tapped him to ask what plane he'd come off of. But Katz didn't answer, he was searching for his buddies.

Down the aisle, Daniel marched into view. He poked his chest out like a proud general who'd just defeated his foe. Behind him dragged his parachute, its outer edges getting caught on chairs and seats, while Scouts scurried to pick it up. Daniel caught sight of a teen costumed in a Minuteman uniform; he looked like Johnny Revv. He saw him leap off the stage and sprint toward a florescent haired kid who was mounting a horse.

A group of Scouts leaned over Adam who lay blinking. One kid moved his hand in front of his face. "How many fingers?"

Adam stared past the fingers, then he felt others grab him and pull him up. Off-balanced, he leaned into a Scout and dizzily gazed about. The fireworks beyond captured his attention so he didn't notice Lakalo, Rubin, Virgil, Spencer, Katz, and Daniel coming toward him. But he did hear Lakalo's voice.

"Hey, Adam!" Lakalo could see Adam was shaken up and came to his side. "How you doing?"

"Woozy."

The Hawaiian took hold of Adam's upper arm to support him, while Daniel undid his parachute. Adam noticed an awkward figure coming down the grassy aisle. It was Israel, moving in his unorthodox gait, his one hand pincered to his chest while his other trailed behind. He looked like a lopsided gorilla, sporting a huge grin. Closing on them, he announced, "Ttttthat was bbbbbad, that was so bbbbbbad."

"Hey, Israel. You see Miami?"

Israel excitedly pointed past them at something coming their way.

They turned to see a gray horse powering up the slope. Its rider, they knew. His one hand held the American flag and his eyes were locked on Daniel's.

Hairs rose on Daniel's arms, and he mouthed, "Montana?" Then he shouted, "Montana Stu!"

Stu pulled Gray to a stop and was immediately surrounded by Scouts.

Daniel eagerly pressed toward the horse but had to fight through the crowd. Unable to reach Stu, he touched Gray's neck. Gray gave a low whinny.

Atop his horse, Stu extended a hand toward him. "Hey, Daniel . . . take my hand." Daniel proudly grabbed it. The Montanan pulled him up.

CHAPTER 30

C ommander Rex and Commander Charles followed a nurse down a long corridor then into a hospital room. Walking past the bed, she flicked her finger toward Junior Commander Alan, then crossed the room and took hold of the curtains. She spread them open.

The morning light exposed Commander Charles going up one side of the bed while Commander Rex quietly neared the other. Though both commanders looked worse for the wear they had a sparkle in their eyes as they gazed upon Junior Commander Alan who was asleep.

Word had come from Jamberama that, except for Joey, the rest of the troop had somehow dropped out of the sky, parachuting in during the closing ceremonies. And although Commander Charles had no idea how he'd explain this parachuting to their parents, minor details didn't concern him now. There was much to celebrate. He was looking upon a healthy Junior Commander Alan.

"Junior Commander Alan?" Commander Rex said.

Alan's eyes flashed opened. The teen's movements were abrupt as he looked about. He knew Commander Rex's voice, but stared past the end of the bed frame to see an arm, someone's khaki shirt, then Commander Charles's round face. His head jerked back in surprise.

Commander Charles couldn't help but chuckle. His chuckle was deep and warm. "Good morning, Junior Commander Alan." Charles thrust his hand forward to shake. Junior Commander Alan slowly moved his palm up.

"Good morning." The young commander's words sounded smeared. He grinned back at them. "I had this dream."

"Tell us."

"I dreamed I went to heaven." He grinned. "It was something." He slowly lifted one hand. "It had this, like, sea of glass that you could walk on, yet see right through. You could see planets and universes. I saw, like, a whirling white Milky Way but bigger . . . huge." He pointed toward the ceiling. "It was right there." He caught Charles' eye. "And different beings, some were huge. And you could talk to everybody, like . . . all at once, even hold different conversations and not get mixed up." He paused. "Everybody . . . you can do back flips while you're talking. You wouldn't believe this song . . . and the angels." He managed a weak chuckle. "Somebody brought this bowl of green Jell-O stuff in a dish and man," he tapped Charles's hand—"I generally don't like green stuff, so I just took a sniff." His eyes rolled. "It was like I could hear a waterfall, just from sniffing it. And feel the mist of a jungle." He became serious. "And felt, like, the Arctic. Oh, man, and all its vastness. It was so cool."

Commander Rex nodded. "I bet it was Gummy Bears."

* * *

Later on that day a special ceremonies was held at Jamberama. Close to ten thousand Scouts looked like an Army unit about to meet the president. They stood at attention, lined up, row after row, dressed in their khaki uniforms. At the podium were Commander Rex and Commander Charles, flown up that afternoon by the Council.

Commander Charles looked sharp as he leaned over the mike, his voice boomed. "Would Lakalo Kealoha, Virgil Calhoon, Israel Rodriguez, Rubin Washington, Daniel McGregor, Katz Schmalenbach, Spencer Grant, Adam Diaz, and Montana Stu please come forward?"

The troop came through the middle, down the long walkway. They looked like polished toy soldiers, decked out in their formal uniforms, all wearing red bolo ties. There was an aura of pride about them. Even Israel looked taller. A rush of excitement rippled through the mass of Scouts watching their approach.

"When I look out on these young men coming my way, I can truly say, God is good." Commander Charles's eyes watered. "Please hold your applause till we're finished." He cleared his throat in an attempt to maintain his decorum while the troop lined up before them with Israel at the head.

"There should be a merit for covering more miles than any other troop via plane, trains, and automobiles." His grin burst forth, and there was sudden, massive applause. Scouts couldn't help themselves. Before them was the troop that had gotten lost in the Texarkana forest, the Commander-less troop that had fallen out of the night sky.

Commander Charles waited for the crowd to settle before continuing, "The first merit I want to hand out goes beyond the arena of simply surviving, of what is required in the survival merit. This merit is for living life powerfully." He gave a half-bicep flex. "I've named it Muscomus."

Stepping toward Israel, he extended his hand. If ever Israel's awkward hand suddenly snapped into position to shake someone's hand, it did it now. His grin broadened, and his legs looked as if they were doing a swing step to a slow dance. Commander Rex placed the medal around Israel's neck.

Commander Charles leaned closer, "Good job, Israel." then adjusted the red, white, and blue ribbon of the medal.

Israel tilted his face in a great grin and slurred, "Fffffun." He chuckled till he drooled.

Commander Charles, grinning, addressed Lakalo, "Good job, Lakalo." They shook hands and Commander Rex placed a medal around his neck. "I hear you were a rock."

"It was good."

"It is very good." Commander Rex liked Lakalo's firm handshake.

Commander Charles swung his focus to Adam. "Good job, Adam." He shook his hand.

"Thank you Commander Charles."

"We'll be sure to get you a Krispy Kreme or two on the way home."

He rubbed his stomach. "You know I'm a growing boy."

Next up was Spencer. Spencer bowed his head for Commander Rex to put the medal round his neck.

"Good job, Spencer. I hear you helped guide the ship."

"Thank you." Spencer adjusted his glasses as he straightened.

Next was the Southerner. "Good job, Virgil." Commander Rex placed the medal over Virgil's neck. "I hear you're quite the woodsman. Remind me when we get back to look into a Cut-and-Chop card."

"You still have my knife?"

Charles felt his pocket and nodded.

While he waited for his medal, Katz felt like his head was going to pop off.

Commander Charles shook his hand. "Good job, Katz."

Commander Rex placed the medal over his neck, and Katz fingered the bronze. His emotions swung hard and he dropped his head as his eyes filled.

Commander Charles reached his hand out to Rubin. "Good job, Rubin."

Commander Rex placed a medal around his neck.

"My uncle is going to be amazed that I survived the Sasquatch." Rubin proudly fingered the merit. "Let alone received the muscle medal." He flexed his bicep.

"That's Muscomus." Commander Charles grinned at Rubin and stepped after Commander Rex who was placing the medal over Stu's head.

"Thank you for helping out with my troop."

"It was great."

"And now young man. I hear you're a bit of a parachute buff who likes to jump out of planes."

Stu gave a slow cautious stare.

"Yes, yes, for you we've made up a new award called a 'Flying-by-the-seat-of-his-pants Award.'" Commander Rex pinned the bronze flying wings to Stu's uniform. "I want you to know these wings came from a World War II vet who flew twenty-five missions over enemy territory."

Stu admirably rubbed his finger over the bronze wings.

Commander Charles shook his hand. "Thank you for helping out with my troop."

"They're the ones that saved me." Stu glimpsed Johnny Revv at the front of the crowd. Johnny gave him a thumb's up.

Commander Charles stepped in front of Daniel and shook his hand. "Good job, Daniel. I hear you're pretty fast along the tracks."

"You should give him an award for singing," Lakalo interjected.

"Singing?" Commander Rex dropped the medal over Daniel's red hair. "I didn't know you could sing, what song do you have for us today?"

Pondering, Daniel looked out over the thousands of men and boys.

Big Lakalo moved in to advise, "Com'on Daniel, you can sing."

Katz added, "Do the Dairy Queen song."

"The one for the lady."

Daniel pulled out his harmonica and gave it a small blow.

Commander Rex asked, "So, you have a song for us Daniel?"

Daniel looked up at Commander Rex, "If you like it, will you take us to the Dairy Queen?"

EPILOGUE

Dear Mom,

I'll never go looking for Sasquatch prints again. On our way to Jamberama we shouldn't have camped at Boggy Creek. Rubin said the Sasquatch take the men at night and come for the boys in the day. We ran like crazy. Spencer don't know how to read the compass and the nine of us got lost, more and more. Virgil got in a big fight with him. It was really bad because the troop split. I was going to starve to death when we see this guy coming down in a parachute and we all think its Army to rescue us but he's only a kid and worse off than us because he hit hard when he landed.

He's all mixed up and thinks he's Montana Stu. We have to join up again just to help him. His hair was so white we called him Miami. He told us about a cabin where we could get food. But what does he know, it was a drug making cabin. I almost died because I hadn't drunken anything for days. Then we had to hide because there were killer dogs and murders there.

Miami said he knew how to drive this old car but he didn't because he ran over a garage then ran over a man then smashed a truck straight off the road. We go on and Miami still thinks he's Montana Stu and gets us to sing for a lady at the Dairy Queen to get some food. She don't have much but after the car runs out of gas we had some beans we got from the cabin.

Virgil sees the train was going to Jamberama and it was taking off so we run like crazy. We all make it but it was so dark in that boxcar and there was this bad person in the other end and we didn't know because it was so dark. He was going to kill us for those beans. I never have been so scared. He came at us and Katz knocked him out the train. Katz cried and cried but it wasn't his fault.

The next day the train went on and on and on and my lips were so dry. I was so hot in that boxcar I thought I was going to die. I'll never take a train like that again. The train didn't even go to Missouri. It ended up in Georgia. It was so bad because it was the last day for Jamberama and there was no way we could make it. This old farmer fed us but he wanted a song too. All these Southerners want everybody to sing to them.

We told him that it was the last day for Jamberama so he called his Army friends, they were all so old and they came over and they got the biggest Army plane ever. It came right out of the barn. He said he was going to fly us to Jamberama.

Miami was afraid of planes and he was throwing up on everything, even my shoe.

We flew over Jamberama right at the end, and that's when Miami goes crazy because he wants to jump out of the plane. They all grabbed on him but they couldn't stop him, and I was the only one that didn't fall out.

Now I'm in Pinewood, Georgia. The old pilot says he'll fly me to California but I won't ever fly again. Please come get me soon because I've run out of songs to sing to this Southerner.

Joey

ACKNOWLEDGEMENTS

I'd like to thank my wife, Elaine, for her tireless work on the editing and critiquing. Honey, you're special!

Thank you to Rod and Linda Allen for your kind critiquing.

Special thanks to Joseph Schmalenbach for his work on the cover. Wow!

I'm so fortunate to have friends like you.